THE PART
OF
FORTUNE

Also by Laurel Goldman

SOUNDING THE TERRITORY

THE PART
OF
FORTUNE

Laurel Goldman

Weidenfeld & Nicolson
New York

Published by Weidenfeld & Nicolson, New York
A Division of Wheatland Corporation
10 East 53rd Street
New York, NY 10022

Grateful acknowledgment is made for the following:

SPANISH HARLEM, copyright © 1960 & 1961 by Hill & Range Songs, Inc. and Trio
Music Co., Inc. Administered by Unichappell Music, Inc. (Rightsong Music, Pub.).
International copyright secured. All rights reserved. Used by permission.
OH BOY! by Sunny West, Bill Tilghman, and Norman Petty. Copyright © 1957 Wren
Music Co. Copyright © renewed 1985 Wren Music Co. International copyright
secured. All rights reserved. Used by permission.
BACK DOOR MAN, copyright © 1961, 1970 by Arc Music Corp. Used with permission.
All rights reserved.
OLE BUTTERMILK SKY by Hoagy Carmichael and Jack Brooks. Copyright © 1946 Morley
Music Co. Copyright © renewed 1974 Morley Music Co. and Frank Music Corp.
International copyright secured. All rights reserved. Used by permission.
LONG TALL SALLY by E. Johnson, R. Blackwell, and R. Penniman. Copyright © 1956,
renewed 1984 ATV Music Corp. All rights controlled and administered by Blackwood
Music Inc. under license from ATV Music (Venice). All rights reserved. International
copyright secured. Used by permission.
I'LL BE YOUR BABY TONIGHT, copyright © 1968 by Dwarf Music. Used by permission.
All rights reserved.
OUR LOVE IS HERE TO STAY by George and Ira Gershwin. Copyright © 1938 by
Gershwin Publishing Corp. Copyright renewed, assigned to Chappell & Co., Inc.
International copyright secured. All rights reserved. Used by permission.
YOU BELONG TO MY HEART (SOLAMENTE UNA VEZ), Spanish words and music by Agustin
Lara. English lyrics by Ray Gilbert. Copyright 1941 by Promotora Hispano Americana
de Musica, S.A. Copyright 1943 by Promotora Hispano Americana de Musica, S.A.
Copyrights renewed. All rights controlled by Peer International Corporation. All
rights reserved. Used by permission.
YOU CAN'T ALWAYS GET WHAT YOU WANT by Mick Jagger and Keith Richard. Published
by ABKCO Music, Inc. (BMI) 1969. All rights reserved. Used by permission.

Library of Congress Cataloging-in-Publication Data

Goldman, Laurel.
  The part of fortune.

  I. Title.
PS3557.0369P3 1987   813'.54   86-11079
ISBN 1-55584-004-3

Manufactured in the United States of America
Designed by Irving Perkins Associates
First Edition 1987
10 9 8 7 6 5 4 3 2 1

For my grandmothers,
Edith Leventhal Goldman
and
Julia Jessel Leon

THANKS TO

Georgann Eubanks
Angela Davis Gardner
Linda Hirschmann
Peggy Payne
And especially to my sister
Terry Vance
and my mother
Ione Goldman.

*"You can't always get what you want;
but if you try sometime,
you just might find,
you get what you need."*

—*Mick Jagger & Keith Richard*

ONE

1

There are as many versions of my parents' deaths as I had hours to invent them. In most they died noisy, heroic deaths; in a few they were craven, sick with dread. In one they sought their own destruction willfully.

I tried several times to reshape the ending, but I couldn't. My art had boundaries that could not be transgressed. The ending was immutable. My mother and father were dead.

In school I was considered odd because I was an orphan and lived with my disreputable aunt. I enjoyed the distinction, and I set about to enhance it. I played rough games with the boys, won every spelling bee, excelled at sums and wore my father's Phi Beta Kappa key pinned over my left breast every day. I was much envied for the tiny gold emblem, and I hinted that it was a source of power. On Thursdays, assembly day, I cinched a pale blue garter of my mother's around my upper arm, which gave me an enviable military bearing.

At lunch I told stories in the school yard. At first I hadn't many serious listeners—three or four at best. But in no time at all I had a considerable crowd. When the bell for class rang, my heroes and heroines would be left swaying over the edges of cliffs, dangling over pits of fire, sweating under the blade of a sword that was already so close it had scraped off the top layer of skin of its victim.

I was never at a loss for words or admirers. But I knew I was odd and I knew I was alone. "I'm alone," I said out loud to the empty yard as the children trooped back into the school. "I know I'm alone." I sang it out as if someone were accusing me of not knowing it, of not having the courage to understand my fate.

* * *

When I was seven my mother and father fell into the sea
when the silver plane they were in blew apart. So I am
spared the possibility of seeing my parents end their days
in a place like this.

My name is Clara Julian. This summer I've been telling
stories to the residents of the Green Mansions Home for
the Elderly. I tell stories everywhere to anyone who'll listen. My Aunt Celia used to say I'd tell a story to a deaf
man, and I would. "You'd tell a story to a stone," she said.
But she was wrong about that. I need a face to look into,
a clue to what comes next.

Occasionally I make a little money telling stories, but
usually, as Celia predicted, I don't. I make my living typing. When I come to a new town, I sign up with a temporary agency. So far I've always found the work I need. I've
even been offered permanent positions with a future. But
I'm doing what I want to do, so a future doesn't tempt
me.

2

"She was about to begin her life," I said, and although this
was the story Johanna had imagined I would tell, she held
her breath. Her pale face grew paler still as she tipped forward, straining to hear what I would say next.

She was about to begin her life when . . . ? What? What happened to her?

But Johanna was not destined to find out because the six-tiered stainless steel cart that held the salmon-colored plastic supper trays was being wheeled in with the usual clatter by Honora Bliss, the head nurse and acting director of the Green Mansions Home for the Elderly.

In the instant it took Johanna to register the disappointment, the lounge of Green Mansions came alive with the only genuine activity of the day. Everyone, with the exception of Mrs. Merriman—who eats glucose all day long from a tube attached to a vein in her arm and nutritional supplements from a tube passing down her nose into her stomach—takes an interest in mealtimes, even Mr. Martin, who since the death of his wife takes an interest in almost nothing. Even Johanna's grandmother, Hannah Jessup, who had a reputation for being an exquisite cook, looks forward to the dehydrated potatoes, the frozen fish sticks, the beige pudding that comes out of a tin.

*   *   *

Three months ago this building and the property on which it stands were sold to a developer who plans to build a condominium complex on its three acres.

Already bush hogs and bulldozers graze in the yard. In the lobby painters are building a scaffold. Gigantic canvas drop cloths, heaped into corners, mound up like desert dwellings.

There isn't any one facility in the area that can handle sixty-five additional people, so the former residents of Green Mansions have been parceled out to different homes as space became available. In the past two weeks all but four of the residents have been moved out. The official line is that the residents who are still here have been, for one reason or another, the most difficult to relocate, but the truth is, Honora Bliss, the director, has kept her favorites back.

Miriam Stone hisses at Dr. Milne, who comes once a week to Green Mansions. He can do nothing for her severe arthritis. Her knuckles are stacked one on top of the other, and her back is bent almost double. She walks with increasing difficulty. Infrequently, in the dead of night, she leaves her wheelchair to ransack Honora's office. She twice destroyed the chart that describes her as disruptive and abusive. She abuses Honora as vigorously as she does everyone else, referring to her as "that ugly Watusi bitch."

Mrs. Merriman is confined to a wheelchair, a victim of a central nervous system disease, which the neurologist speculates had been lying in wait for her since her probable exposure to an epidemic of encephalitis when she was a child. She has not spoken for as many years as Honora has been here and no one knows how long before that. Virginia Merriman is locked in her silence "like a bird locked in a cage," Honora says, "but sometimes I think maybe she's flying around in her mind, and I picture her mind like a big open space and her thoughts are as large as clouds." The other patients shun her. "Who does she think she is?" Mrs. Stone says. "She never opens her yap."

Except for his seriously deteriorating eyesight and a chronic, not very serious, irregular heartbeat, David Martin, the sole male resident of Green Mansions, is ambulatory and in good physical condition. In fact, there is something exaggerated, extravagant, about his physical presence in this house of women. He is too tall, too broad-shouldered. His grey hair is too thick.

At ninety-three Hannah Jessup, Johanna Green's grandmother, is the oldest resident of Green Mansions. Han, as her granddaughter calls her, has been confined to a wheelchair for almost nine months following the fall that shattered her hip. Since the accident she has become increasingly confused and forgetful, and in the past few months she has developed circulatory problems.

* * *

If I were making up a story about the three old women, each one would be a queen in exile and each would tend a garden.

Virginia Merriman has been in exile so long that her arms and legs have turned to stone. Her strong hawk's face has the fine, greasy shine of old marble. Her garden is spare and dry as a desert. Strange yellow-grey blooms rise out of the sand on long, rigid stalks. Visitors to the garden shudder and move on without speaking to Mrs. Merriman. They assume she is a particularly austere example of a certain kind of stone angel, which, along with naked cherubs pissing, is a popular garden ornament in this country.

Miriam Stone has mixed feelings about being in exile. There are days when she'd rather not be found by any would-be rescuers. She squats on a stump. Knobby and gnarled, hacking at the rocky soil in her winter garden, she might be one of her own vegetables, a turnip, a rutabaga, a parsnip. "The sonsofbitches will never find me," she mutters to herself. No one, herself included, knows if this is a complaint or a dare.

The long years of exile have not diminished Hannah Jessup's beauty. To this day the king who abducted her suffers jealous rages imagining, incorrectly, that she is pining for her husband. Still, it would be worse to think that she refuses his repeated offers of marriage for any other reason. He follows her as she roams through her exquisite garden tipping her sterling silver watering can. The gorgeous blooms, pink and scarlet and cream, are the same heart shape as her face.

* * *

I have been making up stories for as long as I can remember. I would sit on my Aunt Celia's porch and watch one or another of her men friends coming up the front steps. While they were inside doing whatever it was they did that left them looking sleepy and well fed, I would invent their lives.

Mr. Berry always wore a yellow tie, and in my stories the yellow tie wound its way through his colorful life like the yellow Ganges wound its way through India in my atlas. When I grew tired of Mr. Berry, I hung him from the yardarm of a pirate ship with that same yellow tie. He continued to visit Celia, but I never again acknowledged his greeting to me, and he complained to my aunt, in my hearing, that I was a snotty little thing.

Mr. Simmons had coal-black hair and sooty eyes and gold-rimmed spectacles that he put on when there was something he really wanted to see.

As soon as he got to the bottom of the porch steps, he'd take his spectacles out of his shirt pocket, push them up on his thin nose, and he'd look up at my Aunt Celia, who was waiting for him on the top step. He'd look at her as if he'd never seen anything like her, as if he'd never laid eyes on a woman before.

Without his glasses he was a sober man, somber even, but as soon as he put on his golden spectacles, his whole face glittered, and his black eyes shone as if they'd been polished.

In my stories Mr. Simmons' spectacles were part of his face. He'd been born with them on, and all his power was in his shiny black eyes. He could see backward or forward through all time, and he could see straight into your heart.

One day Mr. Simmons came earlier than usual, before Celia was through with her bath. I watched him coming up the road, and when he got to the bottom of the steps, he fished in his front pocket for his spectacles. He drew them out so slowly, I held my breath. He slid them carefully onto his nose, and he looked up at me for a long, slow time, and he said, "You look nice, Clara." His eyes shone so brightly that they gave me a headache. I got up off the step and stuck my head in the front door and yelled to my aunt that Mr. Simmons was here, and she yelled back to send him on in.

That day in my story Mr. Simmons tried to see too far into the future, past all the stars in all the galaxies to the very end of time. And just when he was certain he was about to see what no one else had ever seen, his glasses shattered in a million pieces.

At that instant he lost all his power to see backward and forward in time. He couldn't tell you what was going to happen tomorrow or remember what had happened yesterday.

The next time Mr. Simmons came to call there was a Band-Aid wrapped inexpertly around the broken nosepiece of his golden spectacles. At supper that night Celia remarked, "Burt Simmons is slowing down, if you know what I mean."

I did know. And I knew that stories that are fashioned with care are likely to be true.

* * *

Honora Bliss told me that in its first incarnation this building represented the Southeast's sole attempt to capitalize on the success of the $1.99 steakhouses which at that time were doing a brisk business in New York City. Only the red-flocked wallpaper in the women's tub room serves as a reminder of those long-gone days that ended in financial disaster.

Soon this old building will be converted into a clubhouse. The colorful brochure promises that the Taralawn

Estates clubhouse will "comprise a viewing room with two Betamaxes for your viewing pleasure, a state-of-the-art video games room and an intimate lounge for impromptu get-togethers."

Green Mansion's lounge is not intimate. The ugly out-sized room swallows up the ill-assorted furniture. The wife of the chairman of the board of Green Mansions donated the dilapidated black stuffed Leatherette couch and the more or less matching armchair. Two dozen orange and two dozen aquamarine plastic chairs with aluminum legs and no arms were donated by a local high school, and two years ago Honora brought in the old brown card table and four folding chairs that her first husband, Monroe, had bought her. On either side of the black couch are two end tables, one wrought iron with a glass top, the other a triangular-shaped wedge of blond wood. On each of the end tables is a large lamp with découpage lampshades. No one knows who made them. "Who would admit it?" Mrs. Stone asks.

3

When I first came to Green Mansions, Honora was reserved. She made it clear that she couldn't pay me for telling stories here, and she said I'd have to fit into the established routine.

When I agreed to all her conditions, she looked at me narrowly. She didn't ask me where I was from, or how long I'd been here, or where I'd worked last, or whether I was married, or how old I was. She could tell from my voice I wasn't born or bred here. She could see I wore no wedding band. She could guess I was maybe ten years her junior, which would make me something close to fifty.

What she asked was, "What do you want to come here for to tell your stories? You could go on up to the YMCA. They got programs like that."

"These people have time to listen to stories," I said.

Honora nodded, but she didn't say anything.

"I've told stories at Ys, Mrs. Bliss. I chose Green Mansions because the people here have lived whole lives, and they have stories to tell."

"I thought you did the telling," Honora said.

"People tell me their stories and I tell them back to them," I said.

"What do you mean?"

"I listen to what they say. I listen so hard I can hear the faintest whisper. But it's not their words I hear, it's the current rushing from their lives to mine. That's where I find the story. That's what I'm listening for—the place where lives meet and are the same."

Honora made a small expulsive noise through her nose as if she'd been holding her breath. "All right," she said, "I'll give you lunch whatever days you come." And then she said, "You could have supper too, if you cared about staying that late."

"Thank you," I said, "but I won't stay for suppers."

*   *   *

The day I told my first story at Green Mansions was the day Johanna and I had our first conversation.

"Your story was about my grandmother," Johanna said. "The beautiful queen in exile, that was my grandmother."

"Did she recognize herself?" I asked Johanna.

"Yes. It made her laugh."

"I heard her," I said. "Her laugh held the story together."

"You know all about her," Johanna said. "How did you know?" And then she told me how her grandmother came to be here.

In the beginning, Johanna told me, everyone in the family had looked on Hannah Jessup's stay at Green Mansions as temporary. Mrs. Jessup was only here in this Southern town because of a sequence of unusual circumstances.

Her fall in the bathtub in her tiny Manhattan apartment came only two weeks after her daughter and son-in-law had sublet their own New York apartment and moved to Belgium for a much-sought-after eighteen-month appointment to the Antwerp office of the firm where Mr. Green had labored so long and so successfully.

Hannah Jessup's hip shattered like a china vase, and Johanna's mother flew home immediately and stayed on a cot in her mother's hospital room, high above the East River. She spent ten sleepless nights staring out at the dark river trying to imagine ways she could manage her mother's convalescence in Antwerp.

"When Han was released they told my mother she could never live alone again. A social worker in the hospital arranged for two women to stay with Han. One in the day and one at night. My mother wired my father that she couldn't come back yet."

For three weeks Johanna's mother stayed in a hotel at night; during the day she stayed with her mother, who signaled her to come into the bathroom, where she whispered that the daytime woman was a thief and the nighttime woman was a drunk.

"My mother called her brother," Johanna said, "but he's got troubles of his own."

Johanna's mother tried unsuccessfully to get Hannah Jessup into a home in the city, near the apartment to which she and her husband would return when the eighteen months was over, but the waiting lists were long. There would be at least a six- to eight-months' wait for an opening in any of the supposedly decent places.

"We got her in here so she could be near me," Johanna said. "There was nothing else to do."

"It's a grave responsibility for you," I said.

Johanna looked startled. "Oh, no. I mean, there was . . ."

"Nothing else to do," I said.

"You don't know all about me, do you?" Johanna asked from behind the tangle of wine-colored hair that hangs over her face like a curtain.

* * *

If I told Johanna's story, the sky would be the limit. That's what she thinks. But she is not ten or twenty or even thirty. Her teeth do not gleam like pearls. She is not a prodigy or a poet.

Still, I can imagine beginnings and middles and ends for Johanna. I can reimagine possibilities no longer possible for me.

* * *

Johanna can't stand to be here and can't wait to go. She frequently shows up just at suppertime, when she knows visitors are supposed to leave.

"Miss Green," Honora said to her yesterday, "how come you always come right when you're supposed to go?"

"I wasn't aware of the time, Mrs. Bliss."

"You got a watch on."

"It stopped. Watches stop on me."

Watches stop on Johanna's wrist. Sound watches, watches she has inherited from people for whom they performed perfectly for years, die on her wrist in a matter of weeks.

4

My father's sister Celia brought me up, or down, according to some people. To support us Celia worked three hours a day powdering donuts at the bakery and three hours three nights a week serving drinks at a roadhouse on the outskirts of town.

Celia had never married but she couldn't claim maidenhood, having lost her head at sixteen, as the local wits had it. Celia frequently lost her head but never for very long. "I'm afraid I'm shallow," she'd tell me when she was about to stop seeing some gentleman. "And well, Clara, sweetheart, once the feeling's gone, why, I'm gone too."

I always assumed that Celia would leave me one day just as airily as she left her suitors. But she never did.

I left her when I was seventeen.

Celia gave me her alarm clock and the beat-up Bible that had belonged to my father to take with me. "He loved it," she said, swatting the dusty black cover with her handkerchief, "and I never look at it. You have it." I opened the Bible. In the margin of the first page my father had written a note to himself: "The best narrators efface themselves."

"I won't write, Clara," Celia said. "You know how I don't

write letters. But I'll be happy to see you any time you want to come back."

I never did want to. I have never wanted to go back anywhere.

* * *

After my third visit to Green Mansions, Honora said, "Hannah Jessup says you're better than TV, and Mr. Martin wanted to know if we had some sort of contract with you and how long it was for. It would be nice if you kept coming. They're used to you."

I told her I would.

"You'll stay," she said.

I could tell by the way she said it that she only half believed me. That day she told me something of the history of Mr. Martin and his wife, Charlotte. It occurred to me as I listened to her that Honora was seducing me. She would make sure I stayed. She would fuel my imagination.

The next time I came she said she'd seen me talking to Johanna. "She's curious about you," Honora said. "She asked me where you came from."

"I take it she grew up in New York," I said.

"Johanna was born and raised in New York City," Honora said, as if she were offering me an exotic fact. "The island of Manhattan."

"She was telling me her grandmother speaks German and French and Russian," I said.

"If you make up another story about Mrs. Jessup you could put that in it."

"Everybody knew it was she," I said, pleased that it was so.

"You told it just the way she talks," Honora said.

"I could tell dozens more stories about Hannah Jessup," I said.

Honora nodded. "There's a lot to Hannah Jessup."
She waited for me to give her some signal that she should
continue. "She's been here awhile," I said.

Honora made a swift calculation in her head. "Seven
months. In the early days she thought she was visiting.
I'd tell her it was time for bed, and she'd say, 'I should be
getting home.' And I'd go along and say it was so late,
and I'd already made up a bed for her, and wouldn't she
please stay. And then she'd say, well, she would then if it
wasn't any trouble.

"Those days she'd speak to the other residents if they
said something to her first, and she talked a lot to Mr.
Martin. They talked about all kind of things. They talked
about singing canaries. Mr. Martin said singing female
canaries will abandon their nest. And Mrs. Jessup said she
would've given anything to be able to sing, and Mr. Martin said, 'But you wouldn't have abandoned your family.'
'I would've abandoned everybody,' she said. 'Oh, if I
could've sung like Maria Callas, I would've abandoned
everybody.' And Mr. Martin said him and his wife loved
the opera. They listened every Sunday to Texaco.

"Later on she was bothered about the aides, and I knew
she was getting worse. 'They come in,' she'd tell me,
'without an invitation. Those girls come in, and they put
their feet up on my table and read magazines. They call
me honey. It's disgusting.' And I'd tell her I'd speak to
them, which I did, but it didn't do any good."

* * *

Every Monday, Wednesday and Friday afternoon, when
Johanna comes to visit, her grandmother has a new complaint about the strangers in her house.

"My God, darling, that woman over there," she says,
pointing to Mrs. Merriman, who stares unblinking at the
ceiling. "She urinates in my living room. I told her, 'My

God, can't you go into the toilet like a decent human being?'
but she doesn't answer me."

As soon as Johanna stepped into the lounge this afternoon, Hannah Jessup cried out, "Johanna, please come. Please. They took away my nice mahogany end table that you always liked so much, and they brought in this terrible furniture that I didn't order. Call Altman's for me right away, darling. Please, darling," she cries, "you have to tell them there's been a mistake."

Miriam Stone is indignant at this display of disorder. "There's been a mistake all right. She belongs in a loony bin."

Johanna is overcome with laughter.

"Oh, my God," Mrs. Stone says, "you're crazy too."

"I'm not crazy. My grandmother isn't crazy either."

"She didn't say one word that makes sense," Miriam Stone insists.

"She's talking in code," Johanna says.

"Like some other people I could mention," Mrs. Stone says, and she swings her wheelchair a half-turn around to fix me with a stare.

* * *

Johanna comes every Monday, Wednesday and Friday afternoon to see her grandmother.

She cannot keep her eyes off the clock. "Mom is coming to see you, Han," she says, looking over her grandmother's head at the dun-colored clock on the wall. "She's coming at Thanksgiving. For two whole weeks. And she'll be home for good in the spring." Johanna watches the punishingly slow sweep of the seconds. "Thanksgiving's less than three months away."

* * *

Johanna has one eye on her grandmother, one eye on the clock and the third eye on me.

"Johanna's studying you," Honora says.

"And I'm studying her," I reply.

Johanna smiles across the room at me. But we say little more than hello and good-bye. Since our first conversations about her grandmother, our longest talk has been about the heat. But when she saw me getting ready to leave this afternoon, she hurried to speak to me. "Last night I dreamed I took a picture of you," she said, rushing the words together. "But when I put the negative in the developing solution, the face emerging was my own." Before I could respond, she said, "We're alike. That's why you've been watching me. Because we're alike."

"But I decided long ago who I would be," I said.

Johanna's face reddened as if I'd struck her. She walked away. I called out to her, but she kept on going.

"I don't feel superior," I said, loud enough so I knew she heard me. "Maybe you've gained something by waiting to decide."

Johanna turned around. "Is that why you're interested in me?"

"I can't imagine my life any other way than it is, but I can imagine all kinds of lives for you. And . . ."

"You can?" Johanna smiled a spectacularly sunny smile. "So can I. If I had three hundred years to live, I couldn't do all the things I want to do."

"And I like you," I finished.

"Oh," Johanna said with a little drop in her voice that could only be disappointment.

"You're naturally curious about each other," Honora said as she walked me to the door. "You're both here. You both got time to be. You neither one has a regular full-time job. You neither one is married. Or has children staying with you. At least, you didn't say so."

"You see us both outside of things."

"You seem to like it outside," Honora says.
"As long as I can look in," I said.

* * *

I imagine Johanna living in a hut in the forest. *She lives frugally but not simply. She eats dark bread and cheddar cheese and cold peas straight out of a can.*

The hut is disordered. Panes of glass are missing from each of the windows. The lock on the front door no longer works. The posts that support the lean-to porch lean so precipitously that it can only be a matter of months before it caves in altogether.

Contact sheets litter the floor. Rolls of exposed film snake around the legs of chairs. Negatives are stacked up in the corners of the tiny kitchen. And the deadly chemicals she uses to develop her pictures line the bathroom shelves, displacing the shampoos and Tampax and the bars of Ivory Soap that once were there.

It is no longer possible to invite anyone to visit her here, and so she spends a great deal of time alone in her hut. It has been so long since she entertained that she can no longer remember whether the wineglass goes to the left or the right of the dinner plate.

5

My coming to Green Mansions when I did was fortunate, for only three days before, Mr. Martin had demolished the TV. It still sits in the middle of the room, a giant console on wobbly legs with a clean twenty-seven-inch square hole where the screen should be.

"Me and Mr. Martin and Mrs. Jessup, we were all sitting here together," Honora explained, "watching this show that comes on every Sunday afternoon about books. Mrs. Stone was watching too. 'Under protest,' she said. 'Even my idiot daughters read books,' she said. "The man who was on every week said this book they were going to talk about was setting the groves of academia on fire. I was about to ask Mr. Martin what exactly that meant,but Mrs. Stone started shouting—'They can read all they want. You notice it doesn't stop them from dumping their mother in this pit.' And Mrs. Jessup said, 'Please, I can't hear when you scream like that.'

"I heard the TV man say, 'It gives me great pleasure to introduce the author of *Life as Metaphor*,' and the next thing I know, Mr. Martin, who was sitting next to Mrs. Stone, grabbed Mrs. Stone's cane out of her hand, and Mrs. Jessup called out, 'Oh, my God, don't kill her.' Before I could draw a breath, Mr. Martin smashed the curved end of that cane right through the middle of the picture. There was this loud popping noise, and all these tiny little pieces of glass fell out onto the floor.

"I didn't say anything at all. Nobody did. Not even Mrs. Stone. It was so surprising. That's what made us all so quiet. It was so surprising that it was Mr. Martin did that. Mr. Martin stood up then, and he looked as tall as a stork looking down at us, and his face was as white as a white sky. 'Please, excuse me,' he said, and he went to his room and stayed there and didn't come out even at suppertime. So I took him a tray to his room, and he was very polite but he didn't say one word about the TV, and I didn't either. I never did say anything more about it. I just cleaned up all the glass. And I got Frank's wirecutters at home that night, and the next day I cut all those hanging wires out."

* * *

For a long time my coming and going at Green Mansions was irregular, frequent but without a pattern. Honora didn't approve. Finally she spoke to me.

"They wait for you now, Clara. Even Mrs. Stone. You come regular so they know they can count on you, or you don't come at all."

It cost her something to make that condition because she wasn't sure I'd agree to it. But she was firm. "You're no good to me if I can't count on you," she said. "I had enough of that with Monroe."

"Your husband."

"My first husband." Honora laughed.

"Were you in love with him?" I asked her.

"Oh, yes. I was just a girl, and he was very handsome and tall, and he had broad shoulders like I like. He had all kind of plans about what he was going to do, and he wrote me letters about how beautiful I was. I was nice-looking. We looked good together, and I liked that. We went dancing, and everybody looked up when we walked into the dance hall. We fit just right for dancing. We might have been one person we fit together so good.

"Monroe and my daddy didn't have much use for each other. Daddy thought Monroe was too raw and flashy. After we was married and I was going on about Daddy, Monroe said, 'He's nothing like what you say. He's just a boring old man who likes to hear himself talk.'

"Daddy died the year Monroe and I got married, so he never did get to see that Monroe got to amount to something. And he didn't get to see that Monroe ran around on me.

"My father ran around on my mother, but still I held him up as an example of what a man should be. The day I left Monroe, he said, 'I don't understand it, Honora. He did worse than I did, and you think he's God, and you think I'm a piece of shit.' Monroe lied a lot but he told the truth that day.

"I hated his lying. It disgusted me to see him squirming like a fish on a hook, making up any old thing that came into his head so I wouldn't be mad at him. The worst thing was I could see he was in a panic. He'd be starting to sweat, hopping around, and it made me want to rip his heart out.

"Everybody thought everything was fine with me and Monroe. He made a lot of money selling shoes for Mr. Lovett, even before he bought him out, and he gave me money to go buy dresses, and we bought a bigger house in the part of town where my folks had their house and a new car and what all. None of it meant anything to me, and that ate at Monroe. 'I don't care about anything you're giving me, Monroe,' I'd say to myself, and he heard me every time.

"But everybody thought we was just fine because Monroe invited all the people at the shoe company to come by for supper all the time, and I knew how to cook, and we had plenty of liquor on hand. And Monroe and me danced together just as good as when I still loved him. When they was all gone, he'd say, 'That was a great party, Honora. Everybody said so, and everybody still says how beautiful you are. Jack Rider came right up to me and said, "Honora's the best-looking black woman in this town, Monroe." ' But he never come near me in the bed after one of those parties unless he was so drunk he couldn't do nothin' anyway.

"When my first baby, Alice, was born, Monroe was in Detroit buying another store. When he got back, he took one look at Alice and said, 'She's got squinty eyes. She's ugly.' He didn't want to hold her.

"By the time we moved to Detroit, Alice was three and everyone fussed over her. Monroe did too, when he was around. But I figured he only liked her now because she was pretty enough to show off. So it didn't make a difference to me. It was too late.

"I hated Detroit. I hated everything about it. It was cold and rainy in the winter and steamy in the summer. It was in Detroit I knew for certain he was seeing other women. I caught him in our bed with some girl from the company. She wasn't as smart as me by half, or as pretty either.

"All night long Monroe said, 'This girl doesn't mean anything to me, Honora. She's nothing to me.'

"Monroe thought that would make it better to me. But it made it worse. He just did it the way you'd eat another piece of pie or smoke another cigarette.

" 'You've got no passion,' I said.

"I could never forgive him for that. So I took Alice and I came home. He begged me to stay. He said he loved me and he couldn't live without me, that everything he'd done he'd done for me and without me there was no point to any of it.

" 'You're all for show, Monroe,' I said. 'There isn't any Monroe for me to stay for.' And I walked out the door."

6

Mrs. Stone almost never speaks to me, but today, when I finished my story, she motioned me to come to her.

"I've heard better," she said, looking up at me. "My father told stories, and so did my grandfather. Stories with plots. Wonderful stories. You couldn't imagine, of course. You're not in their league. But that's not what I wanted to tell you. Sit down, why don't you, Clara. Sit down beside me."

She waited for me to pull a chair over, and then she said, "I wanted to tell you my Uncle Jacob was a storyteller too, and he ended up in jail for perjury."

"That's extremely interesting," I said, enjoying myself.

Mrs. Stone smiled. "I thought you'd think so."

* * *

Sometimes Celia would tell me what it was like when my father and she were children together "in this very house."

"Your father told a lie every chance he got, Clara," she said. "The more trouble he thought he was in, the better the lie was.

"One time he was kept after school for cutting up in class, and he walked in the house at five p.m., and before my mother asked him one solitary question, he launched into this story about how Mr. Ferris, the assistant manager at the Missouri Midland Bank and Trust, had passed him on the Mill Road on his way home and asked would he like a ride in his bright blue Ford. 'Well,' your father said, 'we hadn't gone more than a mile when the left front tire blew out.' The car wobbled all over the road, he said, and Mr. Ferris started to sweat, and turning the wheel this way and that he brought the Ford to a stop, but not before they had gone off the road with their back end in a ditch. 'I asked Mr. Ferris did he have a jack,' your father said, 'and a spare, and he said, very snappish, "Of course," and he got out and opened the trunk.'

" 'I know,' I said to your father, 'there wasn't any jack and there wasn't any tire.'

" 'Of course there was a tire and a jack,' your father said. 'The point is that shoved way, way back in the corner was this green strongbox with a fancy lock, almost like a jewel. Mr. Ferris saw me look at it, and he said, "There's nothing in there, just tools." But he said it too fast, if you know what I mean, and he tried to shove that box even farther into the corner, and his hand was trembling.'

"Well, Clara, your grandmother couldn't hold back anymore," my Aunt Celia said. "She burst out laughing. 'An hour ago in the market Mrs. Ferris was complaining to me that Mr. Ferris had been out of town all week and wouldn't be back till Friday,' she said.

"Your father I could see was halfway between being insulted that your grandmother didn't buy his story and relieved that the truth was out," my Aunt Celia said. "But he didn't miss a beat. 'Mom,' he said, lowering his voice, 'Mr. Ferris is no more out of town than I am. But you have to give me your solemn word you won't tell Mrs. Ferris what I'm about to tell you.'

"That particular night after we had done our homework and were on our way up the stairs to bed, I said to your father, 'You're the best liar I ever met.'

" 'I'm not telling lies, Celia, I'm making up the truth.'

" 'Well, you sure are good at it.'

" 'You got to put in a lot of details,' he said."

7

The black Leatherette couch is so caved in, so low to the ground, so miserable, that even the découpage lamps on top of the end tables lean away.

"Who ordered it?" Hannah Jessup asks. "It doesn't go with any of my pieces."

Since no one ever sits on it, Honora and David Martin and I shove the couch into the darkest corner of the room, near the supply closet.

"The end tables too," Mrs. Jessup instructs, "and those hideous lamps."

The couch is mine now. Stuck away in the corner I can range and roam and meander and drift. I can dream, I can fly. I can hear hearts beating and watches ticking. I can see.

* * *

Johanna's walk is disconcerting. Her head, like the head of an eager bird, tilts forward on her long neck. The rest of her body is pulled back. Unseen hands clutch at her ankles, dragging her away.

"Are you coming or going?" her grandmother asks.

"I'm not late, am I, Han?" Johanna rushes forward then stops short, balancing on one leg, looking over her shoulder as if there were something behind her urging her back.

Rapunzel could never make up her mind whether to let down her long hair or to pin it up in a bun at the back of her head, whether to fish or cut bait . . .

Johanna lunges for her accustomed chair, and the chair topples onto its side.

"Is she coming or going?" Miriam Stone asks.

"Who is that?" Hannah Jessup demands. "That old woman repeats what I say, and I never saw her before in my life. I wish you would pull your hair back off your face, Johanna. I can't even see who I'm talking to."

Johanna rights the chair with undue deliberation and settles herself squarely on the plastic seat.

"What does your mother say about it?" her grandmother asks.

"About what?"

"Your hair."

"She likes it."

Immense scorn vibrates Hannah Jessup's nostrils. "She likes that mop in your face, and she said it all turned out for the best that I came here. She said I'd like the warmer weather. She said it would be so nice to be with you."

"She writes you almost every day," Johanna murmurs in a little bleating voice.

"Who writes me every day?"

"Mom does."

"Oh, her. I'm tired. I have to take a nap."

Johanna springs up. "I can stay if you want." She leans forward, and her dark hair swings exuberantly on her neck. "I could stay while you sleep."

"It's silly," Hannah Jessup says.

"Well, I'll see you Friday then. I'll stay longer to make up for today."

"She trips over her own feet rushing to get out of here," Mrs. Stone says. "I watch her every day."

"Did you invite her?" Hannah Jessup asks her granddaughter.

"Not I," Johanna sings under her breath. "I never saw her before in my life."

*   *   *

What interests me about Johanna's looks is their instability. She looks, in general, younger than her thirty-eight years, but sometimes she looks as worn as a woman well past middle age. She is conventionally pretty most of the time, but there are days when she is spectacularly ugly. There are days when her eyebrows grow together like a forest and her eyes sink back in her head; days when her long electric hair short-circuits, plastered to her skull like a rubber bathing cap. Her plump bosom is flat as a plate, a hump rises across her shoulders and her modest nose sprawls across her face like urban blight across the nation.

Her outfits are unremarkable—faded blue jeans, an old shirt, running shoes. But sometimes she achieves a demented effect, as if she had stood blindfolded and pulled clothes at random out of someone else's closet; clothes so big only her fingertips and her eyes are visible; clothes so small she is strangled by them; shoes so run-down at the heels that she shuffles along like an old crone.

Occasionally she is stunning. Her nose narrows, her lashes thicken, her chin lifts, and she smiles a satisfied smile.

*   *   *

"I see you got scalped," Mrs. Stone remarks as Johanna skulks into the lounge.

"It's not what I wanted," Johanna cries, tugging at her wine-colored hair as if she could restore the lopped-off inches. "It's not what I wanted at all."

"It's out of your eyes," her grandmother says, "that's the main thing."

Every time Johanna goes to the beauty parlor, she expects that this is the haircut that will perfectly frame her face and alter her life. She approaches the movie theater with a thrill of expectation. This is the movie that will delight and inspire her. Each new year she is certain will be her year. She goes to sleep with high hopes and a rapid pulse. Tonight's dream will reveal me to myself. Tonight's the night.

No matter that the haircut is indifferent, the movie dull, the dream a dud, the year a bust. Johanna has always another to look forward to.

8

Mrs. Merriman had been a resident of Green Mansions when Honora first came four years ago. She was the only resident who predated Honora's arrival, and there was nothing in her chart to give a clue to her history, only the scrawled notation "No known family." She wore a gold band on the third finger of her left hand so it was assumed that she was married or had been.

The former director of Green Mansions thought she remembered that Mrs. Merriman had been brought in by a neighbor, a Mrs. Garner.

Honora went through every Garner in the phone book, which took in three counties, but no one knew a Mrs. Merriman.

"I thought if I just knew where she came from or who her people were I might do more for her," Honora explained to me now, three years later, spreading the file open on her lap to show me there was nothing there except the sheaf of physical workups and recommendations that grew steadily and never said anything different.

"If I knew she had children somewhere, I might have talked to her in a way that would matter to her. Or a husband with a particular name. A husband dead or alive. If I just had a name to say aloud."

But Honora had never been able to turn up anything. After the futile search for the right Mrs. Garner, Honora called every social service agency in the book. "I thought Mrs. Merriman might have applied for assistance some time—Meals on Wheels or something like that. My daughter, Alice, was visiting then, and this particular afternoon

I was going to carry her to the station so she could get her bus back to Philadelphia. While she was finishing packing up, I got on the phone to an agency in Raleigh about Mrs. Merriman. When I hung up the phone, Alice was standing in the doorway with her suitcase beside her. She was standing there so stiff you could've cracked her in two with a look. Before I could open my mouth to ask what was wrong, the words came flying out of her. 'You're going to let me miss my bus while you carry on about that old woman, that old white woman who can't even talk.'

" 'We'll make it on time,' I said when we got in the car.

" 'That's not the point.' She shouted it at me. 'You're obsessed with her.' Then she said, 'You could've come in and talked to me while I packed. You could've called about her later.'

"When we pulled up to the bus station, her bus was just pulling up, and I said, 'Alice, I'd do anything for you. I love you more than I love anyone.'

" 'I have to fight so hard for everything,' she said. I didn't know if she was confessing to me or blaming me."

Honora looked toward the door as if she expected to see Alice standing there. "I thought once I had something," she said, turning back to me. "An LPN at a home in Zebulon had known a Mrs. Virgie Merriman. I remember exactly what she said, the exact tone of her voice, because when she said Virgie, I thought, it's my Mrs. Merriman. But what she said was, 'I had a Mrs. Virgie Merriman to die on me. She was a big old rawboned woman and she had leukemia so bad she shrunk away to nothing. A puff of wind would have blown her away.' "

9

On the morning of my eleventh birthday I asked Celia if my parents hadn't left me some message before they died.

I had cherished this belief for a long time. I imagined they had given the message to Celia for safekeeping, and that it was in a vault in the bank awaiting my maturity, which I fixed at the advent of my eleventh year.

"A message?" Celia asked.

"To be delivered to me by you."

"No, sweetheart."

"Maybe you're not supposed to tell me yet. Maybe I have to be thirteen."

Celia shook her head.

"Are you positive?"

"Clara, honey, they didn't *know* they were going to die in that airplane."

I went out to the porch then and sat on the front steps. Celia didn't disturb me, and when it got too cold to sit out there any longer, I went up to my room, where I tore a sheet of paper out of my school notebook and wrote myself this message from my mother and father.

Dear Darling Daughter,

On this your 11th birthday you are grown up enough for us to tell you what we want is for you to be a warrior. This takes a long time honey and a lot of training. You must be as patient as the woman Penelope in that story by Homer the Greek, but you can't sit and do nothing. You have to be ready at all times to do what

is called for even if you're ambushed. Last but not least you have to be lighthearted but not silly and don't think everything that happens to you is a big tragedy.
We know you will make us proud of you.

Your Devoted Mother and Father

When Celia called upstairs to ask was I planning on having supper, I called back an enthusiastic yes. She yelled back "good" because she had a special dessert. She had made us each a chocolate cupcake and had stuck eleven candles in mine. We ate our birthday cupcake before we ate our chop suey.

When we were through with dinner, Celia gave me a jackknife for a present. "You didn't ask for it," she said. "But I thought it might come in handy."

"Oh, it will," I said. The jackknife Celia gave me was the best, the most fortuitous gift in all the world.

* * *

At lunch today Mrs. Stone threw her bowl of butterscotch pudding on the floor, remarking on its resemblance to dog shit. She followed up that observation with a string of epithets cataloging Honora's resemblance to a large black turd. She concluded by damning me as worse than a turd. "You, Clara," she snarled at me, "you're a purveyor of twaddle."

"You're not alone in that judgment, Mrs. Stone," I said.

"Of course I'm not," Mrs. Stone yelled. "It's common knowledge."

After she had wiped up the pudding, Honora motioned me to follow her into her office. It is a small room that functioned as a staff lounge and nurses' station in the days before Green Mansions was sold. The remaining residents' charts are still in their metal rack. Occasionally Honora notes something about changes in medication or sleep disturbances on the charts, and she writes down anything she wants to tell or ask Dr. Milne when he makes his weekly visit. But she refers almost daily to the large accordion file with the shoestring tie, where she keeps letters written to her by members of the residents' families.

"Listen to this," she says. "They wrote me this just about this time last year.

" 'Dear Ms. Bliss: It is our understanding that you have given our father reason to believe that you are not convinced of the necessity of our mother being in a home, despite her severe arthritis, because she is ambulatory. Ms. Bliss, she is too ambulatory. Last year she would walk downtown, two and a half miles from our home, attired in a flannel nightgown, rubber galoshes and the mink coat our father gave her for their silver wedding anniversary. She accosted total strangers to complain that our father abused her, which he never did, being always very understanding of her many eccentricities, which we have all had to put up with. Way before she started walking all over kingdom come, she stopped doing housework and accused the maid of having an affair with our father. On top of everything else, she began to say completely incomprehensible things like a totally crazy person. The following is a direct quote witnessed by my sister and myself and screamed at us for no reason: ''Your father wants to give the world a Coke and keep it company.''

" 'I hope this letter will make it perfectly clear that at this point in time our mother has serious problems which no one in their right mind could expect our father to put up with—or us either. Both of us are married and have children and our own lives to lead, and we do not even reside in this state anymore. Barbara and her husband, Paul, live in Chevy Chase, Maryland, and I live in Minneapolis, where we moved two years ago. Before Barbara and I even got married, our mother was hostile and abusive. She called and still calls my husband, Vaughan, *vontz*, which is the Yiddish word for bedbug, and at a public dinner party she told Barbara in front of everyone that her then fiancé, Paul, had no guts, which is a complete and total lie.

" 'Despite all this my sister and I have, of course, every intention of keeping up with our mother, and naturally we will visit when we can, although pressing activities prevent us from getting down as much as we would like.

" 'We sincerely hope that this clarifies the situation, and we regret that you will soon see for yourself how necessary it is that our mother not be out loose on the streets wrecking havoc on innocent bystanders.

" 'Cordially, Gail and Barbara Stone.' "

"Have they ever come to see her?" I asked Honora.

"Once," she said. "They stayed fifteen minutes."

"She's better off without them."

"That's what I decided," Honora said. "But I'm not sure I'm right."

The last time Vernon Stone came to see his wife—"That was two weeks before you came, Clara," Honora explained—she told him, "If you ever come here again, I'll chop your head off."

"He turned white as a sheet," Honora said, "and he stood stock still like he was growing up out of the floor. Mrs. Stone got up out of her wheelchair. She took up her cane and she thumped across the room to the TV, and she turned it up as loud as it would go and stood there in front of it, all bent over, leaning on her cane.

"So I went over to him and told him it might be better if he didn't come around for a little while."

"Naturally, if it's upsetting her, I won't come," Vernon Stone had said to Honora.

When he'd gone, Honora said, Mrs. Stone turned off the TV. "And she said out loud—I was halfway across the room and I heard her clear as a bell—'You don't have to tell me what he said. He said, "Naturally, if it's upsetting her, I won't come." ' "

* * *

"My husband, Vernon, doesn't visit me anymore," Miriam Stone tells Johanna and her grandmother. "He doesn't want to upset me."

"I have no idea what she means," Mrs. Jessup says to Johanna. "What is she talking about?"

"Lost love," Mrs. Stone says grimly. "Like one of Clara's stories."

Hannah Jessup closes her eyes. "Her stories have some point."

"You did love him once then," Johanna prompts.

"That was so long ago," Mrs. Stone says. "I was sixteen."

"And he loved you," Johanna persists.

"I was pretty, believe it or not. He never saw anything beyond that."

"Maybe you're not giving him credit."

"Everyone gives him credit. He's got enough credit to buy Fort Knox. He doesn't need more from me. I loathe him. I've loathed him for forty years. Everything I should have had he gave away to strangers. He would rise up out of a deep sleep at four in the morning and drive thirty miles in the pouring rain to help a stranger who dialed by accident, but he wouldn't come with me to see my mother when she was dying."

"It's not our affair, Johanna. Why does she tell us such intimate things?"

But Johanna hardly hears her grandmother's protests.

Her pupils are glassy and fixed as stars. "Why did you stay with him? How can you stay forty years with someone you hate?"

"It's a basic laziness in my character. I inherited it from my mother. I didn't have the stamina to change everything all around. It would've been a mess with the children. And you have to sort out who gets what and go talk to the lawyers and make a big to-do with the whole family and his mother and my mother. Oof." She sighs deeply, as if the thought still exhausts her. "The only lawyer I knew was Roger Fine, and I didn't like him. About twenty-five years ago I actually did call him, but his secretary put me on hold. I stayed on hold for five minutes, my heart in my mouth, waiting for him to come on the line. And then I remembered I had a pot roast boiling away on the stove. I could smell the meat beginning to burn so I hung up. And that was that."

* * *

"I never met a woman," my Aunt Celia told me, "who didn't know the score. Even Annie Settle, who had a neck as long as a telephone pole and blue eyes as big as saucers. Even Annie, who sniffed poems as if they were flowers and never knew what day of the week it was, even Annie Settle was born knowing love doesn't conquer all.

"Men are the romantic ones, Clara. That's why we fall in love with them and why we feel superior."

* * *

Honora showed me a newspaper photo of the construction at Green Mansions. The caption said, "New condominiums, Taralawn Estates, to rise on rest home acreage." Beneath the picture was a line or two about the Dixieland

Construction Company's other major projects, and at the end of the story, Harley Creech, the foreman of the project, was quoted. "This heat's pretty terrible, but we're sticking right close to our projected timetable."

Privately Harley Creech told Honora he considered the conversion of Green Mansions into a clubhouse for Taralawn Estates "ill-advised. You can't make chicken salad out of chicken shit, Mrs. Bliss. Any fool knows that."

Twice a week when Harley comes around to supervise the progress of his crew, Honora goes out to badger the foreman into another equivocal concession.

"He says this heat can't hold," she says. "Not this late in September, this hot and not a drop of rain. A serious rain could hold him up for a good long while, that's what he said."

Still Honora dreams, she says, of old men lying by the side of the road and boarded-up houses with Xs on the windows.

10

When I was thirteen I surprised my Aunt Celia gazing at an old picture album. "You're always lurking," she accused me, slamming the album shut so dust sprang out and made her cough.

"I am not lurking," I replied. "I am practicing blending in."

"What do you want to blend in for? The thing is to be

noticed," she said, and she shook her fresh-washed hair for emphasis.

"Did you know," I told her, "that ermines and snowshoe hares change color according to the season? In winter they are snow white and in the autumn they are leaf brown."

"Is that really right?"

"Flounder and halibut can change their color and their pattern too. If you saw them on the bottom of the sea you wouldn't even know they were there."

"Not much chance of my spending any time at the bottom of the sea," Celia said, and yawned.

"If an octopus is swimming among clumps of orange sargassum, it will turn orange."

"I don't know what sargassum is, Clara. If we're going to talk in this vein, I'd appreciate knowing what we're talking about."

"It's an algae and it floats in the water like a waving weed and it has spore-bearing structures on it."

"Oh," Celia said.

"As the octopus moves through the sargassum weeds, it only uses two of its arms," I continued. "It holds the other six up over its body so it looks like a waving weed too."

"You can't see a crab-spider if it's sitting in the middle of a sunflower," Celia said. "Your mother showed me that one day."

"Yes, yes. That's it exactly. And there's chameleons and sloths. Sloths have very thick hair and they have symbiotic green algae living in their hair so the sloth's hair looks green to match the jungle, and no one knows they're there."

Celia looked straight up at me then. "Clara, do you think someone's hunting you down or something? Stalking you?"

"I am stalking," I explained. "If you are real quiet and blend in, you can see things. You can understand. As soon as you're noticed, you might as well forget it."

"Stick this back up in the closet for me, will you?" Celia said, handing me the album. "Way up on the top shelf. Just move that junk out of the way."

When I had secured the album, Celia said, "Do you remember that artist fellow, Gerald? He used to watch me so close it made me crazy, and then one night I caught him rummaging around in my drawer where I keep my letters. Just watch out you don't turn into a sneak."

*   *   *

A few days ago I asked Johanna if she would bring in some of her photographs.

"How did you know I take pictures?"

"She's an undercover agent," Mrs. Stone said. "Clara Julian is not her real name."

"You told me yourself," I answered Johanna. "Don't you remember?"

"My wife took pictures," David Martin said. "She was very good."

Mrs. Stone mimed someone writing on a pad. "A reporter. A snoop doing an exposé on nursing homes. Why does she bother with Johanna? She should interview me."

"What kind of pictures do you take?" Honora asked Johanna.

"Portraits. Faces," Johanna told her.

"Please bring them," Honora said.

"I haven't worked seriously in a long time," Johanna hedged.

"You think I'm kidding?" Mrs. Stone continued. "I'm not kidding. What do we know about Clara Julian? Nothing. Zilch."

"I'm not an agent, Mrs. Stone," I said. "Or a reporter. But I would like to interview you."

"Hah!" Mrs. Stone snorts. She wheels herself out of our

little circle. "Who could believe a storyteller," she calls back over her shoulder.

After lunch I asked Mrs. Stone if I could interview her at her convenience.

"Well, it's not convenient now," she said. "I nap after lunch, as everyone knows."

"Perhaps when you get up," I said.

"Perhaps," she said. "You want some background stuff on me. Right?"

"Yes," I said. "That's it exactly."

"I thought so," Mrs. Stone said. "You might want to make up a story about me someday."

"I had thought about it, if you have no objections."

"I wouldn't object," Mrs. Stone said, "as long as it's tasteful."

* * *

At some point every day Honora sits down to talk to Mrs. Merriman. She tells her what day it is and what month and year. She explains that all the racket outside is the workmen building the condominiums. She tells her what she heard on the news that morning.

"You're wonderful to her," I said to Honora. "You seem close to all of them."

"I don't know what good it does," Honora said. "Used to I wrote down what each patient liked and didn't like. I wrote down their favorite foods and what they didn't have a taste for. And their favorite magazine stories and books. And what colors. And radio and TV shows and what kind of music. I asked them and their families all these questions, and I wrote it all down. But I couldn't make it work. I couldn't get everyone their favorite food. I couldn't see that each one had something their favorite color in their room. I couldn't even switch the TV right at the right times so everyone got a turn to see the show they like best."

Unemployment is rising, Honora tells Mrs. Merriman this morning, and embassies are burning, but there's a man in Seattle who risked his life to save a woman he didn't know from drowning, and a little girl in Iowa is thriving on a kidney her older brother gave her. Clara's going to tell a story before lunch, and Johanna will be coming later to see her grandmother, and she's promised to bring her photographs to show everyone. Mr. Martin got a postcard from his son with a Turkish postmark.

*   *   *

Johanna's photographs are startling. There is nothing between the viewer and the face Johanna presents. It is like looking into the clearest of mirrors and seeing yourself with someone else's face.

In her pictures Johanna's sense of proportion is exact. She knows what must be forward and what in the background, what in light and what in shadow, what weight to give to what. In her life she does not discriminate so nicely. "My car won't start," Johanna cries across the parking lot. "Sonofabitch, oh goddamn sonofabitch. The engine won't turn over." She slumps across the steering wheel, defeated by all the machinery of her stalled life.

"And my tub won't drain." *The water, stagnant as her life, stays, reproaching her. Nothing new can come in, she thinks. In a day or two there is a fine, scummy film on top of the water.*

The pipes freeze and her heart turns icy cold. If they burst, she thinks, holding one pale hand over her breast, I am a goner.

The toilet overflows, and she sees the porcelain bowl can no more contain its deposits than her heart can contain its sorrows. I can't contain my sorrows, she thinks, watching with dismay as one tiny, sorrowful turd slips over the edge of the toilet.

11

Week after week Johanna sits in her accustomed chair and waits for something to happen. She doesn't move a muscle, yet the curtains flap, the floor squeaks and the old walls groan. The goatish reek of her dissatisfaction shrivels Honora's fern, which is all the way across the room, and when Johanna sighs the lights flicker.

. . . *Anomie picked up an old* Road and Track *magazine that had belonged to her daddy and riffled through it.*

"We could take in a flick," the young man said, sitting down beside her.

Anomie groaned and tossed the magazine on the floor. "Oh, Sal, please, not another movie."

"We could go dancing or driving or stay here and talk."

Anomie drummed her fingers on the arm of the sofa. "It's past time for my nap."

"You don't seem to care if you hurt people's feelings."

"Fillings?" Anomie pronounced the word in an odd way, as if it were foreign.

"Yeah, you know, feelings," Sal said. He got off the couch and went to stand by the open window. The smell of new-mown grass came in on the breeze. "I can smell the grass," he said. "We could go on a picnic—burgers and fries, blue skies, a little vino." Sal smiled at her, and his smile was so warm she could feel its glow clear across the room.

Anomie felt a tiny icy stab of fear in the middle of her backbone. Sal was coming toward her.

She heaved a sigh at him but he kept on coming. In desperation she yawned.

Sal stopped dead in his tracks. "I woke up this morning," he sang so sadly, *"blues walked 'round my bed."* He held up a hand. *"So long, babe."*

"I went to eat my breakfast," Sal sang as he went, *"the blues was all in my bread."*

*   *   *

"You never married," Miriam Stone calls out to Johanna, who is on her way to ask Honora for a cup of tea for her grandmother.

"What?"

"Why didn't you get married?"

"I have to get my grandmother some tea. Would you care to join us, Clara?" Johanna calls to me.

"She's evasive," Mrs. Stone remarks to Johanna's retreating back. "Like a criminal."

Perhaps, Johanna thought, my life will begin when I marry. But the first time a man asked Johanna to marry, she broke into a sweat that was so profuse the man floated out of her vagina and off her bed. With the next man she temporized, "Well, uh, maybe later." Later he married someone else. The third man she left before he fell in love with her. That seemed to work out best. No one gets hurt this way, she thought.

The comfort was cold. Still, when she looked at the marriages of her friends, she doubted, after all, whether marriage would be the beginning of her life.

In the middle of our tea Johanna says suddenly, "Will my life be wonderful, Clara?"

"Why are you asking her?" Hannah Jessup says.

"She said she could imagine all kinds of lives for me."

"I'd be happy if you'd pick one," Mrs. Jessup says.

"I don't know how your life will be, Johanna. Your grandmother's right."

"Of course I am. Your mother made a few mistakes with you, Johanna. You should have had a brother or a sister. I thought so years ago, but I didn't want to interfere."

"Is your life wonderful?" Johanna asks.

"Are you speaking to me?" Hannah Jessup says. "I hope you are not speaking to me."

"I was asking Clara, Han. I want to know. She seems satisfied with her life."

"I want to know too," Hannah Jessup says. "I am very interested." She leans forward in her wheelchair. Her face is so lively she looks quite young.

"I've always thought it was," I say.

Hannah Jessup sits back in her chair and smiles at me. It is a smile I cannot fathom.

* * *

When Johanna left this afternoon, I asked Mrs. Jessup if I might sit with her for a while.

"I'd be delighted," she said, gesturing for me to sit down.

"I'm sorry I haven't even a little sherry to offer you," she said as soon as I was seated.

"I don't care for any anyway," I said.

"No, of course you wouldn't care for sherry. I can't imagine what I would serve you."

"I like almost everything."

"How terrible!" Hannah Jessup said, and she laughed and I laughed.

"I didn't do what I wanted to do," she said suddenly, with an urgency that suggested this is what she has wanted to say to me all along. "I didn't even know I wanted it."

"What did you want?" I asked her.

"You could say adventure. Or freedom. It doesn't matter anymore. I had a lot of good things in my life. I only wanted to tell you that I can imagine giving up the things people prize for the joy of singing or painting or telling stories, I can imagine being free as a bird." She leans forward. "I wanted you to know I understand you."

"I'm very glad," I told her.

But I was more than glad, I was grateful.

We fell into an easy silence.

"You are lost in thought," Mrs. Jessup said after a while.

"I was thinking of something I dreamed last night."

"Was it a good dream?"

"I don't know."

"I'll decide," Hannah Jessup said.

"All right," I said. "In the dream I entered Green Mansions through an unfamiliar entrance that led into the supply closet."

Hannah Jessup smiled. "It's a bad dream."

"My Aunt Celia, much aged, was sitting on a pile of sheets. She was looking into a dusty black book and she was laughing to herself."

"She was laughing to herself?"

"Yes."

"It's a good dream," Hannah Jessup said, and her head dropped and she was fast asleep.

"I looked over Celia's shoulder," I told the sleeping old woman, "and I read, 'The best narrators face themselves.' "

12

The old air conditioner is sweating. At irregular intervals it makes a sound like an airplane losing altitude.

"They won't fix it," Honora says, coming to join me at the window. "They said it's too old to fix and they can't buy a new one when we're closing down so soon. That's why they wouldn't get us a new TV after Mr. Martin busted the old one. They said get along the best way you can. We will get along," she says. She yanks the window up.

Two young men, one tall and one short, are hosing down a newly poured length of concrete walk. "My second husband, William, was nothing like Monroe," Honora says, watching out the window. The water hits the concrete in long steaming arcs, and the concrete hisses like a snake. "He was small and stringy and to himself, and I liked that about him. Monroe's opinion was the opinion of whoever he last sat down with, but William didn't have much use for other folks' opinions. He puts me in mind of my mother that way. I never thought of it at the time we were together, but later it occurred to me how much William was like my mother. I couldn't shake him out of a bad mood any more than I could her. When I was little I'd act foolish to get Mamma to smile again, and it wasn't my nature to be foolish even then. I hated doing it. But I did the very same thing with William. I'd dance around and be silly, and I could see he didn't like it. But once I started, it was hard to stop. It just made him go further into himself. And I thought, I'm William's Monroe. But I never thought how he was like my mamma till after he passed.

"William and I had one baby, a son, Benjamin. I wanted to name him after my father, but William didn't want that. He had nothing against my father—he died way before I knew William—he just didn't think you should call a baby after anyone. Benjamin was born in the county hospital—the hospital where I was working by then. He was a little underweight, but he was nursing just fine. But we never got to take Benjamin home. He didn't live but two days.

"William didn't want any children after that. 'Leave well enough alone,' he said. 'It's not meant to be.' He thought something went wrong between us—something in our union that wasn't right. But it wasn't that. What wasn't right with William and me didn't poison Benjamin's cells or make his tiny heart stop beating. God did that. And he don't intend to tell me why either.

"William stayed even more to himself after Benjamin died. Except that he made time for Alice. He always had been good to Alice, but now he sought her out. Alice was crazy about William. She'd crawl all over him and pester him to death, and he'd smile at her. Alice could make him smile. My little brother could make Mamma smile. I thought of that looking at Alice and William.

"William gave up his job selling insurance the day after Benjamin died. 'There is no insurance,' he said. And he went back to being a roofer, which is what his daddy had been and what he'd done as a young man.

"I wanted to be a comfort to William. I wanted him to be a comfort to me. But that's not how it was. Alice says I never understood William. I say he never understood me. He thought I wasn't a serious person.

" 'Why did you marry me?' I asked him one night in the bed.

"Sometime in the middle of that long night, he gave me my answer. 'I am truly sorry, Honora. I don't know why.'

"We neither one of us slept the rest of that night. We lay in the bed, still as corpses, self-conscious of our breathing.

"Just as the sun was coming up, I said, 'I don't know why I married you, William.' That was the first and only time I made William laugh. I made myself laugh too. We laughed so long and so hard we almost fell out of the bed. Six months later William had a massive coronary, and he fell off the roof he was working on and smashed his skull and died on the spot where he landed in some white lady's yard.

"A young boy, a young white boy with long blond hair

like a girl's, came to tell me. He was some sort of apprentice. 'Oh, man,' he said, 'I don't know how to tell you this.'

"So, of course, I knew William was dead. I invited the boy in and I gave him some lemonade, and he threw up, which gave us both something to do. When he left I went into our room and I put on the fan from Sears, and I took off all my clothes and I laid down on the bed, William's and my bed, Monroe's and my bed, and I let the cool air blow over me, and I made myself come with my hand. I wasn't thinking about being with William or Monroe or anyone. I just did it, and then I fell deep asleep."

* * *

"The last of the night staff quit," Honora told me this morning. "That Gloria. She said, 'The front yard is all tore up, Mrs. Bliss. I could kill myself just trying to get in the door. I been here all by myself for the last week. No one can expect someone to work at night all by theirselves.' And then Gloria said right up in my face, 'They're closing you down anyway.'

" 'Not yet,' I told her, and I dismissed that young woman, and I drove home and dragged out the cot that was stuck away in the closet under the stair, and I told Frank what had happened and that I was going to have to sleep here for a while.

"I think he was proud of me for taking my work so serious. 'We'll manage,' he said, and he put both his hands on my shoulders. It touched me that he put his hands on me like that and that he was proud of me. I took his big hands and put them around me so he was hugging me, but he was just stiff like a board and it was all spoiled for me then. I could feel it spoiling. Driving back here I thought how what I really wanted was for him to say, 'I don't want you to be away for even one night, Honora.' And I thought how Frank never gave me what I want when I wanted it.

"And then I lay up in this skinny cot all night long and I could feel Frank's big hands on my shoulders like a weight in my heart. And I thought, you don't give him much, Honora, and what little you give, you take away.

"I know why I married Frank," Honora said. "It was so I wouldn't go back to Monroe. Monroe had got word from someone that William had died and he started writing me, and when I didn't answer his letters he commenced to call. He said he loved me and he wanted me and Alice and him to be a family again.

" 'We were never a family to begin with,' I said. 'You got a convenient memory.'

" 'You got a hard heart, Honora.'

" 'Then you've got no reason to want me, Monroe.'

" 'Shit,' he said, not in a mad way, in a sighing way, and he hung up.

"But he called back. 'I need you,' he said. 'Honora, I need you.'

" 'You're doing fine without me, Monroe, from what I hear.' Monroe was doing very well in Detroit with his shoe company and his real estate investments.

" 'Did you want me not to do fine? Would you have come back if I hadn't done fine?'

" 'No.'

" 'Why won't you come back, Honora?'

" 'You don't know me, Monroe, that's why. You don't know who I am.'

" 'Couldn't you tell me?'

" 'No. I want you to know. That's what I always wanted. You lived with me eight years and we went together three years before that, and you don't know me any more than one of those ladies you knew for a night or a day.'

" 'Oh, fuck you,' he said so low I could hardly hear him, and he hung up and he didn't ever call back.

"I could've called him. I thought about it. I hardly thought about anything else. But I couldn't do it. It was easier when Frank started coming around. He was a widower with grown-up children. He was William's supervisor when William first got back into roofing so I had known him a little and I had even met his wife.

. "I fixed him some good barbecue chicken one night after we'd been seeing each other about three months, and when we were through, he said, 'I had a lot of respect for William. He was a good worker.' And then he said, 'I have the highest regard for you, Honora. I'd be very pleased if you'd consent to be my wife.'

"Frank's a big man, tall as Monroe but much heavier. He's got a big belly, but I never did mind a big belly on a big man, and he's bald but I don't mind that either. He's got a nice shape head, and it suits him not to have anything on top of it.

"Frank is a hard worker. You want the job done right, you get Frank to do it. Everyone says that. Black and white. And he's just so about his charges. He never overcharges anyone by as much as a penny. He liked William because William was a hard worker too. 'But William didn't want to do anything the easy way,' Frank would tell me. 'William wanted to figure out some new way to do what I could do just fine the old way.'

"Frank has no interest in a new way for anything. We make love two times a week—once during the week, generally Wednesday night, and then Saturday morning before we get out of the bed, and Frank is always on the top. That's all right. I don't much care who's where, but he never says my name. He never says anything. And then right after, he'll get up and go into the bathroom, and I always hear the water running a long time. He's washing himself off.

"Monroe never did anything around the house in the way of fixing anything. I did all that. And William could do it but it didn't interest him, unless it was so complicated it required taking the whole house apart. Frank is always fixing something in the house. His face lights up when the toast doesn't pop up or the windows won't shut tight or an old chair loses a leg. He lines up his tools all in a row and he's happy as a clam. And God knows why I begrudge him that, but I do. All I can think of when I see his wrenches all lined up and all those tiny nails and screws all in little boxes according to their sizes is how he gets up out of the bed to wash our sex off him before he can sleep."

13

Since Vernon Stone's banishment, Johanna is the only visitor to Green Mansions, unless you count me, which Honora doesn't. ("You're not a visitor." She laughed. "You're what I got them instead of the TV.") Mrs. Merriman has no one, and Mr. Martin's wife died here last year. His son, a news photographer, is assigned to foreign wars.

Recently Mr. Martin has expressed an interest in seeing *The New York Times* and *The Washington Post* so he can look for his son's pictures.

"It seems like a good sign," Honora says. "I'm going to ask Johanna to pick up the papers on her way here the days she comes."

Every Monday, Wednesday and Friday afternoon Johanna comes in with the out-of-town papers and delivers them to David Martin.

"I appreciate this," he tells Johanna every time, and every time she says, "I'm happy to do it."

The print, it turns out, is too small for Mr. Martin, and he scans the papers looking for his son's name with a magnifying glass Honora found for him among her late husband William's effects. Today when Johanna handed him the papers, he asked, "Would you mind looking for me? Even with the glass, I'm not doing so well."

"I'd be delighted. I'll just tell my grandmother, and I'll be right back."

"I don't mind," Mrs. Jessup says. "Why should I mind? He's a cultivated man."

"Now it's beginning," Mrs. Stone warns obscurely. "You'll see. I know what I'm talking about."

"Well, I don't know what she's talking about." Mrs. Jessup laughs a light, girlish, pealing laugh.

Johanna laughs with her.

"My father laughed all the time," Mrs. Stone says darkly.

Every Monday, Wednesday and Friday afternoon Johanna sits with Mr. Martin and looks through the papers for his son's pictures, which are never there.

"He doesn't cover important wars," Mr. Martin says when Johanna finds nothing. "I'm quoting him. 'I'm assigned to wars that never make the big time.' He called me last Christmas from Paris, and he said, 'The sons of bitches won't let me in on Lebanon.' "

"He wants to be where the action is," Johanna says.

Infrequently David Martin gets messages from his son, dispatches from the war zone, too brief to properly be called letters, with postmarks as various as the papers he writes on—backs of menus in ancient languages, sky-blue tissue paper, theater programs, the front page of a Damascus telephone book.

Now when the messages come, it is Johanna, instead of Honora, who reads them to Mr. Martin.

" 'Dear Dad,' " Johanna reads, " 'Nothing going on here. The guerrillas, if they exist, are lying low. Glenn.'

" 'Dear Dad, You and Charlotte seemed to read each other's thoughts. I get it wrong every time. If a woman wants me to go, I stay. If she wants me to stay, I go. Glenn.' "

"He blames me," Mr. Martin says, looking down at his large, surprisingly squarish hands, which are folded in his lap.

"Blames you?"

"Oh, well." He shrugs, dismissing inquiry.

But Johanna is intrepid. A little dot of perspiration gleams above her upper lip. "Who is Charlotte?"

"My wife."

"Do you have a picture of her?"

"No. She used to laugh at the way she looked in pictures. She was right to laugh. She looked so intense, as if she might fly off the paper and ravish you. Pictures never caught her beauty," he says.

He stretches his long legs away slowly, as if the long, easy glide could take him away somewhere where he wants to go. "I suppose Charlotte wasn't beautiful in the ordinary way of speaking. Taken singly Charlotte's features were not remarkable, but she was the most beautiful woman I ever knew, and I was far from the only man who thought that. Why is it, I would think, watching her, why is she so extraordinary to look at? And I did figure it out finally. It was because every nuance of feeling showed itself. It was all always in her face. She was indifferent to nothing. Everything seemed to excite her curiosity, to challenge her, to touch her sympathy or scorn, to make her laugh or cry.

"She fascinated me. I could never get to the bottom of her, and, of course, I didn't want to.

"She took pictures—like you. She took pictures of the woods in back of our house. For fifteen years she took pictures of those same woods. She would tramp through the woods for hours with her camera and her light meter hanging around her neck. Often she'd sit on a certain fallen log, waiting for something, the light I suppose, and she'd gaze out at the trees as if she were the victim of some enchantment.

"And I thought, the woods are to her as she is to me. She sees the woods as I see her.

"I'd look at her pictures, and I'd think, how is it she found that? 'Charlotte, is it really there?' 'Yes,' she said. 'It is. It's just a picture of what's there.'

" 'You see the woods as I see you,' I said.

" 'I love you more than I love the woods,' she said. 'I love you more than anything.' "

*   *   *

If my Aunt Celia had a best friend it was Letty Dundee, who had apricot-colored hair and a handsome husband named James Croyden and her own name. "Dundee is my maiden name," Letty explained when I asked her how come her name wasn't Mrs. Croyden, "and I kept it."

Maid Marian, I thought, and pictures of Robin Hood and Friar Tuck and Little John roaming the cool green forests rose up in my mind. I saw myself among them deep in the shadowy forest. "I will have a maiden name too," I said. It seemed the only kind of name ever to have.

Outside of my Aunt Celia, Letty Dundee was the only grown-up I told my stories to.

Celia was a very attentive listener, but she'd always want to nail me down. "Wait a minute, Clara," Celia would say right in the middle of a narrative. "I don't see how come Edward didn't think to bring some sort of knife with him in the first place if he's supposed to be so smart."

Letty Dundee always sighed when Celia did that. Letty

cried in the sad parts, and she'd grab hold of Celia's arm in the scary parts. Once she jumped right out of her chair and clapped her hand over her mouth.

When I was through telling my story, Celia would say it was wonderful except Meryl couldn't possibly have escaped from the Hill Knaves the way I'd said she had, and Rotterdam would never have married Mariette given what Mariette had done to his only brother.

Letty Dundee never said a word at the end of a story. She'd close her eyes as if she were in a trance.

Watching her I thought, Letty Dundee is the most remarkable woman in the world, and I wished fervently that I had apricot-colored hair instead of plain brown hair like my Aunt Celia.

14

"Is there some particular reason," Mrs. Stone challenges Honora, "why Mr. Martin is singled out for special treatment?"

"What do you mean, Mrs. Stone?"

"I mean the papers. He gets two papers hand-delivered to him every day. On top of that she reads to him."

"I'll be happy to read the papers to you when Mr. Martin's through with them."

"Leftovers," Miriam Stone sneers. "After Johanna's smeared them all up with her dirty fingers. She crumples the pages up. I used to read the paper on the subway, folded into little sections. When I was through it was as good as new.''

"Well, I don't think Mr. Martin would care if he got them before or after you.''

"I don't care about first or second, and my eyesight is fine. I'm the only one in this place who sees Clara crouching there in the corner. I see like an eagle, and I don't need you or Johanna to read to me.''

"Okay.''

"What I need is a red pencil and a scissors. I want to cut out certain things.''

"But you can't use a scissors.''

"Of course I can't use a scissors. I haven't used a scissors for five years. I want her to cut them out for me.''

*   *   *

"I'm the last,'' Mrs. Jessup says when Johanna has finished cutting articles out of the paper for Mrs. Stone.

"Mrs. Bliss asked me to do it, Han,'' Johanna says, pulling a chair alongside her grandmother's wheelchair. "Just a few minutes a day. It won't take long.''

"It doesn't matter,'' Mrs. Jessup says.

"I could come a little earlier,'' Johanna says, shifting her weight from side to side, swaying like a mourner. "I'm through at the lab by noon.''

"My uncle had a laboratory in his office—microscopes and little dishes and jars. I remember it very well. On the Gartenstrasse in Frankfurt. We visited him every summer until Elise died, then we didn't go anymore.''

"It's where I work, Han. The photography lab, I told you. I'm through by noon. I'll come early and we'll have more time.''

"I have too much time,'' Hannah Jessup says. "There is too much time.''

* * *

Johanna gathers up her purse, sets aside her chair, kisses her grandmother on her forehead. She looks on the verge of tears.

I stop her at the door.

"I think my grandmother wants me to come more often," she says.

"What do you want?" I ask her.

"I want it to be like it used to be. I want to visit her in her apartment on the twenty-first floor. I want to sit by the window with her after dinner and watch the city light up and talk till we're both too tired to talk anymore."

"Johanna."

"I don't want to hear it." She moves to go.

I hold the door open for her.

"She was a refuge for me when I was little," Johanna says. "She took me wherever she happened to be going— to the vegetable market, to Central Park, to the shop on Madison Avenue where she bought her hats, to Carnegie Hall. And she wanted my opinion. She'd ask what I thought of the red hat and the broccoli and the new young pianist. She wanted to see my pictures. When I was with Han I could imagine that I wouldn't be stuck in my anxious childhood forever. I would have a life of my own some- day."

"I can see why you love her so much," I say. "I like her immensely."

"She's slipping away from me," Johanna says. "If I let go now, I'll never get her back."

* * *

When I was ten and recovering from influenza I asked my Aunt Celia, "Could you sit on my bed till I fall asleep?"

"The secret to life, sweetheart," Celia said, dashing great puffs of powder over her décolletage, "is to want what you can get." She came over to me and bent down and planted a warm, wet kiss on my clammy forehead. "You can see I'm getting ready to go out."

* * *

Johanna has started coming every day.

"Such a wonderful girl," Mrs. Stone praises Johanna to her grandmother in Johanna's presence. "She reads to Mr. Martin, she cuts out things for me, and now she comes to see you every day. A remarkable girl. I wonder why she never married."

Johanna looks up at Mrs. Stone.

"I can assure you it wasn't because she wasn't asked," Hannah Jessup replies.

"How do you know I never married?" Johanna asks. "I could be divorced."

"You've got a look on your face. Hopeful. A little dumb. That goes away with marriage."

"I notice you don't wear a wedding ring," Johanna says.

"I threw it down the toilet."

"*Ach!*" Hannah Jessup exclaims. "I don't want to hear it."

"Vernon had been out all night. Supposedly," she says with relish, "at a poker game with some business associates. He still wasn't in the bed when I woke up the next morning. I was furious. I went into the bathroom to brush my teeth. And there he was, naked as a Greek, happy as you please, reeking of sex, pissing in my toilet."

Hannah Jessup clasps her hands together. "Oh, my God."

"I pulled my ring off."

"I never take my wedding ring off," Hannah Jessup says.

"Never. Under any circumstances. I wouldn't dream of it."

"I walked right over to the bowl," Mrs. Stone goes on, "and I threw the ring right smack in the middle of his stream, and it disappeared down the hole. That stopped him. It stopped him in mid-piss."

"We don't have to listen to this," Hannah Jessup says, half rising in her chair. "We'll leave at once, Johanna."

"What did he say?" Johanna asks.

Miriam Stone smiles a seraphic smile. "He was speechless. I never saw him speechless before. That was the only time."

*   *   *

Johanna sits very close to her grandmother. She touches the hem of the old woman's dress. "Do you remember the days we spent together, Han?"

"I remember," Hannah Jessup says.

"We walked downtown," Johanna says. "We went inside the museums and looked at paintings and went for pastries after. We listened to the opera on your old radio, and you told me what the stories were about."

"I remember," Hannah Jessup says. "I remember everything."

*   *   *

"What do you remember most about your mother and father?" I ask Hannah Jessup as we sit together waiting for the tea Honora has promised to bring us.

"I remember as if all those days were still happening," she says, "as if my mother and father were with me still. Every evening after supper Mamma would sit in the chair with the plum-colored cushions and read. I can see her so clearly, leaning over her novel in the lamplight. I remember just how the light fell across the side of her face. After a while Mamma would put down her book and take Elise and Susannah and me in to bed. Then my father would come in to say good night. His beard always scratched my cheek as he bent to kiss me good night, and every night his silk handkerchief fell out on my bed. I see the big white square of silk fluttering down. I hear Pappa's growly laugh and smell his tobacco."

"Did his tobacco smell good?" I ask her.

"Oh, my dear," Hannah Jessup says, "nothing ever smelled so good again."

*   *   *

"Here's a good one," Mrs. Stone exults, brandishing a page of the newspaper at Johanna. "Last year improperly installed wood- or coal-burning stoves were responsible for starting 130,000 residential fires, $264 million in property loss, 2,760 injuries and 290 deaths.

"That cabin he dragged me to every weekend has a wood stove. Cut it out and make an envelope. Vernon Stone. 1249 Magnolia Circle. Magnolia Circle," Mrs. Stone scoffs. "He brought me to Tara. And now we got here Taralawn Estates."

Johanna giggles. "Clark Gable would turn in his grave."

"Don't tell me about Southern men," Miriam Stone says.

"I wouldn't try to," Johanna says, addressing the envelope.

"They'd like you to think their charm is an affliction, something they were born with and aren't responsible for. Something their mothers stirred into those revolting grits."

"I love grits," Johanna says slyly.

"I'll tell you the truth, he charmed me. Vernon Stone charmed me. The first time he laid eyes on me I was typing in the office of the man he'd come to do business with, and he walked right up to me and he said, 'Why are you so pretty?' "

Johanna makes a deep diagonal slash in the newspaper with Honora's gleaming scissors.

"And when he called that night to ask if he could take me to dinner, and I said I couldn't see him till the next night, he said, 'I don't think I can wait that long.'

" 'You have a line as long as AT&T's,' I shot back to let him know I was nobody's fool.

" 'I'm just trying to tangle you all up in it so you can't get away,' he said.

"Well, he did, and I didn't. I came home with him to visit at his mother's house, where they had two meats and five vegetables and three pies and ice tea every noon, and I watched him charm his mother and his aunt and his sister and the cook. 'They'd commit serious crimes for your chicken in New York, Sudie. They'd pillage and plunder and rape to get a taste of your birds.'

"And Sudie and his mother and sister and aunt would all feign shock that he slipped rape in there, but they loved it.

"Vernon told telephone operators they had alluring voices, and he told the checkout girl at the market her new glasses made her look sultry.

" 'You're making a fool of yourself,' I said.

" 'You don't think she looks sultry? Maybe I was wrong. Maybe I need glasses. But one thing I can see is how good you look. And he grabbed me and kissed me and stuck his tongue halfway down my throat right there in the market in front of everyone."

15

Outside Green Mansions the steaming day roils and boils like a stew on a stove. I can hear it through the open window, over the drone of the invalid air conditioner. Honora sniffs the heat as if it were a beast tracking her.

"Time is running out, Clara, and I haven't found places for any of them."

16

"What are you thinking, Han?" Johanna asks her grandmother. "You're smiling to yourself."

"I was thinking about Ascher and William and Rupert." She shakes her head. "What an unlikely trio they were."

"Did I ever know them?"

"Of course," Mrs, Jessup says, still smiling. "In London that summer."

"I've never been to London, Han," Johanna says.

Hannah Jessup looks at her granddaughter. "I thought you were someone else," she says.

*   *   *

Johanna sits with four letters from Mr. Martin's son on her lap. The letters come in batches and they are frequently as much as two or three months old.

"I imagine his letters piling up in some dusty post office in a crumbling banana republic," Mr. Martin says.

"You could write him back," Johanna suggests. "You could dictate to me."

"He moves from one country to another. I don't know where to write."

"He must have an American Express address or box number or something."

"If he does, he didn't give it to me."

"The next time he calls, ask him for an address."

"Next Christmas."

"That's only four months, more or less."

"Ah, God, four months."

"Maybe he'll call before then."

"It isn't that," Miriam Stone snaps, rolling herself in between Johanna and David Martin. "It's all that time. All those days and weeks to live through."

"Why, yes," Mr. Martin says.

"He's surprised I know," she says to Johanna. "In three months, excuse me," she runs on before Mr. Martin can demur, "we could all be dead from those supplements Mrs. Bliss gives us. Vitamin C damages the genes. They discovered it in Canada. It could cause birth defects or cancer or both."

"You'll have to pass that on to Vernon," Johanna says.

"Naturally," Mrs. Stone says. "You'll cut it out for me. Well, I won't keep you, Mr. Martin. I see you've got a lot of letters from your son."

Johanna draws out the first letter.

"Gail and Barbara, thank God, don't write. When they were in camp they wrote every day. Someone forced them, and Vernon and I had to . . . Your son must write hot stuff," Mrs. Stone says. "She's blushing like a radish."

"What is it?" David Martin asks Johanna.

"I'm going," Miriam Stone says, maneuvering herself a clear path. "I'll sneak away like a thief."

"Do you want me to read it?" Johanna asks when Mrs. Stone has rolled herself away.

"What is it? What's wrong?"

Johanna takes up the letter. " 'Dear Dad, A very beautiful woman took me in her mouth tonight . . .' "

Mr. Martin flings himself out of his chair. "Don't continue. Who does he think he is?" he demands, bearing down on Johanna.

"I don't know," she says. "Shall I read the other three?"

"No. I don't know. Yes. Read it. Read them all."

" 'Dear Dad,' " Johanna reads, " 'A very beautiful woman took me in her mouth tonight, and with infinite patience and exquisite expertise she worked for an hour to rouse me and couldn't. I kept her there by force of my boredom. Perhaps her vanity exceeds even mine.' "

"What does he want from me?" Mr. Martin walks back and forth, back and forth, pacing the small distance between his chair and Johanna's. At last he sits, slumping in his chair as if he were suddenly exhausted. "We were so different, Charlotte and I," he says finally, looking away from Johanna, "but we were terribly close. Sometimes I think it was terrible. It was perhaps terrible for Glenn. We did battle for her, he and I. And in the end he believed she chose me."

"Do you believe that?"

"I only know that in my heart of hearts I wanted her to choose me." He closes his eyes.

"I'll go," Johanna says.

Mr. Martin goes on as if he hadn't heard her. "Before Glenn was born I used to do a bit of furniture-making. I'd learned it from my father, and it gave me a great deal of

ʒ

pleasure. I liked everything about it—the time it required, the patience it exacted. I loved what seemed to me the slow unfolding of the vision that was waiting to be released, the dream that was hidden in every finishing nail I drove through the wood, in every joint I cut.

"It aroused me too—touching the wood, smelling it, the cool feel of metal in my hands, a hammer or a plane or a saw. Charlotte used to say I was never more passionate than when I'd been making something.

"I never made anything elaborate—a cedar chest that was supposed to be for storing blankets that ended up a toy chest for Glenn. A little square table that Charlotte piled her pictures on. The nicest thing I ever made was a bed-side table for Charlotte with two drawers in it. I made it out of rosewood, and I was very pleased with the way it turned out. Rosewood is difficult to work with. Charlotte loved it.

"I didn't make anything more after Glenn was born. It seemed there was always too much to do and not enough time. But there was time. I gave it up for some other reason. I gave it up for a sacrifice nobody was requiring. I gave it up for spite."

*   *   *

When I was fourteen Letty Dundee had a heart attack and died. She and her husband, James Croyden, went walking after supper, as was their custom, and Letty keeled over dead.

"She's had a bad heart since she was a girl," my Aunt Celia said when she got off the telephone with James Croyden. "She knew she had a bad heart," she shouted. "Goddamn her," Celia yelled, and she ran past me without a word and went up into her room and slammed the door. She cried all night long.

The next morning Celia knocked on my door and came in before I said come in. Her face was so swollen that her eyes almost disappeared, and her hair looked like a rat's nest. "Did my crying keep you awake?"

"Yes."

"I'm sorry about last night, Clara." She sat down on my bed. "I know you loved Letty too."

The day after the funeral Aunt Celia invited James Croyden over for supper. I ate next to nothing, but Celia and James Croyden both had second helpings of the knockwurst and the cabbage. They sat around over their coffee telling stories about Letty and laughing. They were laughing, and they were holding hands across the table.

I excused myself and went up to bed, although it was only eight o'clock. I don't know what time James Croyden left because I put cotton in my ears so I wouldn't hear them laughing. Before I went to sleep I promised Letty Dundee that I would never tell another story.

And I didn't tell another story for almost five months.

Celia noticed sooner than I thought she would, which gratified me. "Clara, honey," she said one Sunday morning, "you haven't told me one of your stories in a long, long time." She looked at me sharply. "Not since Letty Dundee died."

"I've given it up."

"You mean you don't tell stories at all anymore? Not to anyone?"

"Not to anyone," I said.

"But why would you do that?" Celia asked, and she seemed, to my satisfaction, genuinely alarmed.

"I have my reasons."

My Aunt Celia never said another word about it, but the first time I told her a story again, she sat all the way through it without stopping me once. And at the end she sat very still in her chair and closed her eyes.

17

"The first time Vernon had to be away from home on business," Miriam Stone tells Johanna, "he called me five minutes after he left the house to say he missed me already." She looks up from the newspaper she is combing for warnings of disaster. "But he was gone a week and he never called again or wrote so much as a postcard. In forty years of business trips he never let me know what train or plane I could expect him back on.

" 'Impossible to say, sweetheart.' That's what he'd say." She drags her crippled hand up and down the rows of newspaper columns. "And I'd say, 'It's not impossible. What do you mean it's impossible? If it's so impossible, don't come home.'

" 'But I want to. That's the fun of getting away—I can't wait to get home to you. All week long I'll be thinking how I'll get home late and slip in beside you in the bed and slide my hand up under your nightdress.'

"I won't say what else he said, but it worked on him and on me too. I admit it. But after that first year I understood it wasn't a love scene we were playing, it was a death scene.

"I found one," she says, pointing so Johanna can see. " 'Alfalfa seeds and sprouts,' " she reads, " 'can cause a syndrome identical to a serious immunological disease, systemic lupus erythematosus.' " Johanna gasps.

"Systemic lupus erythematosus," Miriam Stone repeats, relishing the luxurious syllables. "That'll get Vernon. Since I'm in here he eats every day at that little place near the campus that serves that stuff. He loves it. It makes him feel young. All those young girls and all that salad."

18

" 'Dear Dad,' " Johanna reads, " 'I took a picture of a little boy with his foot blown off. I looked through my lens and I framed it up just right, and I thought, this one's a winner.' "

"Goddammit," Mr. Martin swears, "I wish he wouldn't write me anymore. And don't give me some horseshit about this being a cry for help."

"I wasn't going to."

"Yes, you were. I can see it in your eyes. Your eyes are too bright. I'm sorry," he says, but he doesn't look sorry, he looks gratified. "It's just that you're too eager, too curious, too young."

"I'm thirty-eight."

"You look like a child to me. Anyway thirty-eight is young. You have no idea how young thirty-eight is. Or how old." He leans backward in the flimsy chair, and the front legs lift off the floor. "When Glenn was born I thought I'd lost Charlotte." He addresses the ceiling, balancing on the hind legs of the aquamarine plastic chair.

"I already know that," Johanna says, emboldened by David Martin's strangeness.

Mr. Martin laughs and guides his chair safely back into position. "In the evening, when I got home from work, she'd say, 'Come sit with me while I feed Glenn and tell me how your day was.' And I'd say something like, 'Paul couldn't say enough about my brief. He's very high on me.'

" 'Is he, darling?' she'd say, and she'd look at me so brightly that my heart sank.

"She can't tear herself away from him, I thought, watching the baby gnawing at her enormous discolored nipples. Her nipples are grotesque, I thought. And all my desire for her and for our life together drained out of me.

" 'I'm so happy,' she'd say, nuzzling Glenn's scalp as he fed. 'Oh, darling, I have everything I ever wanted.' "

Mr. Martin looks at Johanna. "Now when I think of the three of us, it's those evenings I remember, and I long to have them back."

* * *

Olga Yogurt grew up on the frozen plains of a very large, very cold socialist country. At night she listened to the wolves howling and the wind blowing and the tree limbs snapping under the great weight of ice. The log house in which she lived with her old grandmother had chinks in it, and although the young girl and the old lady spent many hours stuffing the holes with old stockings and caps, the bitter cold got in anyway.

In order to keep herself warm and to entertain her old grandmother, Olga began to tumble. Her routine grew more and more elaborate as the winter wore on. She did double and triple and, finally, quadruple somersaults in the air, landing gracefully on her small flat feet. She laid a broom across two chairs and tied one end of the broom to one of the chairs with a length of old rope. To make it sporting, her grandmother sat on the other end of the broom. Then Olga would jump from the floor to the broom and run lightly back and forth across the handle. She got bolder and bolder. She hopped on one foot. She jumped up and spun around in the air. She executed perfect backbends. Occasionally Olga's old grandmother got so carried away, she would clap her hands and bounce in delight. Then the end of the broom she was sitting on would fly out from under her, and Olga would be dumped on the floor. When that happened the young girl and the old woman laughed till they cried.

So they passed the endless winters. The blood coursed warmly in their veins, and no one in all the land had rosier cheeks or better appetites than Olga and her beloved grandmother.

But even in this immense cold land winter finally ends. In the spring Raskal Raskalnikov, who called himself a personal manager, blew into town with the pollen to offer Olga a position on the country's foremost gymnastic team.

Olga's grandmother pleaded with her not to go to the city. Olga argued that she would be able to bring back from the city whatever was needed to patch the house to make it snug for the next winter. The old lady had it on the tip of her tongue to say "But then we won't need to play to keep warm, and we will be bored and unhappy," but she kept her mouth shut.

Olga was an overnight sensation. The crowds jammed the palaces of physical culture to see the charming young girl from the country defying gravity. Although Olga was only one member of a remarkable team of gymnasts coached by the great Fydor Fydorovitch, it was she who most dazzled the eyes and stirred the imagination.

Two years passed, and Olga, who had gone home to see her grandmother every three months the first year, had not been home for over six months. She wrote a lot though, carefully laying the groundwork for the letter which would explain to her grandmother that Raskalnikov and she were flying to a large Western democracy, where her team would compete in a world championship gymnastic meet.

The mails being what they are, Olga's grandmother did not get the letter until Olga had already landed in the huge city on the eastern seaboard of the great country.

Olga had been warned that the people in this city might be cold and unfriendly, but the first week she was there the mayor gave her the key to the city, and a chain of hamburger joints named a burger for her.

One lovely spring day, responding to the promptings of construction workers, who yelled down at her from their steel perches, she hopped lightly onto a low beam and climbed to a high girder, where she performed her latest routine, modifying it only slightly in the interests of safety.

Her exploit made the six o'clock news and the eleven o'clock news. When she came a few minutes late to the next practice, she imagined some of her teammates were surly. Her esteemed coach, Fydor Fydorovitch, spoke to her sharply for the first time. Raskal Raskalnikov pooh-poohed Fydor's cluckings, and then he told Olga that a famous film impresario wanted her for the female lead in The Idiot. Olga had some doubt that the officials in her country would sanction such an enterprise, but Raskalnikov said détente was making a comeback and anything was possible.

Since the meet was to take place in the movie capital, and the team was right then packing up to fly there, it would not be a great problem for Olga to meet the impresario without Fydor Fydorovitch's knowledge. "No real reason we shouldn't tell him," Raskalnikov murmured, "but why bother him before the meet?"

The meeting with the movie mogul was held at the edge of an enormous swimming pool. Although her command of the foreign language was by now not half bad, Olga was distracted by the beauty of the lifeguard who dangled high over the aquamarine water in his little white tower. His teeth were as white as the white tiles that lined the pool, and his glittering skin was the color of the thin gold chains the movie mogul wore around his thick neck.

Olga's adoring glances warmed Hank Glider's heart as the sun warmed his golden back, and sitting up in the sky in his white tower, he determined to make her his own, though he was only an itinerant surfer and she was a world-famous gymnast.

The story ends as you might expect. Olga helped her country win the gold medal in the gymnastic meet, and although the audiences cheered her as ardently as ever, Fydor Fydorovitch saw clearly that she had lost something.

The movie deal fell through. Raskal Raskalnikov went home to write a book which argued that East is East and West is West *and never the twain should meet. But as he himself had prophesied, détente was making a comeback, and all four thousand copies of the book were remaindered.*

The day after the world meet, Hank Glider drove Olga to the beach, where he made love to her in the creamy surf and so persuaded her to defect.

Olga Yogurt and Hank Glider live in a modest ranch house about a mile from the ocean. Marriage has been a sobering experience for Hank. In her last letter to her grandmother, Olga explained that he surfs now only on weekends. During the week he sells life insurance to other surfers.

Olga is content with Hank. She has had her days of glory. She is satisfied to wheel her cart through the supermarket. There is a baby on the way, and the days are all, one after another, sunny and warm. The nights too are mild, all the year long. But often at night, Olga yearns with all her heart for the sound of the icy wind beating up against the little log house, and in her dreams she sees herself tumbling to keep warm and she hears her grandmother laughing.

19

Miriam Stone hands Johanna a page of the newspaper without comment. "Which one?" Johanna asks.

"You'll see it."

"What is the purpose of all this?" Hannah Jessup demands. "You're wasting my granddaughter's time."

"I'll be through in just a minute, Han." Johanna runs a

long finger up and down the newsprint. " 'Accidents with steel-belted radial tires stir fears . . . "

"No, no. There's a better one."

"This." Johanna has it. " ' Enhanced risk of mouth and throat cancers if cigarette smoke and alcohol are held in mouth for as long as ten seconds.' "

Mrs. Stone smiles complacently. "You're a nice girl. You have a smart granddaughter," she commends Hannah Jessup. "Not like my daughters. I never know what they're talking about. They talk about nothing. They discuss silverware. Which silverware pattern, what face cream."

"Johanna won't even use a face cream," Mrs. Jessup says. "She's not such a young girl anymore after all. She should start."

"Vernon and I used to talk about interesting things once upon a time. Things in the world."

"My husband was a brilliant man," Mrs. Jessup says. "He could have been the physicist in Clara's story. He had ideas in his head like nobody's business, and he could dazzle you with words."

"It didn't last," Mrs. Stone went on. "I got so I could predict our conversations. I had no idea how to stop it. I'd say my lines and he'd say his.

" 'I require some peace and quiet, Miriam.'

" 'What about what I require?'

" 'You require I earn a good living and sit by your side and hold your hand while I'm doing it.'

" 'You're never there when I need you. I get nothing from you.'

" 'What do I get from you? Civil war. Bloody fucking battles.' "

Johanna looks over at her grandmother.

" 'You don't mean anything you say.' " Mrs. Stone gestures in the air with her gnarled hand. " 'You never kept a promise in your life.'

" 'I promise you this, Miriam, I'm weary of this.' "

" 'Don't threaten me. Are you threatening me?' "

" 'I'm telling you.' "

" 'I'm telling you, Vernon. I'd go in a minute.' "

" 'Go,' he would say. 'Go with my blessing. I'll get your trunk down from the attic.' "

"But he didn't get my trunk down and I didn't go."

"I know she didn't go," Mrs. Jessup complains to Johanna. "She tells me over and over the same story."

"It's the only one I've got," Mrs. Stone says, "and if you don't like it, you can drop dead."

* * *

It was the custom in the sixth grade to attend Miss Garnett's ballroom dancing class. I wasn't interested in going, but my Aunt Celia said, "Be a sport, Clara. Give it a try."

When I got home after the first class, Celia took one look at me and said, "Didn't any boys dance with you?"

"They danced with me, but I couldn't think of anything to say to them. Two boys in a row said, 'You sure are quiet.' "

"Did they?"

"Then Matthew Graves asked me to dance. I said I didn't want to, but he grabbed my hand and started to dance anyway."

Celia smiled. "Has to be Saul Graves' boy."

"Matthew looked right at me while we danced. I had to say something. So I asked him a question. As soon as he answered, I asked him another. We danced four dances one right after the other, and I kept asking him questions."

"Matthew must've been enjoying himself to dance all those dances with you, Clara."

"He quit looking at me after a while. I don't think he knew who he was talking to anymore."

"Oh," Celia said. "I see what you mean."

The next morning at breakfast, Celia said, "You know what your father once said to me, Clara? Your mother had gone up to bed, and we were sitting at this very table where you and I are sitting now. Out of the blue your father said, 'The thing I do best is listen.'

" 'When you were a boy, making up stories was what you did best,' I said.

" 'Oh, Lord, Celia,' he said, 'it comes to the same thing.'

"What struck me was the way he said it—it was half a brag and half an admission of failure."

Celia got up from the table and carried our cereal bowls and the jelly out to the kitchen. In a minute she came out. "Clara," she said, scooping up our napkins, "did you get any story ideas listening to Matthew Graves?"

"Maybe," I said.

Celia shook out the napkins. "Everything's good for something," she said, watching the toast crumbs fall to the floor.

20

Only once in all this time have Johanna and Mr. Martin found a picture by Glenn Martin. It's not a very good picture. It's possible it's not even Glenn's. It's a blurry shot of a kid in cutoffs standing in the middle of a muddy air-strip somewhere in, one assumes, Central America. The cutline underneath it says, "Hot spot heats up."

"It must be a mistake of some kind," Mr. Martin said

when Johanna read it to him. "A switch of some kind." But the picture bore Glenn's credit, and Mr. Martin cut it out and put it in his wallet.

Mr. Martin has received no letters from his son for some time. He draws out the packet of old letters and asks Johanna to read them again. Some she has read so many times she knows them by heart. " 'I've fallen in love three times in the past six months,' " Johanna recites, barely looking at the smeary paper in her hand. " 'The last woman looked like a young boy. In certain lights I thought she looked like pictures of me as a kid.'

"What does he look like?" Johanna wants to know.

"He looks like me," David Martin says. "At least he did when he was a little boy. Everyone said how much he looked like me, and no one said it more than Charlotte. In a dream I said to Charlotte, 'I wish I were him,' and I woke in a panic. I jumped out of the bed and my knee hit the edge of the bed table, and the tiny sterling silver box where Charlotte kept her earrings clattered to the floor. 'Goddammit,' I said.

"Charlotte sat up, startled out of sleep. 'What's wrong?'

" 'There's too much clutter in this house,' I yelled. 'That's what's wrong. Jesus Christ, Charlotte, why do we have all these goddamn little pieces of shit cluttering up our lives?'

" 'Glenn, for instance,' she said, and she laughed.

" 'It isn't funny,' I said. But, of course, it was."

*   *   *

For years Johanna had been living in an abandoned theater, watching old movies of her life. In all the films, no matter how small her part, Johanna was the central figure. Whatever happened happened because she did or didn't do it. Every action was a reaction to her.

Glenn, the projectionist, with whom Johanna had fallen in love in the days when he couldn't wait to see what she was going to

do next, *finally tired of the spectacle. "How about James Bond?"*
he would yell down from his booth. "Or Wild Strawberries?
National Velvet? Day for Night? *In the end he would happily*
have settled for an old Gidget film, so bored was he.

In order to divert himself, Glenn began tampering with the
speed of the films. He slowed them down so every move of every
character resembled those lyrical runs that enjoyed such popular-
ity for a while. But that soon palled.

Speeding the film up was more successful. Johanna, who was
herself beginning to tire of the films, found the speeded-up ver-
sions irresistibly funny. Though tears that fell with the speed of
light were not as satisfying as tears that slid slowly down a cheek,
though betrayals accomplished in the blink of an eye did not wound,
though sexual couplings that were over before you could say boo
did not inspire lust or longing or regret, they did make her laugh.
And when she laughed out loud in the darkened theater, Glenn,
who had thought he could never again be aroused by the flesh-
and-blood version of the image he was so bored with on the screen,
fell in love with Johanna all over again.

*　　*　　*

Johanna and I leave at the same time today. We walk onto
the wide front porch of Green Mansions, looking out across
the lawn at the workmen who are wrapping it up for the
day, hauling tools into the backs of their trucks, coiling up
cables to stash out back in the trailer that stays there all
day and all night, dragging cinder blocks out of their way.
They move as if this day has aged them, as if their weari-
ness can never be assuaged. They call back and forth to
each other, drawing out their syllables so there's time to
rest inside each one.

Someone pops open a beer. Johanna leans out over the
porch railing as if there is something important out there
she could see if she looked hard enough.

"Why did you come here, really?" Johanna asks me.

"I think I wanted to know what it's like to look back over the whole length of a life so I could imagine what I might feel like looking back over mine."

One of the men laughs, a large, reckless laugh that foretells some reviving joy in the night to come.

Johanna shivers in the sun that will be shining yet for another hour. "You said you'd always thought your life was wonderful," she says. "Do you still?"

Johanna leans so intently. What is it she sees out there? Is it the joy that's coming?

"Clara?"

"I don't know, Johanna. Maybe I chose who I was going to be before I understood what I'd have to forfeit."

"Oh," Johanna says, as if she understood much more than I have said. She looks over at me, and I have the impression she is seeing me for the first time.

One of the men catches sight of us and waves.

"At least you chose, Clara," she says, waving at the man who is smiling up at her. "That counts for something."

21

When Johanna came yesterday, Mr. Martin handed her two letters that had arrived in the morning mail. On the back of one of the envelopes was a box number care of American Express.

"I knew he'd send it," Johanna cried. Her eyes are shiny as new dimes.

"Why don't you read me the letters."

Johanna tore open the first letter. " 'This place is a hole. Nothing to do but drink and jerk off. They're moving me out in a week. I'll be glad to go.' "

She opens the second letter. " 'I dreamed I was high as a kite on high-grade cocaine,' " she reads, " 'and my tongue was as stiff as my . . .' "

"Oh, damn," Mr. Martin says.

" '. . . cock,' " says Johanna. " 'The woman underneath me came and came and came, and the last time she called out my name. And precisely at that moment I couldn't remember who I was with. Glenn.' "

Today Johanna sits in front of Mr. Martin, balancing a large legal pad on her lap.

"Dear Glenn," Mr. Martin dictates, "my failing sight necessitates that your letters be read aloud to me. In future I request that . . . You're not writing," he says to Johanna.

" 'Dear Glenn,' " Johanna says.

"Dear Glenn," Mr. Martin says. "Dear Glenn . . ."

* * *

"What were you doing there so long?" Hannah Jessup asks her granddaughter.

"I'm sorry, Han. Mr. Martin wanted me to write a letter to his son."

"Why should you write his son? You never met him."

"At one time I had five young men writing me letters," Mrs. Stone says, "but my father didn't like any of them. He didn't like any of the young men who courted Trudy or me. 'What does his father do?' That's what he wanted to know."

"He wanted me to write a letter *for* him," Johanna explains. "What did you say, Mrs. Stone?"

Hannah Jessup removes a white handkerchief from her sleeve and dabs at her nose. "He's an educated man, Johanna. He doesn't need you to write a letter for him."

"And even if I'd said, 'His father is the king,' " Mrs. Stone goes on, "it wouldn't have been enough."

"He can't see to write, Han. His eyes are very bad."

"Did you tell me that once before?"

Mrs. Stone smiles, showing her teeth. "She's told you everything once before."

"Poor man." Hannah Jessup doesn't look at Mrs. Stone. "My eyes at least are fine."

"Ditto," says Mrs. Stone.

"What were you saying about a king, Mrs. Stone?"

"I'm falling on deaf ears. They've destroyed your ears with their bedlam out there."

"It's nice and quiet today," Johanna says, smiling at Mrs. Stone.

Sweet Acidophilus never had a bad word to say about anyone, but her thoughts, which she kept to herself, were as black as the coal her husband hacked out of the mines every day. . . .

Mrs. Stone doesn't smile back. "They'll be back tomorrow," she says, severe as an oracle. "I can hear their hammers in my sleep."

"My parents didn't want me to marry the boy I loved," Hannah Jessup says, wrapping the thin handkerchief around her wedding ring.

"Crash, bang, boom!" Mrs. Stone says. "Not even that racket from the air conditioner can drown them out. What do they have out there? Goliaths, they've got, to mow us down. Let sleeping bags lie, you cowardly scum," she excoriates the phantom workers. "This isn't the walls of Jericho. This is my home."

"Everything is upside down," Hannah Jessup cries. She claps her hands to her head, and the handkerchief dangles over one side of her face like a veil. "I can hear their hammers in my sleep."

Johanna covers her grandmother's hands with her own

and teases her head from side to side. "You used to say I made such a racket you could hear me twenty blocks away in your apartment."

"What are you doing?" Mrs. Jessup protests, freeing herself from her granddaughter's clutches. "You hurt my hand."

Mrs. Stone slides her chair closer to Mrs. Jessup. "She got her dirty fingers all over your nice clean hankie," she says. "She's not a careful person."

*   *   *

"Dear Glenn," Mr. Martin dictates to Johanna, "you imagine because Charlotte took you for granted she didn't love you. She took me for granted too. Her sister always said, 'Charlotte has a dreadful assurance about everything.' And it was true in a way, and in a way it wasn't true at all. It was a kind of faith she had.

"She'd wake me sometimes in the middle of the night. 'I might never have had any of this,' she'd say. She was terrified. Her teeth were chattering, and she was drenched in sweat. And I'd hold her and calm her, but I was glad she was afraid because I was swamped with fears and had no faith.

"I couldn't believe how casually Charlotte slung you around, what prodigious risks she seemed to take with your life. When you were only weeks old, she'd stick you on top of our old dresser, where she changed you, and she'd leave you there naked as a jaybird and so tiny you were dwarfed by our wedding picture in the sterling silver frame. She'd leave you there while she roamed around the room hunting the diaper pin she'd misplaced.

"Finally I couldn't stand it, and I'd leap out of bed and put a trembling hand over you to anchor you. 'Charlotte, for God's sake, if he fell from this height he'd be killed.'

" 'Oh, David, he isn't going to fall,' she'd say from inside the closet, where she was on her hands and knees searching for the missing pin. 'He can't even roll over yet.'

"And later, when you were starting to walk, you'd stagger off into the woods, and she'd smile after you and continue digging in her garden. I'd see all this from the window of my study, and I'd race out and chase after you and tackle you, and you'd bawl because I'd startled you so.

" 'Can't you relax?' she said over and over. 'Can't you just please relax?' But I never could. It seemed to me I had an embarrassment of riches, and it was only just, I thought, that sooner or later it would all be snatched away from me."

*　*　*

"Your grandmother's getting sleepy," Miriam Stone says. It is what she says whenever Hannah Jessup is quiet for longer than two minutes.

"Are you sleepy, Han?" Johanna asks. "I can go if you're sleepy."

"Don't go," Mrs. Jessup says dreamily, gazing out over her granddaughter's head. "I never see you."

"She won't mind if I tell you some things," Mrs. Stone says graciously. "She's in another dimension. Like Clara." She looks over her shoulder at me and smiles with her mouth closed.

Turning back to Johanna she says, "My sister, Trudy, who died a long time ago, swears that my father was a devoted husband and father and a religious man. 'He knows the Talmud inside out and backward,' Trudy would say, as if that was proof of anything.

"I know all about my father and the Talmud. Every time my mother accused him, he'd fall on his knees at her feet, and he'd say exactly like I'm saying it now, 'Oh, my sweet darling, the Talmud says in the place where a truly repentant person stands, even the most saintly cannot enter, because the penitent has at his disposal not only'—at this point my mother, who from years and years knew it by heart, joined in, shaking her head back and forth from side to side to get him to hurry up—'the forces of good in his soul and in the world, but also those of evil which he transforms into essences of holiness.' They recited the last part together.

"At the end of this performance my mother, whose sense of humor ruined her life, always hiccuped, which is what happened to her when she was caught between a sob and a laugh.

"Of all the stories about my father, Vernon liked that one best. Naturally."

* * *

Mrs. Stone wheels up beside me. "Did you get all that?"

"What?"

"What? As if she doesn't hear every word everybody says. About my father and the Talmud and my mother."

"Oh, that. Well, yes. I did hear what you said to Johanna."

"Good," Mrs. Stone says. "You can add it to that other background material I gave you."

"To tell you the truth, Mrs. Stone, I'd already thought of that."

"The last word she has to have. It's not a becoming trait. No wonder you're a spinster."

22

Sometimes at the end of the day, before I go, Honora sits with me on the old black Leatherette couch. "It will take me all night to get back up again," she said the first time she joined me.

"Where is it you go to, Clara?" Honora says this evening, after a long, companionable silence, she in one corner of the couch and I in the other. "You never have said."

"I have a room in a house not far from here. That's how I found Green Mansions."

"Do you have some sort of part-time work in town somewhere?"

"I'm listed with a temporary agency. I type."

"I don't see how you live on that."

"Well, if you're fast and accurate, it pays quite well. If I'm hard up, I can usually work a week or two at a stretch. And occasionally I get paid to tell stories at libraries and schools and once in a while a museum."

"Where were you before you came here?"

"Another room in another town."

"You mean you just move from town to town?"

"Yes," I said.

"I can't imagine it," Honora said. "I can't even imagine it. How long have you been doing like that, moving from place to place?"

"Since I left home, since I was seventeen."

"You never thought about staying somewhere?"

"I've thought about it since I've been here."

"What do you mean?" Honora asks.

"I mean someday I'll have to stay if I live to be as old as Miriam Stone or Mrs. Merriman or Hannah Jessup."

"But haven't you ever *wanted* to stay somewhere?" Honora says. "What are you smiling at?"

"I just remembered a poem I wrote when I was eleven.

> *"Here I sit by my fireplace*
> *with some food and a bed close by*
> *And yet as I look upon the night*
> *and see the star-filled sky*
> *I cannot help but wish*
> *that I was on a dusty road*
> *that leads to who knows where*
> *and adventure yet untold.*

"I have this dream, Honora. I've had it ever since I left home. In the dream my father asks me why I wander. My answer is always the same. For danger, I tell him, for joy, for my freedom."

Honora sits up straighter. "What about love?"

"I have loved, Honora."

Honora looks into her lap. "You never said anything at all about any of that."

When I don't respond, she says, "I can talk to you about anything. About me, and all of them, Johanna and Mr. Martin and Mrs. Merriman and Mrs. Stone and Mrs. Jessup, and you seem to see what I see. But then when you say about yourself, I know I don't understand you. I don't understand you at all, Clara."

"I don't know what to say."

"Maybe I said too much," Honora says.

"Other people have said the same. I was very much in love with a man named Aaron, and he told me he couldn't love me anymore because he didn't understand me. He said, 'I can't love someone I have no hope of understanding.' "

"Well, I don't know he was altogether right," Honora says. "Look at Alice and me."

I laugh. "He wasn't altogether right. I told him that."

"What happened to him?"

"Aaron got married two years ago," I said. "He wrote that his wife looks a little like me."

"Don't you wish he had understood you?"

"I'm not sure."

Honora looks over at me as if there is something more she would like to ask, but she doesn't ask it.

We are silent again for a long time. The lounge is almost empty. Mrs. Merriman and Hannah Jessup are napping in their rooms, and Mrs. Stone has nodded off in her chair over her newspaper. David Martin has stepped outside, though the evening is sultry and still.

"Sometimes," Honora says, "sometimes, Clara, I wonder what I would have been like if I hadn't ever married or had a child. Where I might have gone. I try to picture me without Monroe. Or William. Or Benjamin. Or Alice. Or Frank.

"Once I had this feeling come over me like they were all so gone they had never been. And right then the telephone rang. It was Alice calling from Philadelphia to tell me I ought to be doing something in the neighborhood to help elect Moses Flood mayor. 'How can you do nothing,' she said, 'when this is the first time you've had a viable candidate?'

"It tickled me that she called right then. It made me love her so much. I laughed out loud, and she got insulted. And there wasn't any way I could explain.

"When Alice comes home, it takes her three days to quit whirling around. Then she'll settle into that old blue easy chair and I'll tease her, 'For an activist you do a lot of laying around.' She never laughs.

"Alice was contrary as a child. 'Where's my duse?' she would say when she was three, and she'd bang her plate on the table, and I'd run out and bring her apple juice in her red cup, and she'd say, 'I want it in my blue cup,' and she'd throw the cup on the floor, and the sticky juice would be all over. 'Now you can have no juice,' I'd say, and she'd scream and carry on till it made me crazy.

"But if Monroe was there he'd sweet-talk her with some story he made up on the spot about a blue girl who lived in a red cup. She listened so hard her ears twitched and she'd laugh till her fat cheeks collapsed."

"I can see her," I said. "I can just imagine how she looked."

"I wish I had that picture my grandfather took to show you," Honora said. "It was Alice and Monroe, and Alice was laughing like that. I found it after I started working here, and I sent it to her in Philadelphia, which is where she moved to. She never said anything in her letter back except she got it. The rest was all about my job.

"Alice thinks I'm doing something bad by working in this place for old white people, Clara. 'What about your own people?' she wrote.

" 'It's the job that came open,' I wrote back, 'and it paid pretty good. And I got tired of the hospital after all those years.'

" 'It isn't that,' she said, when she came back the next visit. She was sitting right up on the edge of the blue chair, as if she couldn't stand to light there for more than a second. 'You like being with those old people, those old white people. It's because you can boss them around,' she said, and her voice rose up so high it shook.

" 'What is it, Alice? What's wrong? It isn't that Carl, is it?'

"She flew off the chair then as if she meant to fly straight at my throat. 'I can't talk to you,' she screamed. 'I have never once ever been able to talk to you,' and she lit out of the room before I could think of anything to say to stop her."

"Was it Carl?" I ask Honora.

"It was Alice and me," she says, and then she adds, "But Carl was supposed to come home with Alice, and he didn't come and he didn't call the whole time she was here and he didn't write."

* * *

Festina Lente and Carmen Ghia were the best of friends, but they were as different as night and day.

They were, their mothers agreed, the best-looking young women in the town. Both had dark hair and dark eyes, but Carmen's skin was deeply bronzed while Festina's skin was white as fresh cream even when the summer sun beat down on the tile roofs and scorched the sandy roads. Carmen's eyes blazed like a bonfire. Festina's eyes were as deep and still as the ancient well in the square, where tourists came to drop pennies and waited in vain to hear the coins hit bottom.

Carmen, who considered her mother's housewifely existence an embarrassment, was determined to be someone by the time she was twenty-five. To this end she took a speed-reading course and zipped through the great literature of the twentieth century in one summer. Festina, who could not imagine being twenty-five (she and Carmen were then nineteen), dawdled her way through a bad translation of Henry Miller's Stand Still Like the Hummingbird. *She thought she might find something in it she could use to fend off her mother's criticism of her "indolence," as that woman was pleased to call it.*

"Why can't you be more like Carmen?" her mother shouted at her.

"Mamma, please," Festina murmured, "lower your voice."

A few blocks away Mrs. Ghia shouted at Carmen, "You run around like a crazed chicken. Why can't you be quiet and nice like Festina?"

One might think that such talk would set the girls against each other, but neither of them listened to what their mothers said.

"Rush, rush, rush," Carmen's mother scolded. *"Where do you think you're going so fast?"*

But Festina loved Carmen's speed. In conversation Carmen dashed from one topic to another, interrupting herself as liberally as she did her listeners. Festina watched entranced as Carmen pumped her arms, waved her hands, twirled her long hair, chewed the inside of her plump cheek. After a few minutes Carmen's other friends grew agitated. But Festina could listen to Carmen for hours. *It's better than the opera,* she thought.

Festina spoke little and considered long before she opened her mouth. *"I'll be dead before you say a word,"* her mother screamed. Her sentences when she did speak trailed off at the end, as did her listeners, except for Carmen, who was convinced that sooner or later Festina would produce a pearl.

Now it happened, as it often does in small towns, that Festina and Carmen fell in love with the same young man, Alfredo Dente, a student of the law. And, as often happens, Al was in love with both of them.

The girls spoke openly, as was by then the custom even in their small village, of their mutual affection for Al Dente. We will both make love to him, Carmen decided, and then it will be clear to him whom he loves.

Carmen's passion was quick to ignite, and Al loved its furious heat, though frequently her calendar was so full that she couldn't make time for him, and when she did, it happened often that he couldn't get her to light long enough in one spot to get so much as an arm around her.

Festina's fires were banked but worth the trouble of stoking. Once lit, she could burn forever with a steady blue flame. Too long, in truth, Al had to admit. He was a young man, twenty-six, but after all he wasn't sixteen anymore.

Despite these reservations, Al was crazy about Festina and Carmen and more hard-pressed than ever to choose between them.

"Men are funny," Mrs. Lente said to her daughter.

"I could tell you stories about men," Mrs. Ghia said.

"No time, Mamma," Carmen called over her shoulder as she

ran out of the house, "I'm late for my date with Al Dente."

The summer was drawing to its close, and Al was still in his quandary, which, by and large, he mused, gazing at the cool green hills beyond the town, was as pleasant a place to be as any he could imagine.

The girls, however, grew testy with each other. "We'll be late for the movie again," Festina complained. "You were only going to buy one little melon, and an hour later you're still rushing from stall to stall like a madwoman, stopping to have a conversation with every idiot who passes by."

"No matter how early we get to the movie you will dawdle in the ladies' room," Carmen yelled, "and when you finally come out everyone will push ahead of you so we will have to sit in the front row and crane our necks like birds."

Then both girls burst into tears, alarmed at the pettiness of their argument and the strength of their anger.

"Something is wrong," Carmen's mother said to her daughter.

"You don't look good," Festina's mother told her. "I don't like how you look."

"I can't help the way I look, Mamma."

"I will throw him over," Carmen promised Festina.

"No, no, I will," Festina said.

But neither of them did.

"No news is bad news," Festina's mother said.

"Right," said Carmen's mother.

Now Al was not a mean man or a dishonorable one, and he saw that Festina and Carmen's friendship was suffering. On top of that he was beginning to have bad dreams. "I will choose tonight," he vowed.

All night he wrestled with his dilemma. In the morning he got out of bed and flipped a coin.

"Will you marry me?" he asked Festina at high noon. Festina bent her dark head and was quiet for so long Al thought she hadn't heard him. Finally she looked up at him. Her smile was as warm as the yellow sun spilling in through the slats of the shutters, but one eyelid, he noticed, twitched.

"Certainly I will, Al," she said. "Someday."

That evening Al approached Carmen. "Carmen, will you . . . ?"

"Yes," she said, springing off the sofa, where he had with difficulty pinned her only seconds before, "I will marry you." She paced back and forth in front of him. "I will enter law school in the fall. By the time you are established, I can join you in your practice. I'll take off a few months when we have our first child, and then we can move to a city."

Carmen was so excited by the details of her twenty-year plan that she didn't notice when Al left. "We could emigrate to Philadelphia," she said into the gathering darkness.

Three months later Al Dente married a young woman from a neighboring village.

"I knew it would come to this," Festina's mother grumbled.

"I told you so," Carmen's mother said.

Both Festina and Carmen found love again in time, Festina several years later than Carmen.

Carmen, who became a medieval scholar, lives with her law professor husband on an old farm in the green hills beyond the town. And Festina, who began welding enormous metal sculptures in her late thirties, emigrated to New Zealand with her psychiatrist husband.

Carmen and Festina have remained as close as sisters though thousands of miles and an ocean separate them. They write to each other frequently and visit back and forth as often as the dictates of family and finances allow, and they both look back with mixed feelings on the summer when they learned that their mothers were not so dumb nor life so simple as they thought it was going to be.

*   *   *

"Did your mother tell you stories when you were little?" Honora asks me. She is pulling fresh sheets and towels from the shelves in the supply closet.

"Well, my Aunt Celia used to read the newspaper to me," I say.

Honora looks over her shoulder at me. "The newspaper. Did you like that?"

"I loved Celia to read to me. Anything would have done."

"I made it a point to read to Alice ever since she was tiny," Honora says. "I read her storybooks, and she liked that fine. But there was nothing in the world Alice loved better than for Monroe to make her up a good-night story."

Honora closes the supply closet. Her arms are piled high with clean linen. She puts her face in the fresh white sheets. "Monroe would be half lying and half sitting with his head propped up against the pillow," Honora says, looking up at me, "and Alice would be leaning against him, her head on his chest. I'd be curled up on the side of him nearest to the wall, and I'd be playing with Alice's feet, which were hanging over Monroe's lap, listening to Monroe spin out his long, drawn-out tales that seemed to have no beginning and no end.

"They were nothing at all like his funny daytime stories. 'It's a whole different animal,' Monroe agreed, 'a good-night story.'

"The nighttime stories went in so many twists and turns I'd lose the threads of the story, how it all connected up. The harder I'd try to keep everything sorted out, the harder it was to concentrate. My eyes burned, and I could feel my eyelids growing heavier and heavier, as if they had little lead weights inside them. I'd force my eyes all the way open. But all the time I'm laying there knowing I'm going to give in soon. It was better than anything, shutting my eyes, giving in at last, when we were all together on Alice's little bed, with Alice's cool foot in my hand and Monroe's thigh touching mine and his steady, low voice like a breath going on and on and on."

23

It will be time for supper soon, and still the sun beats into the lounge.

Hannah Jessup has fallen asleep in her chair, and Johanna stands by the window with David Martin.

"They cut down that stand of loblolly pines," he says. "They cut down the shade."

For an instant the light, like a ceremonial robe, blazes over his shoulders, and his grey hair catches fire.

"Your hair in this light," Johanna says, "it's like copper. I'd love to take your picture right this instant," she says. "In this wonderful light."

"I grew to hate the light," he says suddenly, but Johanna is not startled. "It seemed to me that all our days were lit with an intense flat glare," he said, "an unnatural light that assigned everything the same value. There were no shadows, no shade, no respite from the brilliant light and Charlotte's strained attention.

"Charlotte had been an efficient but haphazard housekeeper, but that year she gave routine household chores the singular attention she had given previously only to her pictures or a favorite book. She started making lists—grocery lists, errands, people to call, people to write, things to fix in the house and in the garden. Nothing at all out of the way except that I had been the maker of lists, not Charlotte. 'Be sure and write down "Make love to Charlotte," ' she said once. So the next time we made love I jumped out of bed the minute we were through, and when she asked me what was wrong, I told her, 'I'm crossing "Make love to Charlotte" off my list.'

"I remembered that incident in the middle of the night, and I almost woke Charlotte to remind her of it, but I thought better of it, and then I wondered why I didn't want to remind her of it, and then I couldn't let go of that memory or my reluctance to speak of it to her. I worried it half the night like a dog with a bone, and when I finally slept I dreamed that Charlotte and I were being menaced by a blizzard of tiny white pieces of paper. But in the morning it was just a dream. My anxiety seemed silly.

"Then at breakfast I said something like, 'Shall I deposit that check from Stuart in the joint account?' And she said, 'Please, David, would you deposit that check from Stuart in the joint account?' And all my anxiety came flooding back. She was, I don't know how to say it, careful of me. She listened to the least consequential thing I said as attentively as though her life depended on it.

"We argued less if anything than we had before, but when we did she'd take such pains to build her case, as if she suspected I was bent on uncovering some flaw in her logic. 'You should have been the lawyer, not me,' I said after one such argument.

" 'I still could be,' she said. The way she said it was so odd—defiant and triumphant. My face must have registered that because she said, 'You're so literal, David. I didn't literally intend to literally get a literal law degree.'

"One morning just after I got to the office, Charlotte called me to say she couldn't find the keys to her car. 'I've looked everywhere, David. I turned the whole house upside down. They're just gone. They've disappeared off the face of the earth.'

" 'Didn't you take the car in to Dewey?' I asked. 'I thought that's where you were headed when I left.'

" 'That's right. I told you, the radiator's leaking.'

" 'He got it back to you already?'

" 'David, what are you talking about?' And then she saw. She saw before I did.

" 'Oh, God. My keys are in the car. My keys are in the car, David, and my car's at Dewey's.'

" 'What?'

" 'I didn't lose the keys. My car's at Dewey's.'

" 'Oh,' I said into the phone.

"There was a very long silence. I could hear her breathing. Finally she said, 'Don't be so serious, David. I think it's terribly funny.' Before I could say anything, she said, 'I've got to go. I'll see you tonight.'

Several months later I came home, and I'd picked up two rolls of the film she wanted, and she was very excited because it was May, and though it was after seven, there was still enough light for her to take pictures. I set the two rolls of film on the kitchen table. She went into the bedroom to get her camera, and she came back and sat down beside me and opened her camera. She picked up one of the rolls of film, and she stared at it for a very long time. And then I knew it was all going to come apart and there wasn't anything I could do. I sat there for so long watching her. It seemed like an eternity. Finally she said, 'Is this a trick?'

"Something in my chest caved in when she said that, something vital just collapsed, and I wasn't sure I was going to be able to get my next breath or to speak. But I did, and I said as steadily as I could, 'There isn't any trick.'

" 'Both rolls are the same?'

" 'Yes.'

" 'They're what I asked for?'

" 'Yes. Tri-X.'

" 'Tri-X,' she said. She put the film back on the table, and she closed her camera and put it on the table. And she looked really hard into my face. 'I can't remember how to load my camera, David.'

" 'I could do it for you.'

" 'No. . . . Don't cry, David. I don't want you to cry.'

" 'All right.'

" 'I'm very tired,' she said. 'I'm enormously tired. Will you come up with me?'

"We went upstairs and got undressed and into the bed though it was still light out. We didn't talk at all. I just held her till she fell asleep. I kept watch over her all night long as if it were a vigil there was some point to."

* * *

"It's the time you usually go," Honora says to me.

"Oh, yes."

"You're a million miles away," she says.

"Mr. Martin was telling Johanna about the beginnings of his wife's illness."

"She died here," Honora says.

"I know."

"He moved in here to be with her. There wasn't any sense in it in a way. His friends all thought he was crazy and so did Dr. Milne. He wasn't sick or infirm or anything. He was just keeping faith with her."

"That's what I was thinking about," I say. "Keeping faith when you're not sure there's any sense in it."

We fall silent, but I'm conscious of Honora watching me.

"What?" I say finally.

"Just the way you look," she says. "You look fierce."

"Fierce?"

"William looked like that when he slept," Honora says. "It scared me. Sometimes I'd wake him up and tell him how fierce he looked, and he'd always say he'd been dreaming hard."

"I guess I was dreaming hard," I say. "Honora, would you have time to listen to a story?"

Honora settles herself on the couch beside me. "I've got time."

Father Mother was scandalized by the street attire worn by so many of the young nuns. He himself dressed in full habit always.

A full wimple covered all but the front of his long face, and his ample black skirts swept the sidewalks clean.

This very outfit had been the cause of his excommunication from the Church many years before. Like St. Augustine he put off the putting off of his bad habit. "I couldn't help myself," he told the bishop in their last dreadful meeting. But in his prayers that night he admitted, "I courted disaster, Lord, because she's so easily won."

He had been saddened by his expulsion from the Church that had been his home since boyhood, but relieved too, for he had wearied of giving the sacraments. Confirmations, baptisms, weddings, all spoke to him of joys that would never be his. He dreaded the last rites. The holy words of comfort turned to mumbo jumbo in his mouth, and he saw himself old and dying and afraid.

He would be glad to give it all up. But he could not bear to think that he might never hear another confession.

He did not listen to confessions in the ordinary way, he listened as if his life depended on it. He exclaimed aloud when some revelation moved him. "Oh, no," he cried, and he jammed his big hand through the tiny window in an effort to touch the confessor. Often he laughed his immoderate wheezing laugh, and sometimes he wept. When the sinner was finished, Father Mother frequently said nothing, so heavily did the sinner's pain weigh on him. Sometimes he would say only, "Ah, you poor fateful sonofabitch." Other times he would assign bizarre penances and acts of contrition.

"Don't bathe for two weeks," he would tell the overbearing, "and your pride will be mortified. Jerk off," he told the horny young boys, "every hour on the hour for three days. Your prick will not fall off, but it will be put in its place."

His unorthodox methods in the confessional alarmed many of the parishioners, though many had great comfort of him. When word got back to the higher-ups, it confirmed their worst suspicions. They bounced him with clear consciences and a great weight of evidence.

After only a week on the streets, Father Mother saw that there was no lack of confessors in the teeming city for one who was ready to hear.

They cornered him in alleys and in public houses. They followed him into bathrooms and lobbies and parks. Pushers and pimps and perverts of every description confessed rages and thefts and unspeakable desires.

There were days when Father Mother rejoiced in his new life. "I am blessed," he thanked God. "I am doing what I want to do." But there were other days and nights especially when he counted himself a failure. "I am a joke," he moaned aloud, studying his long horse face in the wavy mirror. "I am alone." In despair he would throw himself onto his bed and jerk himself off. The semen spurted onto the barren mattress, and he had no release for his hungry spirit.

Once he almost cried out, "Oh, my God, why hast thou forsaken me?" but some sense of proportion held him back.

He was not a young man anymore. He was, in fact, a great deal past middle age. The spongy black hair that had covered his body like moss was white and sparse. His eyes were watery, and he did not see as sharply as he once had. There were days when he felt stiff in all his parts and he walked the streets with a great effort, leaning on a stick.

But he could still hear a pin drop on Broadway at midday, and he could hear the faintest whisper of the most shamed confessor. It seemed to him that he heard more now than what was said. He heard what was not said. And all the pain and the bad jokes sounded in his ears like a tragic symphony, and he fell asleep at night with the cello's deep, sorrowful hum vibrating all through his long, tired body like the humming of the trucks on the avenue outside his window.

When he was hearing a confession, his concentration was seamless and complete. But when he was alone, his mind wandered. I would have borne children, he thought, following the progress of the Good Humor truck up the crowded street, if only I had been a woman. But then I would not have been a priest, and hearing confessions is what I love to do. It is what I do best. Perhaps I hear nothing except the sound of my own voice. Perhaps it has all been vanity and delusion. So he reflected as the shadows lengthened and the whores came out on every corner, like gaudy blossoms, he thought tenderly, wondering how he might have looked in red satin.

Passing his reflection in the pawnshop window on his way home, he stopped and stared. "Is it me?" he wondered aloud. "I am bent over and stooped. All the sorrows I have heard press on my shoulders and bow me down like an old man. I am an old man."

When he climbed into his bed that night, he asked God to forgive him for wasting the gifts he had been given. "But I have to say," he added, "you didn't give me a whole lot to work with." Just before he drifted off, he prayed, "Sometimes when I am hearing confession, I imagine I hear you singing in my ear. But more often I wonder, is he there? Where is he? Why does he hide from me? And I want to yell out, 'Show yourself, you sonofabitch.' "

In the dream that came to him just before dawn, he saw himself down on his knees in the middle of a busy street. He saw himself, an old man in a full habit with a long face like a horse, bent over with his nose in the gutter. The traffic was bearing down on him, rushing at him with the force of an avenging army.

I'm too heavy to get up, he thought. I'll never make it. But the cello sounded its purest, most sorrowful note in his ear, and he felt himself rising up. Up he went, light as a feather, up and up. And he knew in his dream with the certainty of death that each sin he had forgiven in his heart had lightened him. He rose straight up into the air over the trees and trucks and buses and cabs. He sailed over the tops of the buildings like the bearded men in a Chagall painting, over the steeple of the church from which he had been excommunicated, over the United Nations building and the World Trade Center. He rose straight up into the blue sky.

In the morning the landlady of the flophouse Father Mother called home came to confess that she had bilked him out of the

*deposit on his room three years before. She found him dead as a
doornail in his bed.*

*"I'm sorry I tried to gyp you," she said aloud. "I been mean-
ing to square it with you." She imagined him laughing his immoderate wheezing laugh, and she felt he would've forgiven her
if he could hear her. She looked down at him for a long while.
"Amen," she said finally, and she made the sign of the cross over
his long body before she went to call the cops.*

"That man listened like you do," Honora says, "and he
loved what he did. He held to it even though it meant he
had to give up things he might have wanted. He held to it
even when he doubted what he was doing or if it was
worth anything at all. You told me a story about you."

24

Honora has been sitting with Mrs. Merriman.

"I was bragging about Alice," she tells me.

"To Mrs. Merriman?"

"Oh, yes."

"You talk to her about real things," I say.

"Well, just now I was talking like everything is wonderful with Alice and me. I left out all the bad parts."

"Like Alice being mad at you because you're here?"

"Alice thinks she's mad at me for all kind of reasons,
Clara," Honora says, "but really she's mad because I left
Monroe and wouldn't take him back and because I didn't
stop William from dying. I said that to her once after she'd

been at me for three hours straight about my lack of social awareness. 'You reduce everything I believe in to something trivial,' she said.

" 'I'm talking about Monroe and William. I'm talking about your father and your stepfather.'

" 'I don't remember my father,' Alice said. 'I don't remember a thing about him.'

" 'You always loved to hear about him,' I told her. 'Even after William was your daddy, anytime you'd be sick in the bed you'd ask me to tell you about Monroe.'

" 'Tell me how you and my daddy used to go dancing,' Alice would say. And I'd say, 'Who said "I'd rather dance with you, honey, than fly to the moon?" ' And she'd say, 'Monroe said that.' And then I'd tell her all about me and Monroe going dancing and how everybody stopped to watch.

"I don't know why, but Alice loves me. She must know I love her. Imagine, she's thinking about running for city council in Philadelphia, and she started out just being my baby that Monroe said had squinty eyes.

"Sometimes I wonder, Clara, if Alice remembers those times I was so bad to her.

"It was always after a bad time with Monroe. He'd have just told me some flimsy lie or been eyeing me all night like he meant business, and then we'd get off to ourselves and he hadn't meant anything. And then putting Alice to bed at night, I'd have trouble getting her arm into the sleeve of the nightdress, and she'd fuss, and then I'd grab her arm and I'd force it the way I wanted it to go. She'd go rigid and scream and she'd get all purple in the face, and I'd tell her to shut up. 'You shut up, you,' I'd say. 'Just shut up.' I'd feel terrible, but I was excited too. I'd feel this surge of excitement because I was so big and she was so tiny. And all the time I was thinking, oh, God, Honora, you are bad. Then I'd hold Alice to me and rock her as if nothing had ever happened, and she'd settle down and fall off to sleep. 'You better not trust me so easy,' I'd warn her.

"When Alice was first born I felt connected to her like I had never been to another soul. I couldn't tolerate loud noises then. People seemed to talk so loud I could hardly stand it, and all the lights were so bright. And I thought, that's how Alice feels coming into this noisy world after being so quiet and dark for so long. It made me feel joyous to feel like her. I thought to myself, I love my baby. I know what love means. And it seemed wonderful to me because I think I'd always been afraid till then that I wasn't ever really going to love anyone.

"I used to love the early-morning feeding. Alice started sleeping through the night when she was about three months so it stopped. I missed it. I missed sitting with her on my breast in the cool darkness before the dawn. I'd sit there and imagine what Alice and me would be doing next year and the year after that and the year after that. Sometimes Monroe would be with us in my mind, but mostly he wouldn't be. Everything seemed so clear in those hours. Monroe won't be here, came into my mind, and it didn't scare me, it was just a fact like any other. And I thought about Alice growing up and leaving, and that was just a fact. Nothing alarmed me in those early mornings. The good or the bad. It was all just what it was."

* * *

"I had a dream," my Aunt Celia told me, "about a month after your father and mother were killed. It was the simplest sort of dream, Clara. My mother sat down beside me on my bed, and she said, 'You miss your brother, don't you?' And I started to cry. I cried terrible, bitter tears because I missed him so much I could hardly stand it. My mother just held me while I cried. Finally I was all through crying, and I was so tired, and my mother said, 'You can go on and sleep now, Celia. You'll wake up in the morning.' "

25

Hannah Jessup takes a bite out of one of the truffles Johanna brought her from the new bakery downtown. "It reminds me of my chocolate icebox cake. You loved that cake, didn't you, darling?"

"Better than life," Johanna says so seriously that her grandmother laughs.

"You used to eat two big pieces one right after the other."

"I'd come over after school to show you my latest photographs, and you'd go over to the window and hold each one up to the light, and you'd tell me which ones you liked best and why. And then you'd feed me something wonderful. Chocolate icebox cake or lemon torte or sherbet you made yourself."

"I was a good cook," Hannah Jessup says. "And you were a good picture taker."

* * *

"My father was already dead when Vernon barged into my life," Miriam Stone tells Johanna. "But Vernon liked to hear me talk about him. 'Tell me about the time Meyer got Mrs. Mendelsohn over the pickle barrel,' he'd say. 'Tell about the time Meyer grabbed the wrong titty in the movie.' "

"I should go sit with my grandmother, Mrs. Stone," Johanna says.

Mrs. Stone continues as if she had not heard Johanna. "His own father had departed, that's how his mother put it, when Vernon was a very young boy, so he had nothing firsthand to tell about him, and his mother never said a word about her dead husband in my hearing. She never said anything in my hearing that was of interest to me, except to tell me about those wonderful girls from lovely old families that Vernon could have married. That was okay by me. I liked it. It satisfied me to hear her go on about them. I was a rock in her way. She could rattle on and on, but she couldn't get past the fact of me."

"My grandmother's waving at me," Johanna says.

"This is the good part," Mrs. Stone says. " 'Vernon, dear,' his mother would say, looking straight across the table at me with those peculiar little eyes she had, like little bright blue marbles, 'do you remember that lovely Elizabeth Crawford, whose daddy was lieutenant governor?'

" 'Elizabeth Crawford,' I'd say. 'Do you remember Elizabeth, Vernon?'

" 'Dimly,' Vernon said.

Johanna laughs.

" 'Well, I know he remembers the time Elizabeth Crawford and Milly Caswell had that terrible falling-out over him,' she said. 'Would you like more pie, Miriam?'

"I said I wouldn't.

" 'I don't recall that,' Vernon said to his mother.

" 'Yes, you do. Elizabeth pushed Milly right off this porch, and Milly broke her ankle and missed her own birthday party.'

" 'Elizabeth Crawford left town five years before I had anything to do with Milly Caswell, Mother.'

" 'I distinctly remember otherwise,' Vernon's mother said, passing me a second piece of pie, 'and I have a memory like a hawk.' "

Johanna smiles at Mrs. Stone. "So do you," she says.

* * *

"Was I a good person?" Hannah Jessup leans so far forward in her chair that Johanna calls, "Watch out!"

"Was I a good person?"

"What do you mean, Han? Of course you were."

"Don't say it like that. You don't tell me anything."

"But you were a good person," Johanna says. "You are. You're a wonderful person."

Hannah Jessup grabs her granddaughter's hand. "I have to ask your mother. I must ask her."

"We'll call her. We'll call her today."

"No, no, no," Hannah Jessup says. "I have to see her."

"She'll be here soon," Johanna says. "She'll be here Thanksgiving."

"Thanksgiving," Hannah Jessup says. She falls back in her chair.

"You don't understand," she says.

* * *

Before I left this afternoon I stopped to speak to Hannah Jessup. "I wanted to say good night," I said.

"Oh, Clara, thank goodness. Have you seen my granddaughter?"

"Johanna left for the day several hours ago, Mrs. Jessup," I told her. "Is something wrong?"

"I was asking her something important," she said. "I don't remember just what." I started to remind Hannah Jessup what she and Johanna had been talking about, but she rushed on. "I always loved her, but when it's time to discuss something important, she doesn't know what I'm talking about. You would have known. You would have understood."

"Maybe she was afraid to talk about it," I said.

"Of course," Hannah Jessup said. "She's afraid of everything real. Work. Marriage. Death. On top of that she exaggerates. She would do something crazy like Mr. Martin following his wife in here. That would be right in her line. Only Mr. Martin was quiet about it. Johanna would make a drama.

"*Ach, Gott,*" she said. To my surprise tears sprang to her eyes. "Oh, Clara, sometimes I wish I'd been more like Johanna in my life—stubborn and foolish and loyal."

26

Tremors move through Mrs. Merriman's body with the regularity of time passing.

"Some days, Clara, I have to force myself to sit with her," Honora says. "I want to run away. But if I run away or if I stay, it's no difference, I run smack into my grandfather. He's sitting on the porch of the old house on Corporation Street, and he's saying, 'Watch for ye know not when your hour comes. Pay attention, girl. Pay attention.'

"One night," Honora says, "I dreamed Mrs. Merriman was a bird, a big old bird, a hawk or an eagle, one, with great wide wings, and she soared over a purple valley, and you and me and Johanna, we were all below watching the shadow of her wings darken the hills."

* * *

Honora wants me to make up a story about Mrs. Merriman. I've been thinking about it all week, and this morning I found my beginning. *Virginia Merriman had a big family and a long memory that could summon the days when they'd all been together.*

27

"I dreamed about your son last night," Johanna tells David Martin. "He looked like you. He was lost in the woods in back of your house."

"Did he find his way out?"

"I woke up before I knew."

"Well, I dreamed there would be a letter from him today," Mr. Martin says, handing Johanna the two new letters from his son.

"You're a seer," Johanna says, carefully extracting the new letters from their thin envelopes. Both letters are written on the heavy white paper butchers use.

" 'Dear Dad,' " Johanna reads, " 'You said, "Your mother suffered significant losses since you were last here." Aphasia, agnosia, apraxia, you said. But you never said, "I have to bolt the doors because your mother wanders deep into the woods in the dead of night." You never said, "She grabs the mashed potatoes off my plate and stuffs them in her mouth." You never said, "She can no longer find the words for what she wants to say." You never said, "Oh, Glenn, she doesn't know my name." ' "

Johanna looks up. Mr. Martin holds a hand up in the air as if to forestall her questions. "Read the other one," he says.

" 'Dear Dad, why did you follow her into the home? The blood was still pumping in your veins. You had a beating heart. You could speak and move and dress yourself and piss in the toilet. You had a son. But you buried yourself alongside your beloved. Why did you do it? Glenn.'

"You loved her," Johanna says.

David Martin takes the letters from Johanna. "I brought her here because she wouldn't eat anymore at home. I was afraid she'd starve to death. But I couldn't leave her in this overheated place that smelled of piss and Clorox. I couldn't bear it. So I stayed."

"You had to stay," Johanna says.

Mr. Martin looks at Johanna. "It wasn't devotion," he says sharply. "Or suicide or guilt or anything I can reasonably name. I just couldn't do it." He stares down at the papers in his hand. "The nerve endings in the outer layer of my wife's brain were degenerating, disrupting the electrochemical signals between cells, and so she asked, 'What day is it today?' ten times in an hour and tapped her foot incessantly and strode purposefully from room to room but had no purpose.

"When I brought her here she was too weak to walk. But at home she walked and walked and walked. She walked and ate and watched TV. We sat in front of the TV for hours and days on end. For a year we watched TV. The sun poured into the room, and it was hard to see the images, but I never thought to draw the curtains. For the most part Charlotte watched without comment, without, I felt, real attention, but if I moved to turn the set off, she'd say, 'It's interesting. It's very interesting.'

"And then she'd make some comment, some observation, and I thought, it's all right, it's all right, she knows what's going on.

"But it didn't last. It didn't last, and watching her strain to understand, I lost my bearings so that finally everything I saw was so jumbled, so without sense or meaning that I sometimes thought I might be hallucinating.

"A pretty woman alluded often to her husband's impotence, and each time the off-screen audience hooted their appreciation. A pleasant-looking man implied you could fly cheaply if you bought a certain camera.

" 'I don't understand,' Charlotte said.

" 'No, no, darling, neither do I. We'll get something else.' On the next channel someone said that dentists recommend that their patients chew gum. I'd look over at Charlotte, and I'd see this terrible tension in her face. So I'd jump up again and switch to another channel.

"A familiar-looking man in a studio spoke to another familiar-looking man on a monitor. I heard the man in the studio say, 'The downside always impacts on the upside.'

"I laughed so strangely that Charlotte put her hand out to me. 'It's all right, darling,' she said. 'It's supposed to be funny.'

"I was staying home for longer and longer periods, and finally I let go altogether of my working life, which seemed to belong to another person in another life.

"Glenn called from halfway around the world somewhere. 'You can't just quit work,' he said.

" 'I'm seventy years old,' I told him.

" 'So what?'

" 'My eyes are very bad, Glenn. They're much worse than when you last saw me, and I've got that irregular heartbeat. I have to slow down.'

" 'You're staying home to take care of her.'

" 'I want to.'

" 'What if I came home? What if I moved in?'
" 'We don't want you to do that.'
" 'You want to be alone.'
" 'Yes.' "

*   *   *

Before she left this afternoon, Johanna asked Honora about Charlotte Martin's death.

"It says broncho-pneumonia on the certificate," Honora said.

"But you don't believe it?"

Honora shrugged. "She was pretty bad when I first saw her. Mr. Martin hadn't been able to get her to eat anything solid for days. She was too weak to stand up on her own, and she already had that infection in her lungs. But she had to eat here, of course. We fed her IV, and she was getting antibiotics IV for the pneumonia. She was picking up a little, and her lungs were a little bit clearer, but after three weeks she got phlebitis at the IV site, so I asked Dr. Milne could I take them out for a while and see if I could feed her water and Ensure with a syringe and antibiotics by mouth. He said okay, we could try it for a few days. And she did it, she took the liquid from the syringe and she was able to swallow the pills. Seemed like to me she was getting stronger. And Dr. Milne said so too. 'She's getting stronger,' he told me. 'There's no doubt about it.'

"A few days after that she stopped eating again. Mr. Martin pleaded with her to eat so I wouldn't have to stick those IVs back in her. But she just kept her head turned away. So I put the IVs in again. She rallied a little the first couple of days."

"Do you think she wanted to die?" Johanna asked.

"She prayed all night long, the last night," Honora said, "and I don't know if she prayed to live or die.

"And all night long Mr. Martin stood by her bed. He wouldn't sit down once. He stood over her like a shadow, and he held her hand so tight it would've hurt her if she'd been thinking of it. You could see by his eyes and the way his jaw was, you could see by the set of his whole body that he was willing her to stay."

"He couldn't stand to see her die," Johanna said.

"He didn't care anymore what she wanted, Johanna," Honora said. "He wanted her to stay. But God didn't ask Mr. Martin what he wanted. He took her and left Mr. Martin behind."

*   *   *

There is another letter from Glenn today.

" 'Coming home was terrible,' " Johanna reads, " 'the hardest thing I have ever done. Charlotte was so silent and remote, and you were crazy, it seemed to me—in a sort of manic frenzy. You spent whole days posting signs: LIGHT SWITCH TO THE LEFT OF THE DOOR. DON'T TURN ON THE STOVE. You had labeled everything in sight—all of Charlotte's drawers, every item in the medicine chest.

" ' "When he puts a sign on the toilet saying this is the toilet, I'm leaving him," Charlotte said one morning, and my heart leaped up and I thought, she's fine. She's just depressed. This is all bullshit. And I said, "He's making you worse, Mom." ' "

Johanna breaks off. "How could he say that to her? You were doing everything and he was doing nothing."

"Please," Mr. Martin says. "Please just go on."

" 'She looked away, past me,' " Johanna reads, " 'the way she had ever since I'd come home. "You don't know," she said. The way she said it made me want to run away. I wanted to jump out of my chair and fly out the door and never come back. But I said, "What don't I know?"

" ' "He has to . . . He has to do that thing . . . He has to . . ."

" ' "What?"

" ' "The thing. The thing you do at night."

" ' "Go to bed?"

" ' "No, no. Before."

" ' "Supper. Dinner? Fix dinner?"

" ' "No, no, no. This." She plucked at the sleeve of her sweater. "This."

" ' "Sweater? Dress? Dress. He has to dress you."

" ' "Yes," she said, and she looked straight at me. "He has to dress me in the morning and undress me at night. He has to do it—all those things." Then she said, "It's okay," and she laid her palm against the side of my face.

" 'That was the last time I ever really talked to her, the last real conversation we ever had, so I go over that exchange. I've gone over it a thousand times trying to extract everything I need. In my best moments I believe she thought I might be as brave as she was and as you were, and I believe she told me she loved me.' "

"May I have it?" Mr. Martin asks after a long silence.

Johanna hands him the letter, and he runs his fingers over every line, as if his son's words were written in Braille, as if he could feel the text.

"Do you want to write him?" Johanna asks.

"Yes. Yes, I do."

Johanna stoops down to her purse and draws out her pad of airmail paper and her felt-tipped pen. Her dark head is bent over the pad of paper. There is a look of ardent expectation on her face, as if the words Mr. Martin chooses to dictate might alter the course of her life.

"Why are you doing this?"

Johanna looks up, startled.

"I don't know you at all. Who are you? Some young woman with purple hair and black eyes. A stranger. A Yankee." He laughs.

"I'd tell you anything you want to know."

"You'll answer questions, you mean."

"Yes."

"It isn't much. Answering questions isn't much at all."

"No," Johanna says. Her black pen drops out of her hand and rolls away across the squares of old linoleum. "I'll get it," she says, but she makes no move to do so.

"It's a sign I shouldn't write today," David Martin says.

"I believe in signs," Johanna says.

"I thought you might," David Martin replies. "You and Samuel."

"Samuel?"

"The fisherman in Clara's story," he says.

"But he misread everything," Johanna says. "Even the tides."

"Sometimes I think you misread everything, Johanna."

"I was wrong about Glenn," Johanna says. "I was all wrong."

"I don't mean that," David Martin says.

"You don't understand how ordinary it was after a while," he goes on. "Just one day after another. You don't understand. Neither does Glenn. You and Samuel and Glenn, you're looking for signs."

*   *   *

When I was in the sixth grade, Celia gave me two yellowing pictures of my father as a boy. I kept them in a special box in my dresser drawer along with a coin from Turkey and my jackknife. She had no pictures of my mother as a girl to give me.

The summer I was twelve, Celia was going through her photo album and came across two photographs of my parents as adults that she said I could keep.

One was a picture of the two of them as college graduates standing in a row with all the other graduates in long black gowns and flat hats with tassels that hung over their faces.

The other picture was a snapshot Celia took the morning of the day they were killed. My father was sitting on a suitcase, and my mother was sitting on my father's lap. "I told them to sit like that," Celia told me. "You can see they're not too happy with my idea."

I could see it. Night after night I pulled the picture out from under my pillow to study it. I was struck every time with how stiff they looked, how tentative—each on his perch, he on the suitcase and she on his lap. But there was something else. They were excited. They couldn't wait to get going.

I saved up my allowance and bought a Quality magnifying glass. "Scientists use this, honey," the salesgirl at Kress' told me. I scrutinized my parents' faces under the glass. Their large eyes looked out at me, but I couldn't fathom what was there.

28

Johanna's mother called Honora last night. "All the way from Antwerp, Clara," Honora said. "She got my letter about us closing down the same day she heard it from Johanna. She said nothing near where she lives in New York has opened up. 'Even if I came home to stay now,' she said, 'it wouldn't do any good.'

"She begged me to do everything I could to see that

Mrs. Jessup gets in a nice place with nice people to look out for her. 'Johanna thinks very highly of you,' she said. 'She says you like my mother.' I told her I do like her mother. And she said, 'She's so proud, you know,' and she started to cry. 'She's pretty too,' I said. 'Hannah Jessup is the prettiest old white lady I ever saw.' Something about that made her laugh. Then she said, 'I told Johanna as soon as she knows when the move will be to let me know, and I'll fly back to the States and help settle her in the new place. I was planning to come Thanksgiving anyway, so I'll just move it up.' I said I thought that would be good. And then she said, 'My mother was counting on me, Mrs. Bliss. She thought I was going to do something.' I said I didn't see what she could do. Then we said goodbye.

"Her voice is a little like Johanna's," Honora said. "Only it's clearer. Even across all those miles, it's clearer."

29

All morning long the fluorescent lights over Hannah Jessup's head sizzle like frying eggs.

She stares up at the rectangular tubes as if she were hearing that sound for the first time. "When is my granddaughter coming?"

"She generally gets here after lunch sometime, Mrs. Jessup," Honora assures her. "Is there something I can do?"

"What could you do?" Mrs. Stone asks. "You couldn't

do anything," she answers herself. "Am I right, Mrs. Jessup?"

"When is my granddaughter coming?"

"They have their own lives," Mrs. Stone says.

"She'll be here soon," I say.

"Clara's right," Honora says. "It will be very soon."

Twenty minutes later Mrs. Jessup asks again. "Where is my granddaughter?" and then again and then again.

"I don't know for certain when she'll be here, Mrs. Jessup," Honora says, "but I know she will be here."

"Johanna comes to see you every day, Mrs. Jessup," I say. "She always comes."

"There's always a first time," Mrs. Stone warns. "They're counting your chickens."

As soon as Johanna steps into the lounge, Mrs. Jessup stretches out her hand, as if she wanted to pluck Johanna up, as if she couldn't wait the time it took Johanna to cross the room. "You're here."

Johanna starts as if she'd been accused. "What's wrong?"

"I want to go home, Johanna."

Johanna stares stupidly at her grandmother.

"I want you to take me home."

"But don't you remember, Han?" Johanna blurts out. "The apartment is gone."

"What do you mean?" Hannah Jessup cries.

"You couldn't stay there alone anymore," Johanna stammers. "You couldn't manage by yourself. We had full-time nurses. You must remember, Han. You hated it. You said you wouldn't have those women in your house."

"You can't take away my home!" Johanna's grandmother exclaims, rising up in her chair. "This is America."

"Hah!" Mrs. Stone says.

Johanna bursts into tears.

Beside me Honora hums, "Oh, no, no." She slides a foot forward as if she means to intervene. But the outcome is inevitable. She can alter nothing.

* * *

The workmen have gone home. Their earth-eating dino-
saurs are ranged about the dusty ground, abandoned co-
lossuses sweltering in the sun. Honora stands at the open
window. "The air-conditioning broke for good last night,
Clara," she said. "And Mrs. Jessup stopped talking."

"Look," she says, pointing. The sun is so hot it has blis-
tered the yellow paint on one side of one of the tractors.

30

The deadly heat outlasts the sun. The days do not end,
they collapse, one on top of the other, like corpses in a
communal grave.

"I can't stand this," Mrs. Stone gasps. "I'm an old lady,
and I tell you I can't stand it." She kicks at the fan (one of
six Honora has bought from Sears and charged to Green
Mansions, although she doubts the board will pay for so
many). "It's blowing hot air at me. What good is it? What
good is it?" She pokes Johanna, but Johanna doesn't feel
it.

"Please talk to me, Han," Johanna says.

Mrs. Stone makes a disgusted face. "Look at her."

Johanna's back is so bowed that her head rests on her
stomach; her shoulders curve in so drastically that they
scrape against each other in front of her sunken chest.

"She's been at it all week, over and over like a parrot,"

Mrs. Stone complains to David Martin. "And in this heat. It's making me crazy. Vernon loves the heat," she goes on when Mr. Martin makes no reply. "He sucks it up like it was gin. He should have left me in Queens."

"My wife's friend Daisy grew up in Queens," Mr. Martin says.

"Where was your wife from?"

"She was from Georgia."

"Oh, well, Georgia." Mrs. Stone sighs. "Georgia's worse. Vernon's mother was from Georgia."

"Oh, really," Mr. Martin says.

"Vernon thinks he did me a big favor rescuing me from Queens, and then he dumped me in a big house with seven fireplaces and one bathroom while he went charging around the country charming the pants off everyone, and he gave me two boring daughters that neither of us like. I take it your son is no great shakes either."

Mr. Martin smiles.

"It was their idea actually, Barbara and Gail, to dump me in this pit. Vernon just went along. That's his major fatal flaw, he goes along. He's got a list of fatal flaws as long as your arm."

"So do I," David Martin says.

"You?" Mrs. Stone says.

"Oh, yes."

Mrs. Stone laughs. "Next time you go out in the world, Johanna, you could bring me and Mr. Martin some nice ice tea. . . . She doesn't even turn her head. I'll ask Clara to do it."

"I'll be glad to," I say.

Mrs. Stone raises her voice. "I said, next time you go out into the world . . ."

"Of course," Johanna says. "I'm sorry."

"Of course, of course. I used to ask Vernon, 'Do you really love me, Vernon?' and he'd say, 'Of course.' When all is said and done, you know who he really loved? Sudie. A black maid. He has dreams about her. Good ones, he says. He's always in a good mood when he has a Sudie dream. He even sings—'Old buttermilk sky, I'm keepin' my eye peeled on you.' "

"Please, please, say something to me, Han."

"She might as well give up," Mrs. Stone tells Mr. Martin. "It's a disease. First her," she nods in the direction of Mrs. Merriman, "now her grandmother. I'll be next. It's the last thing they can do to me. They'll shut my trap."

"She can speak," Johanna says.

"Well, she won't. Anyone can see she's through with it. I'm sorry for you, but I can't get too worked up about it. How many times has anybody said anything you really wanted to hear? Your grandmother never talked to me anyway. But Mr. Martin talks to me. We spoke last night."

"We were talking about your father."

"See, he talks to me. But I wasn't good enough for your grandmother to talk to. She thinks I'm not refined. I'm refined. I'm refined as they come."

Johanna gnashes her teeth so hard that sparks fly out of her fillings and land on Mrs. Stone's green blouse, singeing a tiny corner of one sleeve. The smell of burning nylon brings tears to Johanna's eyes. She brings a finger to the inside corner of each eye and wipes it along her lower lashes, drying the tears and slanting her eyes shut. Inscrutable as a Chinaman, she flattens her spine against the back of her chair and disappears. Only her breath remains.

A fugitive breeze lifts the leaves of a mimosa tree. A faint smell of lemons comes in at the window. A smell of new sawdust and fresh-poured tar. And the strong smell of the young men whose chests and backs are slick with sweat.

"Do you remember, Han?" Johanna says at last from behind her closed eyes. "Do you remember, you used to have me for Sunday breakfast, and we'd spend the whole morning together, and you'd tell me how it used to be when you were a girl in Germany. You told me about the summer evening promenades. I could see you strolling down the wide tree-lined avenues, walking on your father's arm or with your sisters. One night a certain young man smiled. But the young man turned out to be unsuitable. He was too young, a student still. 'I loved that boy,' you told me. But you married my grandfather, who was ten years older than you and established at the university in Frankfurt with a better job at a bigger university waiting for him in America and galley proofs of his first book being set at the printer's in Stuttgart. 'I admired him greatly,' you said. 'He was terribly smart and so witty and attentive, and it all happened before I had my bearings. Before I understood that it was more than a summer's afternoon dream, more than a novel I was reading that I could put aside if another was more to my liking.' "

31

Johanna comes earlier and earlier to sit with her grandmother.

"What did she do?" Miriam Stone demands. "Did she give up her job?"

"She told them there was an emergency," David Martin explains.

"They'll fire her."

"I'm not sure she'd care," I say.

"For once Clara is right," Mrs. Stone says. She lowers her voice. "In my opinion Johanna's obsessed."

David Martin laughs strangely.

"You think it's normal to sit for hours and hours, for days and weeks on end babbling God knows what to someone who doesn't answer?"

"She understands everything Johanna says to her," David Martin says.

"How do you know?"

"She decided not to speak, Mrs. Stone," I say.

"That doesn't mean she understands."

David Martin colors. "You can't just write someone off."

"Mr. Martin," Miriam Stone says, "there's nothing in Mrs. Jessup's face. It's blank like a check. There's nothing in her eyes. Not a flicker."

"You told me about your sisters, Han," Johanna says. "Don't you remember? You and Susannah and Elise in the big house that your father was on the way to losing with his harebrained architectural schemes that everyone but he could see would never work. He had been trained as a lawyer, but the law couldn't contain him, you said. His fledgling practice dried up in less than two years. He bought a department store on the Kirchgasse. 'I'm going to gut the interior,' he said one night at dinner, 'and make an arcade of little shops.' And you and Susannah and Elise gaped as he pushed napkins and knives and forks and saltcellars around the big table to demonstrate his idea.

"But the interior of the store remained intact, you said, and the store's sales plummeted while your father sat in his big office drawing elaborate plans for futuristic cities with freakishly tall buildings connected by silvery bridges miles high in the air. You never knew your pappa was going through a fortune and ruining the business. 'Mamma's family money cushioned all the blows,' you said, and, in fact, it was precisely your father's visions of underground railways and floating parks that had so entranced your mother to begin with. Until Elise's death she encouraged his dreams. 'The store is just something you have to do now, darling. It won't always be that way.'

"But it all changed, you said, when Elise died. Everything changed.

"Elise, the first born, died of a lung disease when she was ten. 'Mamma shut up her room,' you said. She burned all Elise's clothes, and she had the piano taken away, even though Susannah wanted to learn. Susannah never forgave your mother for taking away the piano. When Susannah was forty-two, she wrote you, 'Elise's death was the central event of all our lives. All the resolutions and irresolutions of all our lives sprang from that event.' And when Susannah was seventy-eight, you said, she still talked about the piano. 'Mamma never valued me or anything I wanted to do,' she said. 'It is why I never married.'

" 'Ach, well,' you told me, 'Susannah was always so dramatic.'

"Do you remember, Han, I was visiting you one day, and Susannah called, and I heard you tell her over the phone, 'Susannah, please. It's so silly. It was so long ago.'

"But when you got off the phone, you said, 'If Elise had lived, I think Mamma would have wanted me to marry my young man.'

"Your mother wasn't interested in your father's drawings after Elise died. She seemed to connect them with Elise's death. You said a year after Elise died your father showed your mother a new drawing for a theater with a roof that opened up to show the stars, and she snatched the drawing from his hand. 'It's all those idiotic papers,' she screamed at him. 'They ruined our lives.'

When you were sixteen and Elise had been dead four years, your mother pulled you into her room. She put her mouth right up against your ear and she hissed, 'When

Elise was sick, Papa forced Dr. Manheim to look at his drawings, and the doctor yawned in his face.' She pushed you up against the door, Han, and she whispered, 'I am convinced, Hannah, that Dr. Manheim's treatment of Elise was never the same after that.'

"And then you gave me a warning I didn't understand, Han. 'Obsession is tyranny,' you said."

*   *   *

Edmund was very attached to his penis.

When the nights were cold, his penis was warm. When the market fell, his penis rose. When the nation's moral fiber went soft, Edmund's penis was still hard.

When Edmund got up in the morning, his cock crowed, and when he went to bed at night, he hoisted his flag and it waved in the breeze that blew in at his window. He was a happy man.

His wife was not so happy. In the early days of their marriage, she had been amazed by Edmund's penis and had praised it unceasingly. But gradually, it seemed to Edmund, she had grown inattentive.

You can't depend on the weather, thought Edmund, or the price of gold, or a wife's love, but you can depend on my penis, and the thought was as soothing as his mother's caress.

Edmund lavished more and more attention on his penis. He anointed it with oils, he sang songs to it and he had its portrait painted by a major artist. Its care and maintenance consumed Edmund's energies. He was in danger of losing his job, his wife and his credit rating.

One night his wife blew up. "You never put it in me anymore. Don't you love me?"

"Of course I love you," Edmund said, absently patting the subject under discussion. "I just like to keep my eye on it."

"Oh, my God," his wife moaned, and the next morning she moved out.

Edmund was distressed by the breakup of his marriage, but he had no time to dwell on it. Word of his penis spread throughout the land, and people came from far and wide to worship at his shrine.

Fame preoccupied Edmund. He burned his morning muffins and charred his evening roast. He neglected his business and his friends. But he gave his all to his adoring fans. UP, he would command his penis and up it would go. STAY, he ordered and it stayed. UP, cried the ladies who came to the matinees from the suburbs, and Edmund's penis ascended. ENCORE, cried the ladies. ENCORE. And Edmund did it again.

Edmund lost his job. "Your mind isn't on your work," his boss said over lunch.

"My penis has become a household word," Edmund replied.

It was true. Edmund's penis was on everybody's lips. And now it was going to be immortalized. The governor had just announced that he would officiate at the ceremony that would celebrate the laying of Edmund's penis in the wet cement outside the Chinese theater.

The great day arrived. Network booms swung in the sky. A band played. "And now," the governor said into his mike (a hush fell over the crowd as Edmund unzipped his fly), "the moment we've all been waiting for." The crowd roared as Edmund's penis poked its head skyward. The crowd went wild, and Edmund's penis rose to new heights. But just as the drummer began his final roll, Edmund's penis fell off.

The crowd was aghast. But strange to say Edmund did not sob or scream or go mad. He smiled out at the crowd in a way no one could fathom, not even the television anchorman who was used to analyzing complex situations.

32

"You described particular dresses to me, Han," Johanna says. Her voice is blurry with fatigue and listless as the fans, which whir and flag and sink and whir again in the muggy twilight. "You had a green velvet dinner dress. 'Exquisite velvet,' you said, 'as soft as butter.' The green was the green at the bottom of the sea, so deep it was almost black. You were wearing it at the opera the night Dr. Hermann fell in love with you, fell so obviously in love with you that you could never have him to the house again.

"When my grandfather was honored by the chairman of his department at the university, you wore a maroon wool dress with long narrow sleeves and a high rolled collar. It had a slender belt with a large tortoiseshell buckle. On the drive home my grandfather said, 'I could wrap one hand around your waist and keep you in this cab forever.'

"The night my mother brought my father home to dinner for the first time, you were wearing a dress of grey silk jersey . . ."

"i . . . zeee . . . ee . . . ee"

The long, drawn-out syllables are so thready, so thin, yet they penetrate Johanna's dream. She sits bolt upright in her chair, and the grey silk dress slips through her fingers.

"i . . . zeee . . . ee . . . ee"

Mrs. Stone cranes her neck. "What was that?"

"It's Mrs. Merriman," Honora says, almost in a whisper.

Johanna gets up from her chair. "It's Mrs. Merriman. Mrs. Merriman spoke."

"She doesn't sound normal," Mrs. Stone says.

"It's all right," Honora says in a more usual tone of voice, but she walks over to Mrs. Merriman with uncharacteristic deliberation, as if she fears she will break something valuable if she moves too fast.

"i . . . zeee . . . ee . . . ee"

The effort to speak pulls every muscle in Mrs. Merriman's face into spasm. "i . . . zeee . . . ee . . . ee"

"What is it?" Mr. Martin asks. "Is it a seizure?"

"She said 'I see,' " Johanna says, looking at me.

"No, no," Honora assures Mr. Martin, kneeling in front of Mrs. Merriman. She takes the old lady's bony hand in her own. "It's not a seizure."

"She said 'I see,' " Johanna says again. "You heard her, Clara."

"Is that what she said, Clara?" Honora looks over at me.

"I thought she said 'icy.' "

David Martin laughs.

Johanna's voice surges up like a wave, rolling over David Martin and me. "I know what I heard."

"She didn't say anything," Mrs. Stone says, exasperated. "It's just noises."

Johanna brushes past me, heading for Mrs. Merriman. "What is it, Mrs. Merriman?" she urges, crouching beside Honora. "What do you see?"

The old woman does not answer Johanna. Her face is all in shadow now in the dusk; she is a long, dark shape. At her feet two rounded forms bend like supplicants.

"I'm going to take her to bed," Honora says at last. Holding on to Johanna's shoulder for leverage, she pushes herself upright. "You go back to your grandmother."

"I will," Johanna says.

When Johanna sits again in front of her grandmother, Hannah Jessup lifts an arm in front of her face as if she thinks Johanna means to strike her. "Han," Johanna says.

"Oh, Han, it's me." She gathers her grandmother's hands into her own. "Your hands are so cold, Han," she says, rubbing them vigorously. "I'll warm you," she says. "It's going to be all right, Han. Everything will be all right."

* * *

The night I told my Aunt Celia I was leaving for good, she told me how she and my father had sat up on the porch talking the night before my mother and father got married. "He said he was too keyed up to sleep," Celia said. "He said he couldn't remember ever being so excited or so scared."

"We talked about everything under the sun," Celia said. "We talked about the election coming up and the stock market and a book he'd just read about the Amazon River. They were playing Tommy and Jimmy Dorsey songs on the radio inside the house, and Bing Crosby was singing. He sang, 'I Wished on a Star,' and we quit talking and sang along with Bing. And then we talked about being kids together and our mother and father, and he said how glad he was I was his sister.

"We talked straight through the night. We talked ourselves hoarse, and there we were sitting on this porch sprawled in these chairs like drunks, half asleep both of us and chilled to the bone. 'We'll see the sunrise,' I said. Just as the sky grew light, your father hauled himself up out of his chair. 'Hope's a thief, Celia,' he said. 'It'll rob you blind,' and he went on in the house without waiting for the sun."

TWO

TWO

33

Now I know the story I want to tell about Johanna.

Stars fell on Alabama the night Johanna was born; but she came backward into the world in a teaching hospital on the island of Manhattan, and the midtown lights were so bright you couldn't even see the stars.

Johanna was plump and rosy, a regular baby. "She is extraordinary," her mother murmured as she rocked her little girl. "She has purple hair as glossy as an eggplant and a very high instep."

* * *

When Johanna was three her handsome father tossed her into the air, but just as she reached the apex of the upward curve, the telephone rang. "That's my office," her father crowed. He ran into the next room to answer it.

"I've been abandoned," Johanna cried, pumping her little arms in the air. "On the other hand," she considered, "I am defying gravity."

* * *

When Johanna was five her mother sat her down and told her the facts of life. There are real men. John Wayne, for instance. Lord Mountbatten. Abba Eban. Adlai Stevenson. Paul Muni. Jean Gabin. There are real men willing to stand up and be counted, to die for what is right. Men who are loyal to their wives. There are real men, but your father isn't one of them.

* * *

Johanna and her mother and father lived on the seventh floor of a twenty-two-story building. When Johanna was seven the super hinted they had a shot at a bigger apartment on nine, but the deal fell through.

"I'll fix that sonofabitch," her father said.

"Every cloud has a silver lining," Johanna's mother replied.

*   *   *

"When I was a little girl," Johanna's mother said, "I was very good at climbing trees. No one could go as high or as fast as I could. Not even your uncle Eliott. My mother used to stand under the elm tree and pretend to gasp at my audacity. Sometimes when my father was home from the university, he would come out from his study to watch me and he'd make a joke. 'She'll go far,' he'd say in a booming voice that bounced around in the treetops and carried me to the uppermost branch."

"When I was little," Johanna's mother said, "my father stayed in his study working on his papers and my mother ran in and out of the house like a breeze blowing."

"The first night of my marriage," Johanna's mother said, "I knew I had made a mistake."

*   *   *

One rainy autumn evening, just before her mother came in to kiss her good night, Johanna heard a man with a very deep voice reciting a poem about Sylvia on the radio. "Who is Sylvia?" the man asked, and his voice vibrated so thrillingly that the little radio skated across the top of her bedside table. "What is she?"

"Good night, darling," Johanna's mother whispered, clicking off the radio.

"Bad night."

"What's wrong?"

"You know. You saw it."

"I saw it?"

"Yes."

"When?"

"All afternoon."

"Oh," her mother said, "you mean Victoria Wheat. You mean Victoria won at jacks."

"Eight games in a row."

"Oh, sweetheart, you can beat her at something else."

"Like what, for instance?"

"Well, I don't know." Her mother was silent for a moment. "Her drawings aren't nearly as imaginative as yours."

"That's not the same," Johanna said, disgusted by her mother's obtuseness.

"Go to sleep now," her mother said. "Don't worry about it." She kissed her daughter's furrowed brow and tiptoed out of the room.

Johanna closed her eyes. After what seemed like a long time of not being able to fall asleep, she imagined she heard someone call her name.

"Johanna," the voice called. "Johanna."

Who's there? she said to herself.

"Sylvia," came the answer.

Johanna sat up in bed. Of course. "It's Sylvia," she said aloud. "It's Sylvia, my baby sister. Where have you been all my life?"

"Can I sit on your bed?" Sylvia asked.

It was dark in the room, but Johanna could see that Sylvia was small. "Sure," she said.

Sylvia curled up at the bottom of Johanna's bed. "Could you teach me to play jacks?"

Johanna considered the request for a long moment. "We'll see," she said finally, sinking down again into her bed and thinking to herself that Sylvia, who looked just the tiniest bit doltish, wouldn't be nearly as good as she was at jacks or pickup sticks or anything requiring delicacy and dexterity.

* * *

When Johanna was nine she and Victoria Wheat were building a birdhouse with Victoria's father's hammer and Johanna hammered her left thumb by mistake. The nail turned black, which gained her some pleasant notoriety on the block. Eventually the nail fell off and another grew in its place, but there were deep horizontal ridges in the new nail. She imagined they would go away sometime in the next year, but they didn't. Every bruise and scratch she had ever had, a considerable number, had healed in time, but her nail stayed the same.

When she was ten and a half her mother said, "The ridges won't go away, Johanna."

"They will," Johanna said. She didn't care how the nail looked. It was the idea that the condition was irreversible that alarmed her.

* * *

Often at night, after her mother had tucked her in and kissed her good night, Johanna would sing to Sylvia. She sang old songs, songs she had learned from cracked seventy-eights.

"You belong to my heart," she sang, and she knew beyond a shadow of a doubt what it would feel like to be in love. Her voice, which was already thin and unsteady, trembled out of control.

"We were gathering stars while a million guitars . . ."

"You could be a famous singer when you grow up," Sylvia said. "In a red dress."

Johanna saw herself larger than life fixed in the spotlight's stagy glow. "Shhh," she said.

". . . were still playing. Darling, you are the one and you'll always . . ." Johanna paused, gathering momentum, noisily sucking in breath and feeling for her finale . . . "belong to my heart." Johanna held the last note for a very long time before she sounded the final t.

"I wish I could sing," Sylvia said.

"I'll sing you more songs tomorrow night," Johanna said when

she got her breath back. She said it indulgently, the way she imagined she would speak to her own daughter if she were a grown-up.

*   *   *

When Johanna was eleven she had more secrets than she could count. She had found an ancient Brownie camera in a cardboard box full of old clothes her mother was saving, and she was teaching herself to take photographs.

She was thinking of becoming a Catholic. Under her undershirt, suspended on a very thin chain, she wore a tiny gold cross that Maureen Gallagher had lent her.

At her parents' last dinner party she had come into the kitchen to get a glass of juice and she had seen Mrs. Willet's long pink tongue disappear down her father's throat.

But the secret she hoarded, the secret she was saving for a rainy day, her best-kept secret, was that one day she would be beautiful.

Gazing at her round face in the mirror, opening her eyes as wide as they would go, lifting her eyebrows skyward, she whispered, "Nobody knows," and she dreamed of knocking them dead.

*   *   *

"When I was little," Johanna's mother said, "I didn't want to be anything when I grew up except a woman."

*   *   *

Crossing the busy avenue on the way home from the dentist shortly before her twelfth birthday, Johanna's father said to her, "I am not seeing another woman."

Taxis squealed to a halt, pedestrians froze in their tracks and a great hush fell over the avenue.

He's lying to me, Johanna thought, bewitched by the weakness revealed in the lie.

* * *

When Johanna spends the night at her grandmother's tiny apartment, she can imagine what it will be like to be grown-up. After supper her grandmother serves her deep, dark coffee in miniature cups of maroon and gold and chocolates from Belgium.

"What is your opinion of the mayor?" her grandmother asks her as they sip their coffee.

She shows Johanna a picture in a magazine. "Do you think this shade of green would be becoming to your mother?"

After they have brushed their teeth and are in their nighties, her grandmother will tell Johanna about the city in Europe where she grew up, about the parks and the promenades and the cafés. She will talk about her family and old loves and what it was like coming to America for the first time.

Johanna sleeps on the couch by the window. I can see the whole city, Johanna thinks to herself, looking out at the glittering lights. I can see miles and miles in every direction. I can see my future.

* * *

One afternoon Johanna's father tapped on the bathroom door. "Johanna, would you come into the living room, please."

In the living room Johanna's father stirs his cocktail with a finger and Johanna's mother blows her nose. "Your father and I are thinking of being apart for a . . ."

"You can't catch me," Johanna screamed, laughing uproariously. She ran out of the living room, raced to her tiny bedroom and slammed the door.

Sylvia leaned against the door, laughing into Johanna's ear. "Oh, boy," she wheezed in between seizures of laughter. "Oh, boy."

Later, when they were getting into their pajamas, Johanna noticed how thin Sylvia's shoulders were and how lankly her dim hair fell against her cheek. She felt a stab of pity for her little sister. But when Sylvia asked, "What are we going to do, Johanna?" Johanna barked at her, "How should I know?"

That shut Sylvia up. In the silence Johanna heard her own heart beat. She drew her little sister to her. Sylvia's tears wet Johanna's cheeks. "You have to get a grip on yourself, Sylvia," she admonished, not unkindly, and she told Sylvia a story about two lost girls who after many terrifying near misses with calamity found their way back to their cozy home in the forest, where their grateful parents fed them steaming hot Lipton chicken noodle soup and tucked them into a featherbed.

* * *

Johanna's father left the apartment Thursday morning, and he was back home Sunday night.

Her parents had explained to Johanna that the length of her father's absence could not be known.

"It might only be a few weeks, sweetheart," he had said, grabbing Johanna's thin hand that was a replica of his own.

"It won't be months though, will it?" Johanna asked. "It won't be till summer?"

"It could be," her father said, turning her hand over palm up and laying his own on top of it.

"It could be forever," her mother said, speaking, Johanna could hear in her voice, not to her daughter but to her husband.

It could be forever.

But her father had been gone less time than he was gone on any of the dozens of business trips he took every year to Washington, to Cleveland, to Los Angeles.

Johanna was not reassured by her father's swift return. She held her breath and waited to see if anything was different. It wasn't.

His homecoming had been, after all, only an answer to her prayers. It signified nothing.

* * *

Johanna's bedroom window opens onto the air shaft. At night she lies in bed listening to the voices that float into her room from the other apartments facing the air shaft.

"Aren't you going to shake my hand?" a woman asks. She laughs so teasingly that Johanna knows she means something more than she is saying.

"Another story," a child pleads. Johanna cannot tell from the small, light voice whether it is a boy or a girl. "Another one, Daddy."

"A great king had a daughter who was very beautiful but so proud and haughty and conceited that none of the princes who came to ask her hand in marriage were good enough for her, and she only made sport of them . . ."

"It's very clear," a smoky-voiced woman on someone else's radio sings, "our love is . . ."

A young man sighs. His longing drifts down from an apartment somewhere above Johanna's bedroom. Johanna feels that she could love that man. His sigh carries her into a dream of love.

* * *

When Johanna was twelve she went to Walgreens and selected a large bottle of toilet water—"Eau d'Amour" the saleswoman said as if it were a guarantee—for her mother's birthday.

"Eau d'Amour," Johanna blurted nervously as her mother unwrapped the violet tissue paper.

"Eau d'Amour," her mother said, and her voice rose so violently that it shattered the blue bottle and the smelly liquid spilled out onto the living room rug.

* * *

In the courtroom where her parents are on trial, Johanna is the star witness, and the attorney for the defense and the prosecution. She is the jury and the judge.

"All the evidence isn't in," she pleads. The jury nods. "The defendant is not the villain he's cracked up to be."

"We know." The jurors nod again. "We know."

The prosecution is more aggressive, better prepared. Sadder. The jury is deadlocked and the judge is wishy-washy.

* * *

"When I was thirteen," Johanna's mother said, "I wanted to be a dancer. I had pink slippers and black tights and a tutu made of tulle."

* * *

The mirrored walls of Victoria Wheat's bedroom created the illusion of great space and a numbing self-consciousness. It was not a room in which you could easily share confidences. It was not a room in which you hid giggling in the closet till whoever was "it" counted to ten. But it was the perfect room in which to act out scenes inspired by the treasures in the rusting steamer trunk that had sailed with Victoria's great-grandmother across the ocean to the Continent.

The girls pulled out balding feather boas, red satin mules with the fabric worn through over the toes of the right foot and silver sandals with impossibly high heels. There was a velvet cloak with the nap worn off, a matched set of Oriental fans as yellow and crumbling as old newsprint, tiny evening bags with jeweled clasps that no longer worked and a lace peignoir with moth holes in it.

"I'll be Grace Kelly," Victoria said, wrapping the sturdy, compact body Johanna so envied in the midnight-blue cloak. Victoria cracked a wispy feather boa like a whip in the air. "You can be my understudy."

"Someone in the audience could shoot you," Johanna said.

"Like Lincoln and John Wilkes Booth."

"Right," Johanna said. "I'll run onstage and leap into the audience and nab him."

"You got to do stuff last time, Johanna. You be Grace Kelly and I'll catch the thief."

"Murderer."

"Murderer."

"I get to wear the cloak then," Johanna said.

"Nothing doing," Victoria said. "There's other stuff in there."

Johanna rummaged in the trunk and dragged out a white organza gown with tiny tears under the armpits and a stain at its hem. She pulled off her plaid cotton shirt and her cotton trousers (as fast as she could so Victoria wouldn't see her in her underwear) and dropped the dress over her dark head.

When she emerged from under the delicate stiffness of yards of organza, she was caught by her image in the mirrored wall. She saw a woman with creamy shoulders and round breasts and hips and a waist. Her face was lit up. It was a woman's face with full red lips and knowing eyes. Off to one side, in back of her, she saw Victoria, who could do everything better than she could, left behind. The unaccustomed thrill of mastery colored Johanna's cheeks like shame.

In the mirror Victoria's pale eyes held her own. A splotchy flush spread over the bridge of Victoria's small nose.

A sudden panic laid itself along the length of Johanna's spine like a cold hand. "It doesn't fit," she said. She yanked the dress over the obstruction of her breasts. She felt the fabric pull and heard the soft tearing.

"You tore it," Victoria said. "You ruined everything."

* * *

Johanna falls asleep listening to the songs that drift into her bedroom from the other apartments facing the air shaft.

A wild man shrieks—"Oh, baby, yes, baby, woo, baby, havin' me some fun tonight."

Johanna looks into his eyes and shivers.

"You don't know what you been missin', oh, boy," another, younger man whispers in her ear.

Johanna doesn't know. But she misses it all the same.

She turns uneasily in her bed.

*   *   *

When Maureen Gallagher explained to Johanna what F-U-C-K meant, Johanna thought it was the least surprising and the most amazing thing she had ever heard. She thought about it for days on end. Finally she told Sylvia about it.

"Are you sure that's what it means?" Sylvia asked.

"Positive."

"You mean Mommy and Daddy do that?"

"They did it to make me," Johanna said.

*   *   *

Sometimes Sylvia popped up where she wasn't wanted.

"Get out of here, Sylvia."

"What's the matter with your voice? What are you doing?"

"Nothing."

"You are so doing something," Sylvia insisted. "The sheet is moving. You don't have any pajamas on," she added suspiciously.

"Mommy doesn't wear pajamas."

"She's married. I'm going to tell on you."

Johanna caught her breath sharply and the sheet grew as still as the lake at the camp she had gone to the summer before.

"Do you promise never to do it again?"

"I promise."

"I don't believe you," Sylvia said, with good reason since already Johanna was breaking her vow.

*   *   *

Along with the snatches of songs and stories and conversations that drift into her room from the air shaft, Johanna hears intimations of her future. Someday, she hears. Someday. Someday. Someday.

My real life has not begun, Johanna thinks to herself.

At first she imagines her life will begin when she gets her period. When it comes she is thrilled. She is certain that the bright crimson blood that soaks into the bulky white pad between her legs is a source of power. The heavy, dragging pull and the surprising severity of the pains that attend the flow confirm the seriousness of the event.

But it's not what she's been waiting for.

*   *   *

Her weekend visit to the suburbs to visit Sarah Bishop, who has recently moved out of the city, frightens Johanna.

"It's a ranch house," Sarah tells her.

"Oh," Johanna says, alarmed that it looks nothing like she would imagine a house on a ranch to look.

The house is large and orderly and all on one floor. A beige carpet runs from one end of the house to the other. Outside the picture window, which extends the length of one whole wall, the lawn is orderly. The bushes are low and trim, and no weeds grow there.

In the living room Johanna sits on a large sofa in the shape of an L and watches two chairs in the shape of Ss facing each other. On top of the two triangular-shaped end tables are sparkling glass ashtrays and large matching lamps with blue glass bases. On the glass coffee table there is an enormous book of color photographs of deserts and another one, equally large and equally heavy, of stars.

Sarah's parents change their clothes for dinner. In between courses they ask the girls questions in low voices as if they are afraid someone is listening.

After dinner the girls watch an old war movie on a giant TV in the family room. The picture is so large Johanna sees more than she wants to.

That night Johanna dreamed that screaming Oriental men with teeth like rodents swarmed over the walls of the sand castle she had built at the edge of the sea.

* * *

"When I was a boy," Johanna's father said, "I had so many brothers I didn't know what to do. We all slept in the same bed, and I always had a hand over my face or a foot in my rib.

"When I was a boy," Johanna's father said, "my brothers went to see Hopalong Cassidy get his man. We bought one ticket for a nickel and we sat one, two, three, four, five on each other's laps. I was the baby so I was on top and I got the best view. I told the others what Hopalong was up to.

"When I was a boy," Johanna's father said, "I stuck my thing in a knothole in a tree and it got stuck. I was famous after that.

"When I was a boy," Johanna's father said, "there were bats in the belfry and rats in the cellar.

"When I was a boy," Johanna's father said, "Cavenaugh and his gang were out to get you on your way home from school. They made Jimmy Kountz kiss Cavenaugh's ass and then they beat him up anyway."

* * *

When she was thirteen Johanna grew silent. She opened her mouth only to say no or to fill it with food. She lay on her bed and thought about what it would feel like to be dead forever and what it would feel like to have a man touch her new sore breasts, which seemed to her to be filled with a yearning so intense that it pushed them forward against her shirt.

* * *

Johanna went with her parents to the capital for a holiday. They stayed in an old, luxuriously appointed hotel with long, deeply carpeted corridors. They had a suite with two connecting rooms.

On the first morning Johanna opened the door and saw her parents sprawled naked, fast asleep, on the enormous double bed. The creamy white sheet trailed onto the floor. Johanna's mother lay facedown with one leg drawn up. Her father lay on his back. He lay halfway down the bed at an angle. His head rested in the curve of his wife's spine, and his long feet hung off the side of the bed. Johanna closed the door.

Dizzy with relief and a sudden, anxious joy that made her legs wobble, she lay down on the single bed in her own room. "They love each other," she said aloud. The large, square, sunlit room received the information with majestic aplomb as if, Johanna thought, it had known it all along.

*   *   *

On the second morning of their holiday in the capital, Johanna's father put his big hand flat against her back and shoved her down the corridor of the hotel. Her breath flew out of her and she stumbled half the length of the hall and fell.

Her father pulled her up. "Why is she mad at me, Johanna? What did you say to her, you little bastard?"

*   *   *

In restaurants Johanna watches the couples, husbands and wives, she assumes, eating and not speaking. They have nothing to say to each other. The ice cubes in Johanna's Coca-Cola rattle against the sides of her glass, sounding a warning.

*   *   *

"Don't tell me!" Johanna hears a man yell down the air shaft one clear, cold night in December. His voice sounds so close, as if he were leaning over her bed, shouting into her ear.

"I'll murder you, you sonofabitch," the woman shrieks in Johanna's other ear.

"Shut up, you cunt. Just shut your mouth, bitch."

There is a loud popping noise like a cork going off, or a gun.

Johanna sits up in her bed, stiff with fear.

The woman screams, a scream like a long fall down the length of the air shaft. There is a burst of loud music, horns, and then a stillness like death or falling snow.

Johanna knows she should wake her parents, get up out of the bed and walk into their room. At least she could cry out and they would come. The longer she waits, the less possible it seems to tell what she heard. She doesn't want to tell anyone, not anyone, not even her mother.

In the morning she runs to the door to get the newspaper. She looks all through the paper. There is no mention of the murder. She is relieved. Later it occurs to her that no one has discovered the murder yet. Still she keeps silent. She checks the paper every day for a week.

*   *   *

I am losing my grip, Johanna thinks at fourteen.

She is gaining weight. The pictures she takes with her camera never turn out to suit her. Her grades reveal that she is seriously defective. She has never been kissed, and every time the phone rings, the hair on the back of her neck stands up and she wishes she were deaf. Her dreams are so fearful that she forgets them as soon as she wakes up. There is only the tension at the base of her skull to remind her of them.

*   *   *

Your life will begin the first time a boy kisses you, comes the whisper from the air shaft. The first time a boy kisses you, Johanna. That's when your life will begin.

But the kiss when it comes is a bitter disappointment. It never occurred to Johanna that a boy she didn't like would be the first to kiss her. You spoiled my first kiss, she accuses Alfred silently and is barely civil to him as he escorts her back to her own apartment building.

*   *   *

One evening in early May, Johanna went with her parents to see a movie about a French artist who was as short as a dwarf.

"That was fun," Johanna's father said. They were walking home from the theater, three abreast in the spring night, which was so full of promise. "We have to do this more often. All together like this."

He took his wife's arm and she moved against his hip. "Oh, yes," she said. "It was a wonderful movie. It was so touching. How did you like it, darling?" She turned her head to Johanna.

"It was sentimental and the photography was gaudy."

"I hate you," her mother shouted, breaking away from her husband.

She slammed Johanna's shoulder with her balled fist.

Johanna's father put out an arm and pulled his wife back to his side. "Fuck her," he said to his wife. "Just fuck her."

Johanna pushed ahead of them, righteous tears stinging her eyes. She rammed her hands deep into her jeans pockets. She felt satisfied.

*   *   *

When Johanna was fifteen she lay on her bed on long, dark Sunday afternoons and listened to the whispers from the air shaft and the top ten songs on the pop charts. They told her the same thing— your life will begin when a boy touches you:

> *There is a rose in Spanish Harlem,*
> *A red rose up in Spanish Harlem*

With eyes as black as coal
That look down in my soul
And start a fire there and then I lose control.

"And then I lose control," Johanna warbles passionately. "And then I lose control."

One very cold day in February, Tony Street took her ice skating at the pond in Central Park. Afterward they sat on a bench away from the other skaters and watched the sky turn deeper and deeper shades of electric blue. Just as the edge of the new moon became visible, Tony unzipped Johanna's parka and laid his hands over her breasts.

Tony's touch moved Johanna inexpressibly. She couldn't fall asleep that night. She lay in bed and thought abut Tony. At two in the morning she turned on her radio. A backdoor man told her, "Well, the men don't know, but the little girls understand."

"I understand," Johanna said. "I am changed forever."

But the next day she spilled marinara sauce down the front of the white silk blouse her mother had bought her at Saks, and she couldn't make heads or tails of the novel she was reading, and she had a raw, red pimple in a prominent position alongside her lumpish nose.

* * *

"When I was eighteen," Johanna's mother said, "three of my professors fell in love with me."

"What happened?" Johanna asked.

"I got As in all three courses and only one of them was deserved."

* * *

When Johanna was sixteen Tony Street told her he loved her. So did Marty Brill and Patrick Sheehan.

* * *

Johanna did not enjoy the love letters and poems that young men sent her. Enjoyment, she felt, would commit her to some drastic course of action.

"It doesn't matter if you don't love him," Johanna's mother said.

"It does matter," Johanna cried. "I don't know what to do."

Nevertheless she kept every last one of the letters and poems, and she read them over and over till they fell apart in her hands and the tatters blew away.

* * *

When Johanna was seventeen her left thumbnail was still marked, but in her heart of hearts she believed she would wake some morning and her nail would be as smooth and as pink as all the others.

* * *

The first time she made love Johanna thought, oh, this is it. This is what I've been waiting so long for, and it's true she had been waiting since she was fourteen.

But still her life did not begin.

* * *

On the senior class trip to the Easter show at Radio City Music Hall, Johanna watches the Rockettes from the third balcony. If only I had perfect thighs, she thinks, I would be perfectly happy.

* * *

Johanna covers the waterfront and the side streets and the back alleys and the wide avenues searching for faces.

With her camera slung around her neck she looks for the one that will cry out, "Look, look—it's all in my face."

She takes pictures of hundreds of faces. For months on end she takes pictures of faces. But when she removes the negative from the solution, it is always the same. The clarity she is looking for eludes her. The focus is too soft, the composition disordered, the knowledge forfeit. She tears the contact sheets into pieces.

Before she goes off to college she locks her camera in the old black trunk she took to Camp Wynoka.

*   *   *

On the drive to the airport for her flight to the state where she would go to college, Johanna was carsick. She hung her head out the window and threw up on the parkway.

Later, when they were standing in line to check her bags through, her mother said, "When you were little you spun in circles till you fell down, you stuck your finger in electrical sockets, you held your breath till you turned blue."

Johanna turned around to look at her mother.

"You wanted to see what would happen."

"When you were very little," Johanna's father said, handing Johanna her claim check, "I slung you around my neck and you and I went off the see the world."

"You can't go with her now," Johanna's mother said.

"Nope," her father said, "I guess not."

*   *   *

It seemed to Johanna that the four years she spent in the small southeastern university had gone by as swiftly as a bird's flight and as uneventfully as the slow unfolding spring.

She remembered little of what had passed in the seminars and lectures she attended, though she acquitted herself well in all but a few required courses. Even the love affairs that had determined the climate of her days and the text of her dreams seemed, looking backward, insubstantial. They told her nothing of what her life would be.

One month before the end of the final semester, she dreamed of leaving right away. The violence of the imagined rupture speeded up her metabolism. She raced across the great Gothic quadrangles. I will do it, she thought. I will perform an action that has consequences.

But the impulse that filled her with new energy and made the days vivid was not the stuff of action. Its death was as circumstantial as its birth. Johanna graduated with the rest of her class in the giant outdoor stadium.

She thought of staying on after school in this familiar town where the winters were short, the accents melodious and all the handsome young carpenters had PhDs.

But the noisy, polluted city of her birth drew her back. Where there is smoke, there is fire, she reasoned. I will throw myself into the fiery heart of life.

*   *   *

The summer after graduation Johanna borrowed the security deposit and two months' rent from her parents and moved into a rectangular studio apartment on the third floor of a West Side walk-up. The apartment had a big closet you could walk around in. Perfect for a darkroom, Johanna thought, though she hadn't taken a picture in four years. Every morning Johanna rode the M104 bus, which crossed 42nd Street, to deliver her to the employment offices on the East Side.

In the fall Johanna got a fee-paid job inserting commas in long sentences, and in the winter she found love.

At first sight of his coarse wheat-colored hair and his unimaginably pale eyes that held the color of whatever he was seeing in his mind's eye, the pulse between her legs beat like a heart.

He had sailed around the world on a tramp steamer and climbed a mountain in Nepal. Everywhere he went he had taken pictures.

It was not what was in the pictures that informed his vision, it was what was missing. The mother without her child, the lover without his beloved, the tree without its leaves. His pictures roused in Johanna an excitement so intense she had to touch them with her fingers.

"It isn't me you love," he said, watching her. "It's my pictures."

"I love you," she said. "I love you, I love you, I love you." And she made love to him with a ferocity he mistrusted.

Now I am living my life, Johanna thought to herself as she rode home to him on the bus. She closed her eyes and saw the breadth of his shoulders and the long, smooth muscles of his thighs and his wonderful pale eyes. She heard the sound of satisfaction he made when he entered her.

He had no family and no past. "I am making it up as I go along," he said.

Now. Now. Now I am living my life, Johanna hummed to herself as she lay on her bed beside this man who assumed he might rest his hand between her legs as he talked far into the night, describing where he was going to go and who he was going to meet.

One night, just before dawn, he broke off in the middle of his narrative. "You never tell me anything about yourself," he said.

"You know my parents' names and where I was born and where I went to school."

He sat up in the bed and looked down at her. "I've told you my future. I've shown you my pictures. I tell you what I dream."

"What are you dreaming now?" she asked, unable to stop herself.

"Oh, you chicken-shit bitch," he said.

Below them in the night they heard a woman say, "But do you really love me?"

"Fuckin' A," her companion replied.

"Fuckin' B," someone called from the rooftop.

"Fuckin' C," the garbageman sang as he rattled the trash cans under their window.

In the morning she got up before he did and brought him coffee in bed. "Do you know how much I hate this city?" he said.

"How much?"

"Do you know how much I hate this apartment? I hate this fucking apartment. I hate you," he said. "I'm going to take pictures of you naked and sell them in the alley. I'm going to truss you up like a pig and fuck you till you faint."

"I'm glad you think I'm trussworthy," Johanna said.

"I don't," he said. "I really don't. But I'm in love with you anyway."

One night he jumped up out of bed. "I'm going to sell my camera. Don't say anything," he said. "Don't tell me how wonderful my pictures are."

He picked a roach up off the windowsill, but he didn't light it. "Maybe it's just being here," he said.

"I can't take pictures anymore." He sat down beside her on the bed, laying the roach on top of the sheet where it covered her breasts. "There are all these countries where people won't let you take their pictures because they think you'll steal their souls. Maybe they're right."

"I want you to steal my soul," Johanna said, and she reached up and drew him down to her.

When she got home from work the next day, Johanna found him pacing the perimeter of the rectangular room. He paced like a caged animal or a madman.

Johanna was afraid to ask, what is it? What's wrong?

In the days that followed he could not turn his back or slam a book down on a table or say "shit" that she did not think, it is I who make him curse and weep. He will leave me.

One night, as the long night was ending, he said to Johanna, "I want you to come with me. I want to marry you."

The only sound between them was the silence and Johanna's galloping breath. "Will you?"

"You won't. You won't come. I knew it all along," he said, and he put her hand on his trembling cock, and he buried it deep inside her.

The next night when she returned from work he had gone. There was a note propped up against the pillow on her side of the bed. "Sorry," it said.

Fully clothed she lay on her bed. All night long she lay there sounding all the permutations, all the infinitesimal nuances of that one word. From her bed she could see out the window. The neon sign on the bar and grill across the street flashed SORRY.

In the morning she called in sick to work, and, still in her clothes, she fell into an exhausted sleep.

She dreamed that she looked out her window, and in a clearing in a forest of evergreen trees she saw a young girl, a cripple, fall down on the ground. The girl struggled to pick herself up. Her mouth was screwed into a grimace of pain, and her cotton shift, soaked with the sweat of her effort, bunched up around her malformed thighs. As last she stood. But she fell down again. She struggled to get up. She grabbed at the air. The veins in her neck bulged, and her mouth screwed up in a grimace of pain. She stood. She stood up, and her cotton shift, soaked with the sweat of her effort, bunched up around her thighs.

Waking, Johanna knew that she was the crippled girl, and she knew she had dreamed this dream before.

The next day she quit her job and made plans to leave the city. "I will live alone," she said.

She rented a car and drove down the East Coast until she came to the state where she had gone to college. There she went into the middle of a pine forest and found a hut for rent.

* * *

For seven months Johanna lived alone in her hut in the middle of the pine forest. She lived on hope and the income from a $12,000 CD, a going-away present from her grandmother. From week to week she saw no one except Raymond, the old black man who came to pick up the garbage in his ancient pickup truck, and the checkout lady at the all-night A&P where she bought her food.

Leaning over the kitchen sink, Johanna dines alone on Fritos and ice cream, scanning the week-old newspapers Raymond kindly brings her. ERECTION RESULTS DISPUTED, *she reads.* UNION TALKS WEDLOCKED. *Johanna sighs. Out of the corner of one moist eye she watches the TV, which she turned on three months ago and never turned off. The commercial messages ensure her evening's misery. Tonight is not special. She has no one to reach out and touch, no one with whom to celebrate the moments of her life. "Cannon has not touched my life," she groans and throws herself down on the bare cot on which she has slept alone for these many long months.*

She dozes fitfully through two sitcom reruns she has seen only days before and wakes to hear the tail end of the news at eleven. "Marijuana affects death perception," the anchorman announces, and an electron microscope's vision of the inner workings of an eyeball flashes on the screen. Johanna closes her own eyes.

"The coast is clear," the weatherman advises. Opening her eyes to make sure, Johanna slides her jersey sweatpants down around her naked thighs. "Let's locate the high pleasure area," the weatherman says, pointing at his satellite map.

"Okay," Johanna says. She slips her middle finger out of sight. "Got it," she says, masturbating without enthusiasm.

"A storm is brewing," the weatherman warns.

"I hope so," Johanna cries out, bringing herself to a feeble climax. Then she falls asleep.

*   *   *

Johanna was an avid dreamer. She believed that the revelations in her dreams might bring her closer to her life.

Every morning she scribbled the messages of the night before onto whatever scrap of paper was handy. Images in excess, profligate images, poured out of her pen. Blood and guts and penises and wise men pointing.

But this night her dreams were straightforward.

In the first dream Johanna was in a dark cave. She listens for the dripping of stalactites, but the only sound is the burbling of a Water Pic. As her eyes become accustomed to the gloom, she sees that she is in a subterranean movie theater. The sound she had identified as a Water Pic is, in fact, the sound of a home movie projector.

The images projected on the cave wall are indistinct. The production values are poor, the focus variable. There is no sound, and the color is so muted she's not sure it isn't black and white. There is no plot, and the film meanders aimlessly backward and forward in time.

Johanna's mother sits on a green slatted bench in the park with Victoria Wheat's mother, while their two daughters play together in the sandbox. The heads of the two women are almost touching, the dark head and the fair head. They are whispering. Suddenly Victoria's mother throws her arms out dramatically and makes a face. The two women burst into laughter. The children look up, surprised.

Johanna's father grins and slams the racquetball across the court. His short-sleeved cotton T-shirt is plastered to his skin. His black hair is slick with sweat. He wants to win. He wants to beat that other guy, Johanna thinks.

Johanna's mother leans over the bed to kiss Johanna good night. Her heavy, dark hair swings across her cheek. She's younger than I am now, Johanna thinks. She's a young woman. Her mother tucks the blanket securely around her small daughter. She moves slowly, steadily. She is not in a hurry.

Johanna's mother and father are lying on Johanna's blue blanket at the beach. Johanna's mother's arm is raised across her eyes, protecting them from the sun. Perhaps she is asleep. Her father's leg is thrown over her mother's hip, securing her left leg to his side. Johanna is out of range of the camera. I am not in this picture. It is just the two of them in this picture.

Johanna and her mother have their backs to the camera. Walking down the street, Johanna has hold of her mother's skirt. She bunches a corner of it into her mouth. Her mother walks on, apparently not concerned that her tottering daughter is chewing her good skirt or that a long length of her leg is exposed.

Johanna's father is looking out a large window onto a luxuriously blooming garden. His hair is beginning to grey. The expression on his face is absorbed and far away.

In the second dream Johanna goes to her refrigerator and opens it. In an earthen pot there is a roast with new potatoes and onions and carrots. There are glass jars of jellies and jams, loaves of dark bread wrapped in clear plastic wrap, golden sticks of sweet butter, apple juice in a blue glazed pitcher. There are great stalks of dark green broccoli and soft feathery clutches of dill and parsley. There is a lemon torte with a zwieback crust. As she leans into the fullness of her refrigerator, oranges and grapefruits and melons and cherries tumble out, falling all around her. She kneels down on the floor, gathering the fallen fruit in her lap. A sweet rush of happiness fills her. My mother did this for me.

In the third dream Johanna's father has his large hands raised over his head, which is cradled in his joined hands. His legs are stretched out in front of him, crossed at the ankles. He has Johanna trapped there, holding her prisoner between his long calves. Every few seconds he springs his legs open and Johanna scrambles madly to escape. He captures her again easily and she laughs uncontrollably. Suddenly the scene shifts. Johanna is much older, a grown woman. She and her father are walking across a green lawn.

"You are my daughter," her father says to her.

"I am not your son."

"No. You are my beloved daughter."

"I am not your wife."

"You are my daughter and I love you."

* * *

Johanna awakened from her dream letting out a long-held breath. In the vapor of that exhalation, she saw materializing before her eyes the figure of an old woman.

The old woman stands over Johanna, breathing her hot breath into her face. In the moonlight coming in at the window, Johanna sees that the woman is tiny and stooped. Her nose and chin come perilously close to touching. There are white tufts of hair sprouting out of her big ears. Johanna shudders at this detail. The woman is dressed in a shapeless black garment; it falls in an uneven line to just above her swollen ankles, which bulge out over the tops of her black lace-up oxfords.

"Who are you?" Johanna demands of the old woman. But as soon as the words are out of her mouth, she knows. "Sylvia?" she whispers. "Sylvia, is it you?"

"Who else would it be?"

"But you're so old. My God, Sylvia, what happened to you?"

"My bosom fell. My gums receded. My hair grew white and thin. My eyes got cloudy. My arches collapsed. My uterus prolapsed. And my hearing is going."

"But how did it happen?"

"I lived my life and I grew old."

"I knew it!" Johanna says. "I knew that's what could happen."

"You were always smart," Sylvia says equably. "Move over."

Johanna did and Sylvia sat down on the bed beside her big sister.

"But what did you do with your life?" Johanna wanted to know.

"I sold seashells down by the seashore."

"That's all?"

"I had a husband and two children."

"Oh."

"My husband left me, but I fell in love again. And then the children grew up and went away, and not long after, my love had a massive coronary and died."

Johanna shivered at the meagerness of Sylvia's life.

"Now I sit and breathe the salty air and listen to the waves."

"Oh, Sylvia, I want much more than that. I want to burn all my bridges behind me and my candle at both ends. I want to live

in every city and make love to every man. I want to write the great American novel and sail the seven seas. I want to halluci-nate and levitate and make the rafters ring." Johanna throws her arms open. "I want to see God in a grain of sand and in a flash of blinding light."

"What did you do today?" Sylvia asked.

"I watched a little TV and I took a nap," Johanna mumbled. "Look, Sylvia, what is all this? Why have you come?"

"Do you believe in magic?"

"Oh, yes," Johanna said, enjoying herself for the first time.

"Well, I have come to grant you one wish."

"Oh, my God, that's wonderful," Johanna said, clasping her hands to her bosom.

"Choose wisely and your wish will come true."

"Oh, Sylvia," Johanna said, "I want to be a singer."

"Sylvia laid one cold, arthritic hand on Johanna's warm shoul-der and whispered into her ear, "Formation transformation the eternal mind's eternal recreation."

The incantation was so thrilling that Johanna felt faint and her breathing grew shallow.

"Before you set off to gain your heart's desire," Sylvia said, "you may choose one of the three talismans I brought to help you on your way." She bent down and reached under Johanna's bed and drew out a Waldbaum's sack. She handed it to Johanna.

Johanna reached into the sack and pulled out three long white hairs.

"These three hairs have been pulled from the beard of your father's father's father," Sylvia said.

Johanna was far from fastidious as one could see all too clearly from the deranged condition of the little hut, but she made a face and turned up her nose in disgust. She dropped the hairs back into the bag.

Johanna plunged her hand into the sack again. This time she drew out a golden egg. She laid the cool egg in the palm of her hand. "It glows," she said. "Maybe I should choose this. But I'll

see what the last talisman is." She laid the egg aside and rummaged a third time in the bottom of the paper sack and produced
a long, black, velvety cape made all of feathers.

"It is the cloak of invisibility," Sylvia said. "It is made from
the feathers of seven and seventy-seven ravens."

Johanna jumped out of bed and ran to the long mirror that was
propped up against a packing crate. She pulled off her T-shirt and
drew the splended cape around her bare shoulders. Her skin against
the blackness of the cape was as white as fresh-fallen snow, and
her dark eyes turned more deeply dark till they were as black as
the cape itself. "Look," she cried to Sylvia. "Look."

"You're invisible," Sylvia said. "But I can guess how it be-
comes you."

Reluctantly, giving herself one last fond glance, Johanna left
the mirror. She walked back to her bed and dropped the golden
egg into the sack.

"You choose the cape then?" Sylvia said, watching the egg's
slow descent into the sack.

"Oh, yes."

"Take off the cloak," Sylvia said, "and get back in bed." Johanna did as she was told.

Sylvia folded the cloak neatly and put it back into her sack.

"If you had been wise," Sylvia said, "you would have picked
the three hairs, for they contain the wisdom of the ages. If you
had chosen the golden egg, you would have been smart, for it is
priceless. You chose the cloak for vanity's sake."

But Johanna was obsessed and heard her not. She was remembering how wonderful she had looked in the dusky cape and imagining how beautifully she would sing on all the stages and in all
the supper clubs around the world.

"Close your eyes," Sylvia commanded. "When you want to be
invisible, repeat this incantation." She laid her hand on Johanna's brow. " 'Formation transformation the eternal mind's eternal recreation.' Now I will give you some good advice free for
nothing," she said, so softly that Johanna thought she might

have imagined it. "Breathe deeply and don't embellish your thoughts."

* * *

When Johanna opened her eyes after what felt like a long free-fall in a dream, she was sitting on a royal blue couch in the reception area of a Midtown theatrical agency. All around her were beautiful men and maidens waiting to be seen. Johanna was by no means the most beautiful of the young maidens, but she was the most ardent. Her desire shimmered around her like an aura. The men on either side of her pressed closer to be near its light.

The hours crept by. Still no one had been seen. Ashtrays were piled high, and the carpet was being worn thin by the pacing of many anxious feet. Miss Fielding, the receptionist, shook her head sadly from time to time. New arrivals tried to pin her down. "When? When?" Miss Fielding shook her head and looked harassed.

As the stroke of noon a squat man with a pudding face, a protruding belly, a receding hairline and rose-tinted aviator glasses came out of his office.

"Oh, Mr. Rumplemeyer," Miss Fielding said, "these people are waiting."

"They can't see me now because I'm going to lunch," Rumplemeyer said. He crosssed the carpeted reception area and pushed open the double brass doors that led to the hall and the elevator.

A great pall fell over the reception area. Inside the portfolios of the beautiful men and maidens, eight-by-ten glossies turned dull and lackluster. Miss Fielding put her head on her IBM Selectric. Tears of vexation wetted her keys.

Suddenly Johanna, who had been as crestfallen as all the others, jumped up. "I am determined to be a singer," she said. She dashed through the double doors. As luck would have it, the elevator was old and slow and Rumplemeyer was still in the corridor.

"Mr. Rumplemeyer," Johanna said, overcoming her natural reticence by a great effort of will, "you must audition me."

"Call my secretary," the agent said, not looking at Johanna, and he stepped onto the elevator, which had, at long last, arrived. Johanna rushed in behind him. "Mr. Rumplemeyer, I want to sing. It is my heart's desire."

"Call my secretary, sweetheart," Mr. Rumplemeyer said, staring indifferently at the lighted floor numbers on top of the door.

"You must audition me," Johanna said again, trembling like half-cooled Jell-O. She reached across Mr. Rumplemeyer's girth and pressed the stop button.

"Sonofabitch!" Mr. Rumplemeyer exclaimed. "Are you crazy or what?"

"I will put my nose to the grindstone," Johanna pleaded, "and my shoulder to the wheel. I will do anything to gain my heart's desire."

"You're a determined little thing," Rumplemeyer said, and he looked at her for the first time.

Johanna was breathless with excitement. "Oh, Mr. Rumplemeyer," she managed to gasp, "please give me a break."

"Are you willing to go la la la every day and do re mi every night for seven long years?"

"Oh, yes."

"Are you willing to give up television?"

"Yes."

"And the movies?"

"I will."

"Time magazine?"

"Yes."

"Your friends?"

Johanna nodded.

"Love?" Rumplemeyer mumbled into his tailor-made vest.

"What?"

"Are you willing to give up love?"

"Do I have to?"

"We're talking serious here, darling. You're either serious or you're wasting my time. Are you willing to give up love?"

"I am," Johanna said. "I will. I do."

Rumplemeyer lifted Johanna's finger off the stop button. "Come to my office at midnight on the dot," he said, "and we'll talk turkey."

*   *   *

Now unbeknownst to Johanna or anyone else, the agent was an enchanted prince. By day Rumplemeyer was an agent, but in the evening he took his proper form again.

When Johanna arrived at Rumplemeyer's office at midnight on the dot, she saw an extraordinarily handsome man dressed up like a prince sitting on Miss Fielding's desk. An actor, she assumed, auditioning for a part.

"Are you waiting for Rumplemeyer?" she asked after a while, because he was staring so.

"No," he said. "I am waiting for you. If you will abandon your dream and be my wife, I will be a whole man again." And he told her how he was Rumplemeyer by day and this prince she beheld by night.

"Even if I believed you," Johanna said, "I wouldn't give up my dream."

The prince sighed. "Okay," he said, "then you must vocalize for seven long years—la la la every morning and do re mi every night."

"And then?" Johanna asked eagerly. "Then what?"

"Then Rumplemeyer will give you your big break."

*   *   *

For seven long years Johanna was diligent. She didn't go to parties, she didn't answer letters or sweep the floor of her hut. Some-

*times she was seized by a violent urge to take pictures, so one
night she buried her camera in a ditch and covered it over with
dirt. She donated her TV to Goodwill, and she told Raymond not
to bring her any more newspapers. She cut the cord of her telephone, and she was the only person in the Western world who
didn't go to see* Star Wars. *She didn't fall in love or make love
or even masturbate. And she burned all her old love letters. She
did nothing but vocalize la la la all through the long day and do
re mi through the long night. And she listened to a lot of music.
She listened to jazz and pop and country and blues. She listened
to New Wave and Old Guard and Punk and Funk. She listened
to acid rock and placid rock and flaccid rock. She listened with all
her heart and soul.*

* * *

*At the end of the allotted time Johanna rode the bus to New York
and came again to Rumplemeyer's office. The agent was older and
even dumpier than before. The rosy tint of his aviator glasses
could not conceal the fact that he now wore bifocals or hide the
longing in his small black eyes.*

*"Hello, sweetheart," he said. "I see you persevered." He led
her into his inner office, which had been redecorated seven times
in the last seven years. Three rosewood walls were covered with
pictures of famous singers and actors and dancers and comedians
with fond inscriptions to Rumplemeyer. The fourth wall was hung
with floor-to-ceiling drapes of gold lamé.*

*Rumplemeyer outlined the media blitz he had prepared to launch
Johanna's debut the following week. "We're liaising with the ul-
tra-biggies. You'll do three morning TV shows, three late-night
shows, including Carson. We're taking out full-page ads in the
trades. Your face will be on the covers of* Time *and* Newsweek
the same week. Hunter Thompson will do you for Rolling Stone,
and we're talking to Mailer for Playboy. *We've got a five-page
spread in* Vogue, *Johanna lounging in Calvin Klein pj's on Hal-*

ston sheets with your head in Michael Jackson's lap and your feet in David Bowie's.''

"But where will I sing?" Johanna wanted to know.

"Shea Stadium," Rumplemeyer said, and he leaned so far back in his reclining chair that all Johanna could see of him was the fine, thin soles of his Gucci loafers. "We want impact."

* * *

The night of Johanna's debut was brilliant and cold. The prince picked Johanna up at her crummy hotel on 34th Street. "You look terrific," he said, gazing at Johanna, who was dazzling in a dress woven of separate strands of silver and gold thread by three Chinese ladies who lived in Taiwan.

He looked pretty terrific himself if the truth be told, Johanna thought. What she said was, "Where's Rumplemeyer?"

"Have you forgotten," the prince asked, "that I am he?"

"I had," Johanna admitted, "in all the excitement."

The prince grabbed Johanna's hand. "There's still time. You can still love me and destroy the spell I'm under."

"But I'm going to sing. I'm going to be a star."

"Renounce that dream."

"Not a chance," Johanna said.

And so the prince, who knew enough of the world not to bang his head against a brick wall, gave up his suit, and, a perfect gentleman, escorted Johanna to Shea Stadium.

* * *

The media blitz had worked. The stadium was overflowing. Waves of manufactured excitement rippled through the crowd of celebrities and regular people and sycophants like waves of anxiety.

All three networks were covering the event, and two pay TV channels. Even the public broadcasting channel was represented.

The great playing field was bathed in multicolored lights that pulsed and throbbed and gleamed. The glow of burning joints lit up the bleachers like fireflies. Luminescent Frisbees sailed through the frosty air.

The hot new Australian band Out Back was tuning up in the bullpen. They had been paid an undisclosed amount of money, which had already been deposited in three Swiss banks, for this gig, and they were coked up and happy as larks.

The restless crowds stomped their feet, impatient for the show. "Johanna Johanna Johanna," they yelled. "We want Johanna."

"Ladies and gentlemen." The MC's mega-amped voice filled the ballpark and bounced off the back wall of the stadium. "It is my very great pleasure to introduce to you the fabulous, the fantastic, the one and only Johanna Green."

The base player sounded the first notes of the song he had written especially for the occasion.

Johanna stepped forward. The spotlights turned her gorgeous dress pink, then purple, then fire-engine red.

Johanna opened her mouth and out came her ordinary little voice amplified beyond all reason. Even at 20,000 watts and 140 decibels it was an ordinary little voice, without color or tone or vibrancy. Without subtlety or range or power. Without magic.

After seven years of no diversions and no friends and no sex and no love. After seven long years of denial and hard work. After 84 months, 364 weeks. After 2,555 days of la la la every morning and do re mi every night, Johanna couldn't sing.

The crowd was stunned.

Despite the three coats of magenta blusher the makeup consultant had slathered on her, every drop of color fled Johanna's cheeks. She was as white as a white sheet. She was afraid she was going to throw up, and she trembled from head to toe, but she labored on to the end of the verse.

Some in the crowd were moved to pity by the naked desire that rose up out of Johanna's aching throat. But none were moved to applaud. All the people in the great stadium looked down at their feet and were silent as stones.

In the hush Johanna heard the meaning of defeat.

The mike fell from her hand like a heavy dead thing.

The band stopping playing and walked off the field.

"Oh, God, let my agony end," Johanna prayed, but she could not move her feet to flee. Then on a sudden she remembered the cloak of invisibility made from the feathers of seven and seventy-seven ravens. "Formation transformation," she whispered, "the eternal mind's eternal recreation."

Lo and behold the velvety cloak of invisibility lay at her feet. She stooped and put it on. Then as no one could any longer see her, she gave way to weeping. She sobbed and moaned and tore her hair.

Then she saw in her mind's eye the figures of Sylvia and the prince. And where the prince's shadow would be if it were daylight instead of midnight, she saw the shade of Rumplemeyer.

"I worked so hard," Johanna sobbed. "I worked so hard and I gave up so much. I worked for seven long years to gain my heart's desire."

"And you broke the heart of a prince into the bargain," Rumplemeyer said.

"It isn't fair," Johanna wailed, sinking to the ground. "It isn't fair."

"God gave you many gifts," Sylvia said, "but a voice wasn't one of them."

"I wanted it so much," Johanna cried, rolling around on the frozen ground. "And I had the feeling for it. I had the feeling." She beat her head against the earth.

The prince stepped forward then and lifted Johanna to her feet. He supported her under the arms so she might not harm herself further.

"You cannot spin straw into gold," Rumplemeyer said, and hearing that, Johanna's bitterness flooded her like deadly poison. Breaking away from the prince, she dashed her right foot into the ground; her disappointment was so keen and her bitterness so great that she dashed her right foot so deep into the ground that

she couldn't dislodge it. Then she was so enraged that she stomped her other foot, and the earth opened like a chasm and swallowed her up in its dark heart.

But Rumplemeyer and Sylvia and the prince took pity on Johanna. They put a spell on her. She would sleep under the earth for twelve years and then, by the grace of God, the earth would open up and she would be granted another chance to choose her life.

"Formation transformation the eternal mind's eternal recreation," Rumplemeyer chanted, and he and the prince kneeled to kiss the spot where Johanna was buried.

THREE

34

Ten years ago, it was just about this time of year, my Aunt
Celia died. I got a letter from a Mr. Tomas Juracek.

Dear Clara,

Permit me to call you how your aunt called you. She is
alredy dead a week by the time you get this if you get
it, which I don't know. Your Aunt Celia was so wonderful woman. I am foriner living in this town only so
long and starting bisness. A tavern. Celia loved it. Many
times in the last 2 years I beg to her marry me but she
is always preferring not. She died eating black cherries.
A pit got stuck a rong way and she turned blue. I grabbed
her and turned her upside and punched her in the
stomach and breathed in her mouth and called police.
But nevertheless anyway she died 15 minutes before
someones comes. I almost kill those mens with my bear
hands, but it wasn't their fault. I am desolate missing
her cheery person.

> Sinseerly,
> Tomas Juracek

The next night I left the town where I had been living for
six months. I walked to the bus station. I had to wait two
hours for the bus I wanted. There were other people there
waiting for their buses, and there were the usual drifters
and drinkers and vagrants who hang around bus stations.
So I had an audience.
  I told them a story about a girl who never knew what

was happening to her until she made up a song about it. A lot happened to this girl, and she made up many wonderful songs. At the end of the story her mother died, but the girl couldn't believe it was true. Nothing could convince her that her mother, whom she loved so much, was dead. Even when she saw the body with her own eyes. She bent over the casket and kissed her mother's blue lips, and she said, "Have a good nap, Mom." After that her gift dried up. She never wrote another song. Worse than that, she never cried another tear or laughed another laugh or loved anyone again.

35

The interminable days are rushing away wreaking their slow, certain havoc. The linoleum is buckling, the plaster is peeling, the summer is dying. The wind is rising, but Johanna doesn't feel the hair blow off her neck. She doesn't see how the hem of her skirt lifts as the cold wind blows.

She sits beside her silent grandmother, clasping the old woman's hands in her own. Her eyes are fixed on her grandmother's face, but she does not apprehend what is there.

She is in a dream, a long, continuous dream that rises and falls with her exhausted breath. She sighs, and the memories quicken and dance like leaves on the ground.

"I never introduced you to Michael, Han. I never introduced him to anyone. And I never met a friend of his. He

was from the West somewhere. I'm not sure he knew anyone here to introduce me to.

"We didn't want anyone else. That summer we roamed
the city like gypsies in our bare feet, knapsacks on our
backs. We had cheese and fruit in them, and books, and
we'd lie in the grass in the park near the governor's mansion or in the park on Riverside Drive. We'd fall asleep in
the late afternoon sun under a canopy of sound, Mozart
and Van Morrison and live bongos and children playing."

"Her grandmother doesn't understand a word she's
saying," Miriam Stone complains.

"I think she does," I say.

"Johanna's talking to herself," Honora says.

"Who else does she talk to anymore?" Mrs. Stone continues. "Not me. She has no time to help me clip my articles. That's fine with me. I don't want favors. But she could
say a word. Even Mr. Martin made a comment how she
doesn't talk to us. She could be civil. You at least are civil,
Clara."

"She's trying to sort something out," I say, "and to bring
her grandmother back."

"Clara," Mrs. Stone observes, "you got an overactive
imagination. That's how come you end up telling stories
for nothing in an old people's home. If you want my opinion, Johanna's on some kind of dope."

Johanna sucks the distant summer in and holds it in her
lungs, expelling what came next in a rush of words that
billows up, blueing the air with old regret.

"He said I was lucky he wasn't a musician otherwise I
might have dismissed him as just another hippie and been
the poorer for it.

" 'I'd never dismiss you,' I said.

" 'Wouldn't you? Are you sure?'

" 'Well . . .'

" 'I knew you'd equivocate,' he said, and he kissed my

eyes closed, Han, so I couldn't see whatever was in his face.

"At night he'd tell me stories about his travels. He'd been all over, back and forth across this country and to Australia and New Zealand and the Far East too. I used to dream about particular places he'd been, he made them so vivid to me, as if I'd seen them through the lens of my own camera.

"When I told him I used to take pictures, he wanted to see everything I'd done, and I told him I'd thrown all the old stuff out.

" 'Well, where is the new stuff?'

" 'There isn't any.'

" 'You don't finish things,' he said. 'It's a bad omen.'

"I asked him did he finish things.

" 'I'm not good at anything so I'm not obliged to,' he said. 'I travel well and I'm good at making love, but they're not the sort of tasks you dedicate your life to.'

"One night I dreamed Michael had put a curse on us, and when I woke up I remembered he'd been wearing my old chenille bathrobe in the dream, and I thought—it isn't him, it's me.

" 'This fan isn't doing a frigging thing,' he said one sweltering night. He sat up in bed and gave the cord a vicious yank, and it sprang away from the socket. 'I just fixed this goddamn piece of shit,' he said. He got up out of the bed and walked over to the small window. He sat on its narrow ledge and tried to ram the window up farther with his shoulder, but the humidity had swelled the wood and he couldn't budge it. 'Sonofabitch,' he cursed.

"He left the window and pulled on the jeans and shirt he'd dropped beside the bed. 'I'm going for a walk.'

"When he got to the door he said, 'Do you want anything?'

" 'No.'

" 'Johanna, do you want to come?'

" 'I'll stay here.'

" 'Suit yourself,' he said, and he banged the front door hard as he left.

"When he came home we made love." Johanna lets go of her grandmother's hands. Mrs. Jessup looks down at her fine-boned hands as if they belonged to someone else.

"We made love all the time," Johanna says, "and each time it was more consuming and more desolate than the time before.

" 'You're afraid of how relieved you'll be when you're gone,' I accused him.

" 'You're talking about yourself,' he said. 'It's the only way you ever do talk about yourself.'

"We went to the movies three and four times a week toward the end of that summer, Han. We went to the movies and we sat side by side in the cool, dark theater and held hands and watched other people's lives.

"On our way to see Richard Chamberlain and Glenda Jackson in a revival of a Ken Russell movie about Tchaikovsky, he put his hand on my shoulder and pressed down; he brought all his weight to bear on my shoulder. 'Sometimes I want to crawl inside your skin,' he said. 'I want to curl up in your cunt. I want to be your only love, the only love you've ever had.'

"But in the movie he was aloof. He withdrew his hand from mine and crouched forward as if he meant to leap up, as if he meant to hurl himself at the screen. Glenda Jackson's face filled the screen. Tchaikovsky hates her. She is feeding off his art. She is sucking him dry. I can feel Michael's hatred of her. It pins me back against my seat. I am her to him. He is Dr. Kildare and I am Glenda, and he despises me.

" 'Jesus,' he said, barely able to contain his excitement when the lights came up. 'That was incredible.'

" 'I hated it.' I spat it at him. 'I detested it.'

" 'Don't snarl at me,' he said, and he pushed past me. 'Don't ever do that, Johanna.'

" 'You bastard,' I said to his back, and I grabbed at his arm.

"He caught my wrist and he held it and turned toward me. 'I can't breathe around you, Johanna. You are using up all my air.' He dropped my hand and walked up the aisle, and when I got to the street he was gone.

"In bed that night I said, 'Go away, Michael. You have to go away.'

" 'I can't,' he said. 'What will ever hold me? I'll blow around and around the world and never light down anywhere.'

" 'Tumbling tumbleweed,' I said.

" 'Yes.'

" 'My tumbling tumbleweed.'

"The last time I saw Michael we pretended not to see each other. I was on my way home from work, starting up our street, and he was coming out of our building heading toward the avenue. I looked away. He lowered his head and crossed to the other side of the street. It's the end now, I thought. I kept my eyes down and never broke stride. This is the end. When he gets to the corner where the coffee shop is, he'll turn and be gone.

"There was no note when I got home, but he'd left a picture propped up on the old card table where we ate. He'd torn it out of one of my photography magazines. It was a very wide-angle shot of a picnic laid out on a white cloth in a vast green meadow. It was a feast—cold meats and salads and wine and a profusion of berries and other fruits—but there was no one to eat it. In all that great stretching landscape there wasn't a soul to partake of the feast."

It is the hottest part of the afternoon. Miriam Stone and

Mrs. Merriman have gone to nap in their rooms. David Martin and Honora are listening to a baseball game in her office while she catches up on some paperwork.

The lounge is empty except for Johanna and Hannah Jessup and me. And Johanna's old loves. They are everywhere. Stretched out on the floor facedown like rugs, lit up like lamps in the corners, stacked like the dinner trays one on top of the other. I can't tell if Hannah Jessup sees them. Perhaps she sees her old love—the young man she didn't marry.

I see Aaron the night he left. "What did you think, Clara?" He shouted it at me. "Did you think I'd roam around the world with you? Sell shoelaces on street corners? Pass the hat while you tell stories to tramps passed out in doorways?"

"I never expected that," I told him.

"What am I asking you to give up?" He paced the length of the small room. "A million little crummy towns, two-day typing jobs, a lonely room in someone else's house and the threat of danger besides. All to tell stories to strangers you'll never see again."

"I love you, Aaron," I said. "You know I love you."

"But I can't love you anymore, Clara," he said. "I can't love someone I have no hope of understanding."

"But you can," I said. "You do."

"I can't," he said.

Johanna's voice rises in the warm room. "A month later I took the vacation I hadn't planned to take until the fall," she says. "I flew to Spain because it was far away and hot.

"I craved the sun. I wanted it to sear my skin. I wanted it to burn straight through to my heart, which was sunk in my chest like a rock.

"But it was raining in Barcelona, and the night I arrived I met Wiley Farrington coming out of customs.

"When he first approached me I thought he was an Indian from Guatemala or Peru or someplace like that. He had the flattened nose and the high cheekbones and the wide, fleshy mouth of an Indian. He was short and muscular and very dark. A thick, straight shock of flat black hair dropped across his forehead and covered his black eyes.

"I was looking for a sign that said BUS when he spoke. 'Are you lost already?'

" 'You're American.' I laughed, hugely relieved. 'You're a Southerner.'

" 'Is that all right?' he said.

" 'I went to school in the South,' I said. I told him where, and he said he would be teaching there in the fall.

" 'That's amazing,' I said.

"He smiled. 'You're easily amazed.'

"Before I could decide whether to be put off, he took my suitcase from me. 'Now that we've established this intimate connection, may I offer you a ride to your hotel and dinner?'

"At dinner he told me he'd grown up on a tobacco farm in the eastern part of the state that linked us.

"About the rest of his life Wiley was voluble and full of funny, telling stories, but that was the only information he ever volunteered about his growing up. If I questioned him his responses were so neutral that I soon forgot what he told me.

"Over coffee he told me he was a writer, a short-story writer. I asked him if his stories were set in the South.

" 'No. Not a one.'

"I asked him why not, and he said he didn't know.

" 'I'd like to read them,' I said.

" 'You might not like me anymore,' he said. But the next morning we walked in the pouring rain to a tiny bookstore sandwiched between a flower stall and a bootblack on a narrow street off the Ramblas, and he bought me a Penguin edition of his last collection of stories.

"The first story was set in an airplane endlessly circling an unnamed airport, waiting for clearance to land. In the second a man and a woman played cards all through the night in the salon of a once luxurious ocean liner in the middle of the Atlantic Ocean.

"Wiley's stories seemed remarkable to me. They were as hard and as brilliant, as polished, as gems. But I always had the uneasy feeling that the characters in his stories had been constrained by his art—that their choices were choices they wouldn't have made if they'd been free.

"The next morning we were walking down the Calle Escudellers past a jumble of bars and restaurants, so close together they seemed to be set one on top of the other like steps. 'Do you still like me?' he asked.

" 'I don't know,' I answered him.

" 'Ah, I knew you'd equivocate.'

" 'Someone else just told me that,' I said.

" 'Good golly, Miss Molly,' he said, 'that's amazing.' He grabbed my hand and stuck it in his back pocket. Even on two days' acquaintance it struck me as an uncharacteristically impulsive gesture. And right then he said, 'I'm not an impulsive man. Not at all. People often think I am, but they're wrong. I'm greedy. It makes me appear to rush at things.'

"I could feel his muscles working as we walked, and I felt a rush of desire that was so strong it made me a little sick.

"I took my hand away and edged as close as I could to the buildings on my side of the narrow street. 'Do your characters ever surprise you?'

" 'I surprise them sometimes,' he said, and he laid his hand across the flat of my back.

"On Saturday the sun finally came out, and we rented a car and drove eighty-three kilometers northeast along the coast to the beach at Tossa de Mar. It was there we first made love. We had stayed out on the beach all afternoon, and we drove back to our hotel through woods of pine and oak and small shrubby trees Wiley said were cork.

"When we got to our room Wiley opened all the windows so we could smell the sea.

"Wiley made love the way he wrote. He pored over every inch of my body the way he pored over his sentences, seeking exactly the right gesture, the right rhythm, the perfect pitch. He was creating a masterpiece. But in the end it was unsatisfactory like the endings of his stories.

" 'I wrote a story about you in my head,' he said when we were through.

" 'Were you in the story?' I asked him.

" 'I'm never in my stories. I called you Isabel.' He gave it the Castilian pronunciation, the *I* sounding like an *ith*.

" 'Ithabel would be thinner than I am and more composed,' I said.

"Wiley laughed. 'Oh, I'll adjust for that,' he said.

"We lay all weekend long on the stony beach and let the sun bake us. I thought about how badly I wanted to take pictures of Wiley. I wanted to know if I would see something with the camera's eye that wasn't clear to me with my own. I didn't understand Wiley's loose-jointed charm. I didn't trust it in this dark man whose body was so compact and dense and whose features were as veiled and flat and archaic as an idol's.

"But I hadn't brought my camera with me on this trip, and I never did take a picture of Wiley.

"I have a tape recording of him singing though. He doesn't know I have it.

"He would never have allowed me to tape him singing. I did it to violate him.

"The song on the tape is 'In the Pines.'

> "*Black girl, black girl, don't lie to me*
> *Tell me where did you sleep last night?*

In the pines, in the pines
Where the sun never shines
I shivered the whole night through.

"He only sang that one song. He sang it in that strange twangy growl of his.

"My husband was a railroad man
Was the best in this high lonesome world
The only thing that he did that was wrong
Was to miss just one little curve.

"You never make a sound when we make love, I thought, listening to him, and you cry out like that in your song.

"My husband was a railroad man
Killed a mile and a half from town
I found his head in an engine wheel
But his body could never be found."

Johanna sits up in her chair. She leans toward her grandmother, who sleeps now, her head fallen to one side.

"Oh, Han, when Wiley sang his song I could imagine that I loved him and that he loved me.

"It isn't true that he never made a sound. Sometimes when he came he made a small noise at the back of his throat. But he never let me make love to him.

" 'I've been working very hard to enthrall you,' Wiley said the night he asked me to quit my job and come back with him to North Carolina. 'My critics say that's what I do best.'

" 'I'm not enthralled,' I said. But I was enthralled—by his mockery that was a kind of flattery and his flattery that was a kind of mockery, and by his ease in the world, the larger world that I had never moved in, and by his love-making, which left me restless and horny and lonely.

" 'You're not indifferent,' Wiley said.

" 'Why do you want me to come with you?' I asked him.

" 'Because I do. It's exactly what I want.'

"And I thought, maybe it will be different in America when it's not vacation anymore. And so I came here with him, Han. I drifted into it."

Hannah Jessup opens her eyes.

"I was as much to blame as he," Johanna says. "I said that to him after we had been living together for three months. 'Blame?' He looked up from the book he was reading and raised his eyebrows.

" 'We're sinning against ourselves in a way, Wiley. In some kind of way.'

" 'Bullshit, Johanna,' he said calmly. 'You're always saying some dumb shit like that, and you can never explain what you mean. You're unreasonably inarticulate.' He went back to his book.

" 'You're unreasonably mean.'

"He laughed then as if I'd said something terribly funny, and he put his book down and came over to me where I stood, and he put his arms around me. I was so exhausted suddenly that I thought I might fall asleep standing up in the dark circle of his arms.

" 'Did you know,' he whispered against my neck, 'that the word *sin* derives from the Indo-European root word for being—*es*. As in *esse, être, ser*. We are all sinners,' he said. 'We're born that way. God intended it that way, Johanna. I don't hold it against you, and you shouldn't hold it against me. *Es* we have no bananas,' he sang, and he waltzed me around the room till I was too tired to move another step.

"The next night when I got home from my job at the photo lab, Wiley was writing, but he shut off his typewriter when I came into the room. He leaned back in the old swivel chair he'd gotten from Goodwill. 'I can see your nipples in that top,' he said.

" 'Wiley, I don't think we should be together.'

"He sighed then and turned his typewriter back on, and then turned it off again. 'It's not my fault you're not taking pictures, Johanna.'

" 'I know that, Wiley. You know I know that.'

" 'In fact, I do, but I find it's always better to assum absolutely nothing with a woman like you.'

" 'What do you mean, a woman like me?'

"Wiley smiled at me as if we were flirting. 'My guess that you're returning to your theme of last night. Am right? You think we're working against the salvation our souls by staying together. If God intended us to sinners then it's all the more imperative that we do son thing about ourselves, that we work toward the good a the holy, that we not drift into unions that do not perf us. Is that it?'

" 'Not everything is funny, Wiley.'

" 'You certainly are.'

" 'Well, what do you see happening to us?'

" 'I don't worry about shit like that. I'm just a ¡ country boy. I worry about where my next meal is con from and who I'm gonna fuck tomorrow night, and i not you, honey, it'll damn straight be someone else.'

" 'That's what I mean, Wiley. I could be anyone.'

" 'You could be Isabel,' he said, 'and I could be chael.'

"We went around like that all the time—the wa talked to each other was like that exhausted waltz.

"The next morning at breakfast he said, 'I don't you have any idea what you want, Johanna. Excep you want it to be large.' He said it quietly with no tr malice. 'Large and vague. That's what you like.' "

Hannah Jessup nods as if she agrees with Wile Johanna doesn't see it. " 'And what you like is to be ing,' I said.

" 'And amused,' he said. 'Don't sell me short.'

" 'I don't,' I said. 'I see much more in you than you see in yourself.'

" 'You see more in everybody than is there. It's a dangerous tendency that ought to be curbed.'

" 'You're right and you're wrong,' I told him.

" 'Well, here's something I'm all right about, Johanna. The truth is, if I was upright and honest and interested in making a lifelong commitment to you, which I'm not, you'd be on the first plane out of here.'

"We hadn't anywhere to go from there, of course, but we went a few more rounds anyway. Just like Michael and me.

"It turned out Wiley had known before we'd been here a month that he'd be moving at the end of the spring. He'd gotten a much more lucrative offer from a private college in the Northeast.

" 'You can come if you want to,' he said over the phone after I had already moved out to my own place.

" 'You don't really want me to come, do you?'

" 'No.' And then he said, 'Johanna, would you have come if I'd said yes?'

" 'No.'

" 'I thought not.'

" 'Were you planning to ask me to come with you before we split up?' I asked him.

" 'I don't know. I thought about it.'

"There was a crackle of static.

" 'Static on the line,' he said.

"And I said, 'Sounds like a country song.'

" 'Static on the line,' he sang, 'and pain in my heart.'

" 'I hope so,' I said.

" 'Well, yeah, you would,' he said, and he laughed and hung up."

Hannah Jessup raises the Formica tray-table that is attached to the side of her wheelchair and locks it into place across the front of her chair.

The click sounds ominous in the quiet room, but it doesn't disturb Johanna. "Wiley did write a story about me," she says, "and he did call me Isabel. The story's called 'The Tired Scalp,' and it's the title story in his latest collection. In the story my 'willful innocence' prevents a dying man from dealing with his fate. The review I saw said it was the most powerful and the best realized of any of his stories, and I thought that too. It was the first story he ever wrote that had an ending."

36

The workmen's blasts explode Johanna's expectations. She had not thought to be jolted from her private reckonings. She had not imagined her grandmother's face could shock her.

"What is it, Han? Did something I say upset you?"

Hannah Jessup stares at her granddaughter as if she were an obstacle in the road, a fallen tree limb or a rock or a cow. She lays her hands palms down on the Formica tray-table she has locked into place across the front of her wheelchair. She lifts up her left hand, holding it away from her. With the thumb of her right hand she presses down on her wedding ring. She presses down as one would press on a sore.

"Does something hurt?" Johanna asks.

Mrs. Jessup pushes the ring up her finger. She works steadily, twisting it up and finally off. Then she shoves the ring, the exquisite oval ring of diamond chips, across the tray-table toward Johanna.

Johanna pushes the ring back across the table to her grandmother. "Put it back on."

Her grandmother blocks Johanna's hand with her own. "For me? You want me to have it?"

Hannah Jessup sweeps the ring off the tray with her forearm. It hits the floor with a tiny noise that stuns Johanna.

Johanna sits stupidly, breathing loudly through her mouth. Then she bends down and picks up the ring. She presses the ring into her grandmother's hands, folding the old woman's fingers up around it.

Hannah Jessup leans across the Formica barrier and jams the ring into the hollow of Johanna's throat.

"No!" I shout.

I jump up, and Honora, who has been cutting Mrs. Merriman's fingernails, swings around. "What's wrong?"

"Mrs. Jessup shoved something at Johanna's throat," David Martin says, halfway to Johanna.

Honora rises in her chair. "What did you say?"

"Her ring," I say. "Her wedding ring."

"Wouldn't you know," Mrs. Stone heckles, "I missed it."

"Are you hurt?" Honora asks Johanna, shouldering David Martin aside.

Johanna shakes her head. She is pale and sweaty.

Honora bends over Johanna. "What happened?"

Johanna shakes her head again. Her breathing is shallow, and she swallows with great difficulty, as if there is something stuck that will not go down.

"Never mind," Honora says. "Never mind. Just tilt your head back."

Johanna obeys, and Honora feels under her chin and up and down the long column of her throat. "You're okay," she says.

"Of course she's okay," Miriam Stone confides irritably to Mrs. Jessup. She maneuvers her chair closer to Mrs. Jessup's. "You can open your eyes. You didn't kill her."

Hannah Jessup doesn't open her eyes. She seems barely to breathe.

"Is Mrs. Jessup all right?" I ask Honora.

Honora puts her hand on the old woman's arm. "She's all right," she says.

"The weapon," Mrs. Stone says. With a nod of her head she indicates the ring, which glitters in the middle of the tray-table.

Johanna watches Honora pick up the ring. She watches it drop into the pocket that rides low on Honora's hip.

She buries her face in her hands.

David Martin stoops so he can put an arm around Johanna's shoulders. "It will be okay," he comforts her. But he looks terrible. He looks like someone who has seen a ghost.

"You pretend she isn't going to die in here," Mrs. Stone says. "But she knows. I'll die in here too. You'll die in here," she informs David Martin.

"No one's going to die in here unless they hurry up," Honora jokes. The joke falls flat.

"I saw it in her face," Johanna cries out loud.

"What? What did you see?" David Martin asks.

"Everything," Johanna says.

"Everything," Miriam Stone snorts merrily. "She saw everything. Can you beat it?"

No one can.

* * *

While Honora took Mrs. Jessup back to her room, David Martin walked Johanna to her car. When he got back, Honora and I were waiting at the door for him.

"Mrs. Jessup is breaking Johanna's heart," he said.

"It's time her heart broke," I said.

He stared at me. "Is that your wisdom or your indifference?"

"Clara's not indifferent," Honora said.

"She makes damn sure she doesn't get *her* heart broken."

The outburst emptied him of anger. He lowered himself into the black Leatherette chair. "I'm a little like Johanna.

"Hannah Jessup doesn't want Johanna to save her," he said.

"Johanna sees that now," Honora said. "That's what hurt her so bad. By the time she comes tomorrow she'll be all right."

"She said she didn't think she'd come tomorrow," Mr. Martin said.

"Oh," Honora said.

*   *   *

I had my old dream again tonight, the dream where my father asks me why I wander. He looked into my face waiting for me to say something, but I couldn't answer him. I turned away and saw David Martin running toward us. He ran past me, hailing my father as if they were old friends. He took my father's arm, and he said, 'Your little girl makes sure she doesn't get her heart broken.' My father looked upset, and I thought, he's worried about me.

37

As soon as I got here this morning Honora handed me the paper, pointing to the headline: GREEN MANSIONS SLATED FOR DEMOLITION. The text explained that the developers of Taralawn Estates had rethought their original plan. "We began to feel," Dallas Bancroft, the senior architect, said, "that the present structure could never have the sweeping feeling, the sense of open space on the one hand and intimate enclosure on the other, that we envision for this leisure complex."

The article went on to assure the reader that demolishing the old structure and starting from scratch would be more economical in the long run. "Oh, no question," Stuart Rich, vice-president of Dixieland Construction, said, "this is going to be a whole hell of a lot more cost-effective." The last line of the piece said that Green Mansions was scheduled for demolition on September 23.

"They're going to blow us up," Honora stage-whispers.

"That should liven things up," Mrs. Stone whispers back, guiding her wheelchair into place alongside Honora and me.

Honora jumps. "I didn't see you coming."

"Evidently." Mrs. Stone is enjoying herself. "Are you planning to tell the rest of them when we're being blown up, or is it a surprise?"

"We have two weeks," Honora says stiffly. "We knew we had to be out soon. It doesn't really make any difference to us if they blow the building up or convert it."

"Certainly not," Mrs. Stone agrees. "Why should we care?" She eases the newspaper out of my hand. "You don't mind if I borrow this, Clara, do you?" She smiles pleasantly at me, then addresses Honora. "You don't mind, do you, Mrs. Bliss? I thought I'd let Mr. Martin see it."

"He has trouble reading the paper," Honora says.

"I'll read it to him," Mrs. Stone replies. "I enjoy reading aloud."

* * *

Johanna called to say she wouldn't be here today. She hung up before Honora could ask her if she's coming tomorrow.

* * *

Honora went out to talk to Harley Creech about the demolition.

When she gets back, Honora says, "He said, 'It's as good as done.' Then he said, 'I got a good one to tell you, Mrs. Bliss. It'll cheer you up. That landscape architect, that Richard Newhouse, he come down here last week telling me all this kudzu's got to be cleared.'

"Mr. Creech did a slow turn," Honora says, demonstrating Harley's moves, "looking all around at that tangled mess of kudzu vines hanging all over the trees." She stops in mid-turn, remembering the sight. "It's like a forest that's under a spell out there, Clara. All those strange shapes the kudzu makes. Like a forest in one of Monroe's nighttime stories."

She sighs, shaking herself free of some enchantment, and sits down beside me on the old black couch. "Mr. Creech said he asked Mr. Newhouse how long he'd been down here," she goes on. " 'I've lived here over three years,' he tells Harley. Then Harley looked at him and he said, 'You don't clear kudzu, Mr. Newhouse, you just hope it don't come after you.' "

"Did Mr. Newhouse laugh?" I ask Honora.

"No," Honora says. "He told Harley he wasn't amused. So then Harley said, 'I wasn't aimin' to amuse you, I was aimin' to warn you.'

"Harley and I laughed at that, and then he said, 'You can't stop the demolition, Mrs. Bliss, and you can't stop kudzu. Not a thing to be done about either one.' "

* * *

While Honora was out talking to Harley Creech, I'd gone into Mrs. Jessup's room. She was asleep, her heart-shaped face very white and still on the white pillow. I pulled a chair up to her bed and sat down. I sat for a long time watching the slow rise and fall of her chest. I sat for an hour hoping she might wake up, but she didn't.

* * *

Mrs. Stone wheels up alongside Mr. Martin. "Hannah Jessup didn't turn a hair when Mrs. Bliss told her Johanna's not coming. I'll bet you five dollars Johanna never comes back."

"She's only missed one day, Mrs. Stone," he replies. "You're the one who thought she was nuts to come every day and stay so long."

"Certainly it's nutty, but you could also say admirable in a peculiar way. Now it turns out she's Barbara and Gail. Almost," she amends.

"She'll be back," David Martin says.

Mrs. Stone pats Mr. Martin's knee. "In time to see the rubble."

* * *

Honora is closeted in her tiny office making her calls. She calls every morning trying to secure places for Virginia Merriman and Hannah Jessup and Miriam Stone and David Martin. She calls the directors of other nursing homes. She calls the social workers attached to the two retirement communities in the area. She calls the chiefs of gerontology at three different hospitals. She calls the local newspaper. She even calls the governor's office.

"Groveling won't work," Mrs. Stone pronounces. "You've got to kidnap someone. Hijack a plane to Havana."

"I wouldn't mind seeing Havana," David Martin says, folding his arms behind his head.

"Of course not," Miriam Stone agrees. "All those gorgeous wide boulevards and Sloppy Joe's bar. I saw it in *Life* magazine. And Castro in my opinion is a very good-looking man. He looks a little like my father in his prime."

38

Vernon Stone appeared on the doorstep first thing this morning with a smear of fresh paint on the sleeve of his oxford-cloth shirt. Behind him one of the painters, who has been dismantling a scaffolding, swears apologetically.

"I've come for my wife," Vernon says, stepping inside. Before Honora can close her mouth or head him off, he swings past her, Duke Wayne heading for a shoot-out.

"Oh, my God," Miriam Stone exclaims, catching sight of the advancing Vernon. "Who let you in?"

"I saved all the articles you sent me, Miriam," he says, stopping squarely in front of her. "I tacked them up over our bed."

"You're crazy. You've got paint on your sleeve," she adds, as if this confirms her diagnosis.

"Last night on the radio this young man was talking about a record album he'd made a while back," Vernon continues, "*Still Crazy After All These Years.*"

"What's he talking about?" Miriam questions her left shoulder.

"Don't look around, Miriam. Look at me. I'm your husband."

"What do you want, Vernon?"

"I'm too old to change horses in mid-stream. I want you to come home."

"You found another horse already?"

"I want you to come home."

"Some invitation."

"I'm bored, Miriam. I'm bored to tears without you."

"You were bored with me."

"Your days here are numbered, Miriam. It's all over the papers. You may not be so lucky with the next place. Who knows what kind of hellhole they'll stick you in. You saw *The Snake Pit* with Olivia de Havilland. We saw it together."

"That was an insane asylum, Vernon. I'm not being sent to the booby hatch."

"You had on that peach-colored dress."

"Do you think you're putting something over on me, Vernon? You're just afraid you'll end your days with Barbara or Gail."

"It's a gloomy prospect, Miriam."

"It looks like you're rescuing me, but it's me rescuing you."

"I wouldn't let just anyone rescue me. I'm not a whore."

"You're trying to make me laugh, Vernon, but I'm not amused."

"Yes, you are. I can still make you laugh. And I'm still attracted to you. Doesn't that count for something?"

"I'm not attracted to you."

"You sent me all those letters."

"Articles."

"I waited for the postman as if you were sending me passionate love letters. I waited as if I were sixteen."

"We made each other miserable for so long."

"That wasn't all of it," Vernon says.

"Neither of us has changed."

"I don't want you changed. I figured it out, Miriam. I never really did want you changed."

"But I want you changed. From day two I wanted you changed."

"I won't see other women."

"Now he can't do it anymore, he'll be faithful," Mrs. Stone informs the ceiling.

"As of Tuesday night, I could still do it, Miriam."

Mrs. Stone brings a hand in front of her mouth to hide the sudden trembling of her lips. An uncontrolled whooping laugh goes off like a small explosion in her chest before it's forced through her lungs into the air. She laughs till tears come into her black eyes. She laughs till she coughs.

"You might as well go tell her," she manages finally, between the spasms of coughing, nodding in Honora's direction.

"I will," Vernon says, looking his wife full in the face before he turns away. "I surely will."

"It hurts when I laugh," Miriam adds after him, holding her pigeon breast and frowning.

* * *

It takes all morning to arrange Mrs. Stone's departure. Honora asks me to pack Mrs. Stone's things while she talks with Vernon about his wife's care.

"I explained the arthritis is getting worse," Honora told me later, "which he can see for himself. I told him one day he'd need someone to help take care of her. I told him she gets five coated aspirins at every meal and five more with her bedtime snack and she has to take a nap in the early afternoon and she's stiff as a board in the morning."

Honora said Vernon looked right in her face as if he didn't want to miss a word, and somewhere in the middle of everything, he said, "You're a handsome woman, Mrs. Bliss."

After her discussion with Vernon, Honora suggests she and Mrs. Stone go back to Hannah Jessup's room. "I'll wake her up so you can say good-bye."

"She couldn't care less if I go or stay."

"Still," Honora coaxes, wheeling Miriam away, "still . . ."

When she and Mrs. Stone return to the lounge, Honora directs Vernon to her office and leaves him there to read and sign the release forms she has prepared for his signature.

"You got a few minutes," Honora says, coming up to Miriam Stone, who is looking at herself in the mirror of a gold compact. There is a small clump of loose powder on the tip of her nose. Honora knees aside Miriam's two suitcases so she can get closer. She brushes a finger over Mrs. Stone's nose, evening out the powder. "You look nice," she says.

"So-so," Mrs. Stone says, closing the compact with some effort.

"You could say good-bye to Mrs. Merriman while your husband's signing the papers," Honora says.

"I don't want to. You made me say it to Mrs. Jessup, who didn't even open an eye."

"But that's it. Mrs. Merriman will know you said good-bye to everyone else."

"What everyone?" Mrs. Stone raises her voice. "There's only Mr. Martin. And Clara." She waves across the room at me. "Bye-bye, Clara."

"Only Mr. Martin?" David Martin calls back, reaching for some final gallantry to please himself and Miriam.

"So," Miriam picks it up, "you wait till I'm reconciled with Vernon."

"A fortunate man," David Martin says, dragging his chair closer to Honora and Mrs. Stone.

"Vernon or you?" Miriam asks.

"Mrs. Merriman will see you're gone," Honora urges.

Miriam raises her scanty eyebrows skyward. "First Johanna and now her. Merriman-Einstein, according to them." She gestures to David Martin. "If I were you, I'd get out of here." But she asks Honora, "What do you want me to say to her?"

"Just tell her you're going," Honora says. "Just tell her good-bye."

Honora watches Mrs. Stone swing herself into position in front of Mrs. Merriman, then ducking her head as if she were avoiding a blow, she turns her back on the little scene she has set in motion, kneeling to open first one and then the other of Mrs. Stone's suitcases, checking to see that everything is there.

Mrs. Stone fidgets in her chair, scowling into her lap. "I'm going home today with my husband, Vernon."

Mrs. Merriman slides one skinny leg out a little farther than the other. Mrs. Stone watches the slow progress of the bony leg. When she speaks again she seems to be speaking to the leg. "Something terrible can always happen," she says. She sits forward a little in her chair. "What if we'd known when we were young . . . ?" She breaks off. "You probably don't know what I'm talking about." She sighs, a long, whistling exhalation. "Who knows what you know," she says. "I don't know what I know so how would I know what you know?" She looks sharply at Mrs. Merriman. Then, concluding her concession to the immensity of possibilities in the universe, she barks out a "so long" and executes a practiced about-face with her wheelchair, turning on her edges like a skater doing figures.

When Vernon comes out of Honora's office with the signed papers, we all gather at the front door. The painters in their white overalls move in and out of the half-painted lobby, hauling away silvery ladders and canvas drop cloths and buckets of white paint and huge tin drums of kerosene. Seeing us, they rush away as if they are afraid or embarrassed. We stand there together, Honora and Vernon and Miriam Stone and David Martin and I, looking out at the bright, hot day. Harley Creech is leaning against his forest-green Datsun pickup truck, which is parked in the middle of the front lawn. He is talking to a small man in a white suit and tugging at his yellow cap. "The one in the white suit is the one in charge of the demolition," Honora says.

Miriam Stone does not appear to be interested in this piece of information. "Well, that's it," she says, rearranging herself in her chair. "Good-bye. Don't forget to put me in a story, Clara."

"I won't forget," I say.

Honora swings Mrs. Stone's chair into position in front of Vernon, turning over the stewardship of her charge to the new guardian. Vernon hands her the signed release forms in exchange.

Miriam tightens her crippled fingers on the metal arms of the wheelchair, steadying herself for the descent down the broad front steps of Green Mansions.

"They've been promising us a ramp ever since I been here, and we never did get one," Honora says. She says it thoughtfully, as if there is much to consider in it.

"Let's go, Vernon," Miriam says impatiently. "I don't

believe in dragging things out," she adds, and then catches herself. She shrugs, acknowledging her predicament, and we all smile.

"You take care of her," Honora says.

"I will," Vernon says. He flushes suddenly, as if he has been caught out in a lie, then turns away and bumps his wife's chair carefully down the steps.

39

Johanna arrives only minutes after Vernon and Miriam Stone have gone.

"Is this a celebration or a wake?" she asks, seeing us gathered together in the middle of the lounge.

"You're back!" David Martin holds out his hand.

Johanna sidesteps him.

"It's both," he answers her then, "a celebration and a wake."

Before Johanna can shape her question, Honora says, "It's nothing to do with Mrs. Jessup."

"Your grandmother's fine," I say.

"She's in her room," Honora goes on, stretching it out a little, enjoying the small suspense she's contriving. "She fell asleep after breakfast so I just took her on back to her room and put her in the bed."

"You missed it," David Martin says, picking up Honora's cue. "You just missed it."

"What? . . . It's Mrs. Stone," she answers herself.

"She's gone," Honora says. She pauses for effect. "Gone with the wind."

Johanna looks to me for confirmation. "He came to get her, didn't he, Clara? Vernon came to get her."

"He did," I say.

"I never said good-bye to her," Johanna says. "I haven't talked to her in days."

"Or to me," Mr. Martin says. "Or anyone."

"I wish I'd been here," Johanna says. "Did she say to say good-bye to me?"

"Oh, yes," Honora says. "She said, 'Say good-bye to Johanna for me.' And she . . ."

"What did Vernon say to her? What did she say?"

"She took him back," Honora snaps, suddenly irritable. "That's what it came to."

Johanna touches Mr. Martin's sleeve. "But what happened exactly?"

"Ask Clara," he says, looking at me. "Clara hears everything."

"She wouldn't tell me what I want to hear," Johanna says.

Mr. Martin laughs.

"Excuse me," Honora says. "I got things to do. Excuse me, Clara."

I move aside to let Honora pass and sit down next to Mrs. Merriman to watch the dust Johanna raises. She grabs two folding chairs from the six that are stacked against the wall, cracks them open with an efficient flick of her wrist, and slides one directly behind Mr. Martin, compelling him to sit.

"Tell me," she prompts, settling herself into her chair opposite him.

"I've never seen you move with such dispatch." He smiles at her. "They had a conversation and then they left," he says.

"But what did they say to each other?"

"I only caught a line here and there. I heard Mr. Stone say something about a whore."

"Are you sure?"

"Yes. He said something about a whore, and not long after that Miriam said, 'I'm not attracted to you.' And he said, 'I waited as if I were sixteen,' and she said, 'From day two I wanted you blamed.' "

"She said, 'I wanted you blamed'?"

"Yes." David Martin leans forward. "You guessed Mr. Stone had come for his wife."

"Now that it's happened, it seems obvious."

"Does it? It isn't obvious to me."

"It changes everything," Johanna says.

"What in the world do you mean?" David Martin asks her.

"It's a happy ending," she answers him. "It proves that anything can happen."

David Martin sighs, and his sigh seems to physically diminish him, to reduce his true height and breadth as if he were releasing substance into the air instead of breath.

"The week before Charlotte died," he says, "I was reading to her. She was in bed, in our old room here. In Green Mansions. She had a very high fever, and she was in and out of a delirium. She was so thin. She was so thin I couldn't stand it. It didn't make any sense, reading to her. But I did it anyway. I pulled up a chair beside her, and I was reading Henry James to her. I'd been doing it all along, way past the time when I had any way of knowing if she was understanding. It was *The Wings of the Dove*, her favorite. '. . . gratefully glad that the southern summer was still in the high florid rooms . . . ' That's what I read. Suddenly she threw her arm out and knocked the book out of my hand." He flings his arm out to show Johanna.

"She hoisted herself up in the bed and she stuck her

face right up against mine. I could see the pulse at her temple beating. 'QUIT BREATHING DOWN MY NECK, YOU SHITASS,' she said. She snarled it at me." He drops his outstretched arm. It hangs off him like a dead weight. "I could feel myself growing cold," he tells Johanna. "And then for some reason I started to laugh, and I couldn't quit. Finally Honora must've heard me because she came running in and pulled me up out of my chair and held on to me.

" 'She introduced me to Henry James,' I told Honora.

" 'It's the disease, Mr. Martin,' Honora said. She was still holding on to me. 'Whatever happened, it's the sickness.'

" 'How can you say that?' I think I was shouting at her. 'You don't know.'

" 'I don't know,' she admitted, and she moved away and went over to Charlotte, who had dropped off to sleep with her mouth open. Charlotte's arm was dangling off the bed, and Honora lifted it and laid it alongside Charlotte's body. I watched her straighten the sheets without waking Charlotte.

" 'She called me a shitass,' I told Honora. I had to make this very great effort to keep from bursting out laughing. I clamped my jaws together and sucked my lips in hard against my gums.

"Honora said, 'You got to get some rest. You got to rest now. By yourself. Go on in 108. I think there's a spread on the bed in there. I'll come get you for supper.'

"So I went and lay down in a vacant room on top of a stripped-down bed that had an awful lime-colored spread thrown across it. I wanted very badly to sleep, but I couldn't. I looked around the ugly room, and I tried to imagine I was in a motel room. But it didn't look like a motel room. They don't have side rails on the beds in motel rooms, or trays you can swing into place over the bed.

I was entertaining myself after a fashion, with thoughts like that, when out of the blue I remembered this conversation I'd overheard fifteen years before.

"It was a Sunday afternoon in the spring, and Charlotte's old friend Daisy came by, and we all sat around and we had a beer together, and after a while I excused myself and went upstairs to sack out before supper.

"When I woke up I heard Charlotte say, 'David made me up. He invented me.'

" 'Men do that,' Daisy said. 'It isn't only David.'

" 'He thinks I'm beautiful so I'm beautiful. He thinks I'm strong so I'm strong. What would happen, Daisy, if I wasn't strong?'

" 'Don't look a gift horse in the mouth, Charlotte,' Daisy said, and the two women cackled together like schoolgirls."

He moves restlessly in his seat. "Did she mean me to hear that? She may have. And I wonder if it was true. And what it meant to her."

"You didn't ask," Johanna says.

"No, I never asked." He stretches his legs out in front of him, then bends over, kneading the long muscles of his calves, first one and then the other, as if they were cramping. He sits up again. "And then all these years later I was lying on an unmade bed in Green Mansions, and my wife was dying a few doors down the hall, and I remembered other words we'd said to each other on particular occasions, and they seemed to carry entirely different meanings than I'd thought they had. And gestures too. Ways we'd touched each other even. I was flooded with all these old memories, but everything we had said and done and been seemed altered and strange and full of dangerous meanings.

"I'd stayed stuck in one spot all my life, Johanna. I'd been crouching in this narrow corner looking at everything from this one fixed point and never any other. And I thought, maybe Charlotte isn't who I believed her to be. Maybe I am not who I believed myself to be."

"I never ask either," Johanna says. She is studying David Martin's face as if she is trying to figure something out, as if she is reckoning the cost of change.

"You can still get up out of your corner," David Martin says. But it is he who jumps up and Johanna who stays, staring after him.

"Johanna looks funny," Honora says to me as she passes.

"You look funny," she says, coming over to Johanna.

"I'm all right." Johanna plants her hands on her knees like an old or an infirm woman and hoists herself up out of her chair. She folds the chair up and drags it back into place against the others at the wall.

"I started to tell you before," Honora says, "Mrs. Stone said to tell you . . . "

"What?" Johanna folds up David Martin's chair.

"She said, 'Tell Johanna not to read too much into this.' "

Johanna slams the chair against the wall, and the whole stack of folding chairs crashes to the floor. "Fuck her," Johanna shouts, turning on Honora. Her face is crimson. "And David Martin and Clara and you, Honora. Fuck you."

"What is it?" Honora asks. "What's the matter?"

"You're wrong. That's what's the matter. All of you are wrong. Anything can happen."

"Johanna," Honora says, "I don't know what you're talking about."

"I can take my grandmother out of here. I am taking her out of here."

Honora stares. "You can't do that."

"I can," Johanna yells. "I will. It's what she wants."

"She wants to go *home*."

"She'll come home with me," Johanna says.

"We'll find a place for her."

"I've heard you talk about those places," Johanna says. "Shit on the floor, that's what you said, Honora. Old men strapped in their beds so they can't cause any trouble."

Honora puts a hand on Johanna's shoulder. "We'll find a *good* place for her."

Johanna moves sideways out of reach of Honora. "It won't be good enough. I want her to sleep in a real bed, goddammit, and sit in a real chair and eat real food."

"She'd need someone there all the time," I say, coming up to them. "You can't go off to your job and leave her by herself, Johanna."

"I'll quit my job."

"Your grandmother wouldn't want that," I say.

Honora moves to retrieve the fallen chairs. "What are you going to live on?" She looks at me as if it is me she's asking. "How are you going to feed her?" she asks, looking back at Johanna.

"I'll fix up a darkroom in my house. I've been wanting to do it anyway. I can get free-lance work. My boss asked me months ago if he could job out extra work to me."

"You can't lift her out of her chair by yourself," I say.

"Honora does it. If she can do it, I can do it."

Honora fits the chairs back to back, one against the other, against the wall. "You can't go out at all," she says, turning to face Johanna. "You don't see what I'm saying. You can't go to the store or to the pictures or to a friend's house for supper."

"Then I'll get someone to come in when I have to go out."

"Oh, Johanna . . . "

Honora does not finish whatever it was she was going to say. Her eyes, so eloquent in her dark face, speak all the difficulties, all the paradoxes, all the sorrow no one can find the words for.

But Johanna is not looking. She is imagining the future. She is changing the world.

40

Honora has been on the phone to the Methodist Retirement Home in Chatam County for almost half an hour.

"It's settled," she tells me when she comes out of her office. She looks as if she's been though a siege. Her hair, which usually lies close to her head, stands out around her ears in unruly spikes. A line of sweat, starting at her temple, streaks across one side of her face. Three dots of black ink like bugs trail across the bosom of her white uniform. "An old man died there last night," she says, "and they were set to take a lady in the county." She lets herself down into the old black couch beside me. "I had the charge nurse on the phone, and she said the director was the one I should speak to, but he was out of town at a conference. I told her the director promised me personally six weeks ago that I could have the first spot that came open, and she said she'd never heard one word about it or seen any mention of it written down anywhere. And I said, 'You can check with Dr. Brandon when he gets back.' His name just flew into my mind that second. And she said, 'Well, I don't know. It's so unlike him. I've only been here six months, but he's generally very careful to write everything down and to tell us about it. He's a very scrupulous sort of person,' she said. 'I know he is,' I said. 'When Dr. Brandon said, "Mrs. Bliss, you have my word on it," I knew it would be so.'

"And then she said, 'Well, what is her name?' I'd been planning all along I'd say Mrs. Jessup because of all this mess with Johanna. I thought if it was all done quick and Mrs. Jessup got settled somewhere it might be all right. But when she said, 'What is the name of the person you wish to transfer?' I said, 'Virginia Merriman. It's Mrs. Virginia Merriman.' And then I told her Mrs. Merriman was a lovely person and she'd been a Methodist all her life and all her family back generations were serious Methodists, and she said, 'That is not a requirement,' so I wished I hadn't made that up." Honora reaches over to switch off the lamp. "I didn't tell her Mrs. Merriman needs a skilled-care bed. I didn't tell her anything about Mrs. Merriman's condition. I thought if Mrs. Merriman gets all the way there, they'll probably keep her no matter what. But if I tell them beforehand, they might have a second thought. I knew the next thing that nurse was going to ask was did she need skilled care. So I rushed everything up. 'I have an emergency situation here,' I said. 'Just please tell me when someone can come for her.' And she said, 'Well, this afternoon, I suppose. Around one. I don't know. This is all so irregular.' And I said, 'Thank you for all your help,' and I said for her to please give my regards to Dr. Brandon when he got back from his conference."

* * *

Honora spends the rest of the morning sitting with Mrs. Merriman. I heard her explain to Mrs. Merriman that she would be leaving this afternoon, going to another place, another nursing home, because Green Mansions was being shut down. "The place you're going to is a lot like here," she said. "It even looks a lot the same. But it's out in the country, and it's newer and they'll be more people. I wrote all how they should care for you on the chart. I wrote down no restraints. There's no reason to think they'd tie you up. You never move from this chair, but I suddenly thought, what if they did it on account of the tremors? So I wrote down no restraints. I wrote it in red so it would stand out. Never under any circumstances. No restraints. I wrote a note to Dr. Brandon too. I told him you like someone to sit with you and visit. You like for someone to talk to you, and you understand it all. Mrs. Merriman understands everything."

Mrs. Merriman's knee jerked.

For an hour now Honora has sat beside Mrs. Merriman, holding the old woman's large hand in her own. Mrs. Merriman gazes at the ceiling, and Honora looks out at the empty lounge. Mrs. Jessup is asleep in her room. Johanna hasn't come yet. Only Mr. Martin is here, sitting by the window, watching the workmen come and go. And I am here in my corner on the old black couch watching Honora and Mrs. Merriman.

"One day," Honora says suddenly, "my mother and father were having an argument inside the house, and my grandfather and I were sitting out on the porch, and my brother was throwing stones at a tin can in the yard. You could see my brother was mad. You could tell by how hard he was throwing and by the way he wrenched his shoulders every throw.

"I was sad and nervous because my mother and father were fighting and because I was too tall and my breasts were too big and because I couldn't say even what I did know when Mrs. Berry had called on me in school that day.

"I kept moving around the porch, sitting down in one spot and getting up and sitting in another. I couldn't stay put.

"My grandfather was swinging back and forth on the swing chair, making this tiny creaking noise that made me edgier than anything else in the world just then. So I'd sigh and get up and move again. But my grandfather just sat there creaking with his eyes closed. I thought he must be sleeping he was like that so long, and then he opened his eyes and he said, 'We all of us got it all wrong. All this

sighing and crying and carrying on. All this *working.*' And
I asked him what did he mean, and he said, 'Oh, it's no
use me saying what I mean. But it's worth applying yourself to it, Honora. It's worth figuring out.'

"Sometimes I think I did figure it out; I see what he saw.
We're all throwing ourselves around, carrying on, fighting
a thousand battles. We're all working so hard. And most
of the time it seems like that's how it's meant to be. That's
the way we learn what we got to learn. That's the way we
come to ourselves. But what if we're not meant to strug-
gle? And what if we just gave it up? What would be there?
And I wonder do you know?"

*   *   *

When I was fifteen a strange gloom settled over me. I sat
for hours staring at nothing. My stories seemed pointless.
I lost my appetite. I minded suddenly that I wasn't pretty
and that my Aunt Celia had a reputation.

In the lunch line at school I had overheard Edna Bittle
tell Louise Dancey that her mother said no nice boy would
ever ask me out because my aunt was "iffy." The year
before I would have punched Edna Bittle in the nose. But
the year I was fifteen I wanted to make my Aunt Celia pay
for what she had done to me.

At home that night Celia was doing the bills, figuring
out what we owed who in town and how much we had
on hand and how much we were short. She was sitting at
the round oak table in the dining room in her red flowered
wrapper that Louise Dancey's father had brought her back
from the Orient the year before.

I sat across the table from her watching her with a peculiar fascination born of loathing. She was humming under her breath as she added up the columns of figures.
"Uh-oh," she'd say, every five minutes it seemed to me.

"Uh-oh. We are in sorry shape this month, Clara." And she'd go back to humming.

Finally I couldn't stand it a minute longer. "What are you so happy about then?" I exploded. "What are you humming for like everything is wonderful?"

Celia pushed both hands against the table's edge and sat way back in her chair and gave me a long look.

"Well, what's wonderful?" I screamed at her. "What's so wonderful?"

"Nothing at the moment."

"That's right," I said. "There's nothing right at the moment. We're short again this month like we always are."

"We are short again," Celia admitted.

"And you don't care."

"I'd a lot rather we had money. I'd a lot rather we were rolling in money."

"I suppose you know you have a reputation?" I went on, leaning across the table.

"I know," Celia said.

"Well?"

"Well what, Clara?"

"It's fine with you, I suppose?"

"No."

I burst into tears. "Then why are you happy all the time?"

"I'm happy when things are going my way, Clara, and I'm not happy when they're not. Just like everyone."

"You're not just like everyone. You're never just like everyone. You're always happy like some idiot that doesn't know any better."

Celia considered it. "You might say I'm cheerful."

"There's no difference between happy and cheerful. No one in their right mind except someone who'd wear a horrible red wrapper that Louise Dancey's father picked out sees a difference."

"Happiness always depends on something or someone,

Clara, but you can be cheerful if you want to be. Nothing else has to come into it. You can be full of joy. Do you see what I'm saying?" Celia asked me.

"Certainly I see what you're saying," I answered her. I didn't, of course. I had no idea what she was talking about.

But that night after I'd cooled off, Celia got it out of me about what Edna Bittle had said to Louise Dancey, and we talked some then about what it was like to be fifteen and strange and living with an iffy aunt.

The next day at school I told Edna Bittle if she ever said another word about my aunt, I'd flatten her.

41

As she had promised when I left home, Celia never answered my letters. But periodically I'd get a brown envelope addressed in her large, looping handwriting. Most of the time she sent clippings from the local paper, or photographs.

She sent a long piece about Edna Bittle's engagement to a Mr. Clyde Whitaker. On the bottom she wrote in red pencil, "Mr. Whitaker is no prize." She sent a notice of the foreclosure of Walter Ferris' farm. Folded up inside the clipping was a note that said, "Walter Ferris is the grandson of the Mr. Ferris from the bank your father put in his tall tale when he got home late from school that time." She sent a picture of herself and Letty Dundee sitting on the hood of Letty Dundee's red Buick convertible.

Once Celia sent me cookies. A battered shoe box was forwarded to me from my previous address. Inside was a pile of hard, dark crumbs.

The last thing Celia sent me was my mother's old blue garter that I used to wear around my arm. Her note said only, "You might want this. Love, Celia."

42

Two young men, one black and one white, are at the front door. The white man holds a contraption of leather and steel under one arm, a collapsible stretcher it must be. A gurney, Honora calls it. There's one like it in the supply room, leaning against a shelf full of draw sheets and disposable paper diapers.

David Martin leads the young men over to where Honora and I stand beside Mrs. Merriman. "Mrs. Bliss," Mr. Martin says, "the men from the Methodist Home are here."

"I'll get Mrs. Merriman's chart," Honora says. She disappears into the office and returns with the chart and a form for the men to sign. The black man signs the paper and hands it back to Honora. She grabs hold of his hand. "Please," she says.

"Ma'am?"

Mr. Martin pulls Honora's hand away. "You better go ahead," he tells the young men. "You better take her."

With a swift, barely discernible contraction of his knees, the white man flips open the gurney. Deftly then, as if they were performing some sleight of hand, as if they were tricking us, the men scoop Mrs. Merriman up out of her chair and onto the gurney.

David Martin and I flank Honora. We are not touching her, but it seems to me we are holding her up.

*   *   *

After a late lunch, which Honora only picks at, David Martin and I persuade her to lie down for a few minutes.

"Mrs. Jessup's asleep again," Mr. Martin says. "There's nothing for you to do."

Honora nods, acknowledging more than Mr. Martin intended.

While Honora naps, the rain begins.

"It's raining," David Martin says. "Thank God, it's finally raining."

The rain pours down, thudding on the roof with a dark, concussive sound. He watches out the window. "They're retreating," he says. "The workmen are leaving the field." Through the open windows we hear the sound of their trucks starting up. The tires crunch the new gravel as they pull away. The rain smells of tar and hot machinery and long sweet grass.

"What about you, Clara?" he says, still looking out the window.

"Am I retreating, you mean?"

He turns to look at me. "You don't know where you're going when you leave here, do you?"

"Not yet."

"It doesn't scare you not to know?"

"I like to be scared."

He laughs. "I wonder if I'm too old to learn to like it."

The rain falls, a steady, soaking rain that fills up the craters the workmen have blasted.

When Honora wakes she tells us she heard the rain in

her dreams. "When I woke up it really was raining, and I remembered like a shock, like I didn't know it already, that Mrs. Merriman is gone."

* * *

The rain stops abruptly. Inside of twenty minutes it is as steamy as it had been before the rain.

Honora seems undone by the heat. "It's too hot to breathe," she says miserably, fanning herself with her hand. "It's the worst it's ever been." She starts for the kitchen to get a drink, but the phone rings.

She gets four calls one right after the other. Johanna is the first, requesting that Honora tell her grandmother she is running late. The next three calls are from Harley Creech, the construction foreman, from Stuart Rich, vice-president of Dixieland Construction, and from Oxford Hayes, chairman of the board of Green Mansions, all to the effect that the premises must be vacated in five days to allow time to set up for the September 23 demolition.

When she emerges from her office Honora tells me that after the four calls, she got back on the phone to the Methodist Home to find out if Mrs. Merriman got there safely.

"I talked to the same charge nurse," she says. "She said it was unethical of me not to inform her of the true nature of Mrs. Merriman's condition. She said just fortunately they had a skilled-care bed, but they might well not have. She said she spoke to Dr. Brandon on the telephone, and he told her he knew of me and he thought he may have spoken to me once years ago, but he had never made me any promise. She said they would keep Mrs. Merriman now they had her and that she was doing as well as could be expected under the circumstances. I asked her what did she mean, was Mrs. Merriman failing, and she said, 'Well, Mrs. Bliss, she could hardly be said to be gaining.' "

Honora presses the heels of her hands to her forehead.

"They tie them up in some nursing homes, Clara. I'm talk-ing about places supposed to be good. Places where only rich people go. I've seen old people naked, tied in a chair, sitting in their own shit."

"Why don't you go home to sleep tonight?" I say. "I can stay."

"No, no, Clara." Honora looks at her watch. "But I thank you."

"Johanna's here," I say. "She's with her grandmother. I told her about Mrs. Merriman, and she said to tell you she was sorry."

"Did she talk to Mr. Martin?"

"No."

"I'm afraid to tell her we've only got five days," Honora says. "I had an idea to call the mother of this girl Alice used to go to school with. I remember once Alice telling me her mother took in boarders. She and her husband. He was some kind of mechanic and got his hand smashed and couldn't work anymore, so he stayed home and they took care of a few boarders, three, I think Alice said, all with disabilities of some kind.

"I don't think they took in white folks," she says help-lessly.

*   *   *

Johanna is rushing through the lounge on her way out when David Martin stops her. "I heard you," he says. "I heard you talking to Honora yesterday." He puts a re-straining hand on her arm.

"Johanna," he says, "you have no legal rights in this, None."

"She wants to come home."

"Johanna, listen to me . . ."

"Why do you think she stopped talking? She can't stand to be here anymore. She'll die if she stays here."

"Your mother is the next of kin. It would be up to her to take your grandmother out."

"She can't do it."

"You can't do it, Johanna. You mustn't try."

"You would have done it for Charlotte."

"She was my wife. I would have been bringing my wife home to the house where we'd lived together for forty-five years."

"You stayed here for her. You would have done anything to keep Charlotte, no matter what it was."

"I would have been wrong."

"You've got no guts," Johanna says.

"Without your mother's approval," Mr. Martin says, "without her express written consent, you may not legally remove your grandmother from these premises."

"Then I'll do it illegally," Johanna vows. "I'm bringing my grandmother home." She swings her purse onto her other shoulder and veers around Mr. Martin, giving him the widest possible berth.

43

The rain began again toward dawn. When I arrive at Green Mansions it is still raining. The sky is low and grey.

There's no one in the lounge except Honora. She is standing in the middle of the room looking all around her.

"There's no one here," she says by way of greeting.

"You look as if you're looking for them," I say.

"Mrs. Jessup went back to sleep after breakfast, and Mr.

Martin is taking a shower," she explains. "A long shower.
He's been in there forty minutes at least. I just talked to
Oxford Hayes," she goes on without a break, "and he said
not to pack anything up. He says just leave everything—
the kitchen supplies and the linen and the furniture and
everything. He says his wife has a committee to come get
all that. He doesn't even care about me boxing stuff up for
them. He said, 'They'll do all that. Don't worry about a
thing, Mrs. Bliss.' "

Honora asks me would I like some tea. When I say I
would, she nods. "I called Frank last night," she says, "to
tell him about Mrs. Merriman. He said he was sorry. And
then he asked had I given any thought to what comes next.
'She'll die,' I said because I didn't want to talk about what
he really meant, which was plans. He meant did I have a
plan about another job. And I don't. It made me mad that
he threw it up to me.

" 'I'm not pressing you, Honora,' he said when I didn't
answer him. 'I just thought it would help you to have
something when all this is over, because it will be over
soon.'

" 'I think I know that better than you,' I said, and he
said, 'I'm tired, Honora. We'll talk another time.' And he
hung up.

"I called him back. When he picked up, I said, 'I'm sorry
I said I think I know that better than you.' And he said,
'Why, thank you, Honora.' And then I told him how that
charge nurse said I was unethical. I told him how I could
hardly stand to let Mrs. Merriman go. I told him I hadn't
called Johanna's mother yet to tell her I don't have a place
for Mrs. Jessup. I told him how I'd never got it right with
Alice, not ever really in all these years. And then I told
him everything. 'I thought there was some place I could
get to, Frank. I thought I could get somewhere where I
could say, here, this is it, this is who I am. This is how the
world is. This is what it means to live a life and die.'

" 'You thought you could do that there in Green Mansions,' he said.

" 'Yes.'

" 'And you couldn't,' he said.

" 'No,' I told him. 'No.'

"And then he said the most surprising thing he ever said to me. He said, 'I love you, Honora.' "

* * *

Last night I dreamed I was on a train rushing through the night. Periodically the train slowed, but it never stopped. I could make out blurry figures, people standing together on the station platforms, as I sped by. I pressed my face against the window. My mother and father waved to me from the platform that sprang out of the blackness. I could see them in the yellow light that flared up for an instant. Then they fell back into the darkness. I looked around in a panic, but there was no one else in the car I was in. I got up and walked through to the next car, but it was empty too. I walked through the next car and the next and the next. Then I ran. I ran and I ran through the long length of cars, but there was no one else on the train.

* * *

When David Martin appears, freshly showered and shaved, it is with something of a flourish. He inhabits his full length; he fills up his frame. He moves with deliberation, like someone who has the habit of intention.

"Johanna is late," he says as he approaches us. "Good morning, Clara."

"Good morning."

"She's not late," Honora says, looking up at him. "It's not even ten."

"I know," he says. "I'm just making conversation."

"You seem different," Honora says, eyeing him.

He puts a hand on the back of Honora's chair. "You sound suspicious. Don't you think she sounds suspicious, Clara?"

Honora edges forward in her seat. "Are you waiting for Johanna?"

He smiles at her, removing his hand. "Yes, I am. I am waiting for Johanna."

Johanna bursts into the lounge, comically on cue. But she is in a different play from David Martin. She is soaked through. Her hair is plastered to her skull, her sleeveless blouse is stuck to her breasts, her blue-jean skirt, faded almost to white, bunches up around her thighs. She looks as if she has barely escaped drowning, like someone dragged up from the bottom of the sea.

"What is it?" David Martin calls, running to her. "What's wrong?"

"It's in the papers," she says. "We have to be out of here in four days. Didn't Honora tell you?"

"You're not in here," David Martin says. "You have a life of your own to live that has nothing to do with this place."

"Oh, you know what I mean." She throws it off impatiently. "Where is she going?" Johanna demands. "I have to talk to her."

David Martin looks back in time to see Honora disappear into her office. "Come on," he says, taking Johanna's arm. "I'll get you a towel and a sweater or something. You're soaked to the skin."

"No," she says, pulling away from him. "I don't want anything."

"Well, sit down at least," he says.

"There isn't any time."

"You don't have a minute to sit with an old man who's been waiting to talk to you all morning?"

"I wish you wouldn't be charming," she says, but she lets herself be steered to the black Leatherette chair. She plops down, and the chair receives her wet body with a vulgar sucking noise.

"Is your son charming?" Johanna asks from the depths of the chair.

"You've read his letters."

"He may have other defects," Johanna says, "but he's not charming. At least not with you."

"It's Glenn I wanted to talk to you about. In a way. I couldn't fall asleep last night. It was all that had happened—Mrs. Merriman going, and Honora feeling so low, and you and me at odds. I lay awake for hours thinking about Charlotte and me. And Glenn. I had this tremendous urge to talk to him. I wanted to talk to him right then and tell him everything I was thinking about. But I have no place to call him. I came very close to phoning you and asking you to come over right away and write it all down for me. I could've sent it to him international express mail. But, of course, I didn't phone you. Finally I fell asleep and I dreamed I was making a cabinet. A rosewood cabinet.

"In the dream I thought to myself, rosewood is so hard to work with, but I had this wonderful picture in my head of what it was going to look like when it was finished, and it was rosewood; beautiful, close-grained, fragrant rosewood.

"It was a funny dream, it was so simple and so real. I went through the entire process of making a cabinet—exactly as I would in real life. I cut dovetail joints. I remember I cut the dovetail with a very fine-toothed backsaw my father had given me. And then I marked the cut dovetail on the mating part of the joint so I could cut it precisely.

"The whole dream was like that. When I was making the corners I was careful to stagger the dowels to avoid splitting.

"It was a long, slow dream. It seemed to take as much time to dream it as it would to make the cabinet.

"When at last I was through I was exhausted. I was sitting on the floor in Glenn's room, and I laid my cheek against the side of the cabinet, and the tiredness ran all through me. And then I backed away to look at it—to really look at it. One of the drawers didn't fit as it should, and there was a place on one side where I'd made a long scratch in the wood with a nail. I looked at the cabinet for a very long time, and I thought, it isn't as beautiful as I imagined it would be. But I was satisfied. And I thought, I worked very hard to make it good, and I'm satisfied. Then I woke up."

"You're leaving," Johanna says, popping up in the chair. "That's what this is all about, isn't it? You're going home."

"Maybe not home. I don't know yet," he says. "Maybe to a smaller place in town. Or even to another town."

"You're saving yourself."

"Johanna," he says, "I can't save your grandmother."

Johanna grabs on to tne arms of the old chair. This is the springboard that will propel her into action, but she has not reckoned on the advancing Honora.

"Wait!" Honora calls, like someone hoping to avert a calamity. "Wait!" she calls again, crossing to them. But all she says is, "You have a call."

"Me?" Johanna leaps up.

"It's for you, Mr. Martin," Honora says.

Johanna sags backward, dropping into the chair. The weight of her sudden lassitude causes the bottom of the old chair to bulge out, dragging against the floor.

"It's from San Francisco," Honora goes on. "Person to person. It's a terrible connection. I didn't get who's calling."

"The only people I know in San Francisco are Daisy and Jack," Mr. Martin says.

"I remember her from when she visited," Honora says. "She had short brown hair."

"They moved shortly after Charlotte died," Mr. Martin explains to Johanna.

Johanna makes a face. "They'll move again before you get to the phone."

When Mr. Martin has gone, Honora says, "Her name was Daisy Plummer. She was Mrs. Martin's best friend." She sits down carefully in the seat David Martin has just vacated. "Johanna, I have to call your mother."

"It's the middle of the afternoon there," Johanna says. "She'll be out."

"I don't mean this minute. I'll call her tonight."

"I don't see what the point is of bothering my mother."

"There's only a few more days," Honora says.

"Four," Johanna says, still sunk in her chair.

"There are people who take in people like your grandmother," Honora goes on, as if Johanna hadn't spoken. "Sort of a boardinghouse situation."

"My mother's never going to go for some junky boardinghouse."

"That's what I mean," Honora says. "I can't just go ahead. I have to see what she wants."

"She wants . . ." But Johanna doesn't say what it is her mother wants.

David Martin is coming toward them, shrugging his shoulders. "I don't know who it was," he says. "I couldn't understand the operator there was so much static. I told her, 'This is a godawful connection,' and then someone else came on the line. I yelled hello about twenty times and got no answer, so I hung up."

"They'll call back," Honora assures him.

"I hope so," David Martin says.

Johanna stands suddenly. "I'm going home. Tell my grandmother I'll be here tomorrow."

"I want to talk to you," David Martin says.

"So do I," Honora says. "We got to talk, Johanna."

They will have to wait. Johanna is leaving. Johanna is going. Johanna is rolling, unstoppable as a wave, toward the door.

44

When Johanna is gone we talk, Honora and David Martin and I, of odd, inconsequential things—the rainfall in other summers, the buttery taste of lettuce grown in a garden, the questionable fate of the tobacco warehouses downtown.

"I heard," David Martin says, "that they're thinking of turning some of them into apartments."

"My grandfather worked in one of those buildings," Honora says. "Did you ever see the ones he means, Clara?" When I say I haven't seen those particular buildings, the ones on Pettigrew Street, she says, "When all this is over . . ."

Her "all this" hangs in the air. David Martin picks it up. "Have you called Johanna's mother?"

"Tonight," Honora says. "I told Johanna."

David Martin pulls at his bare chin the way some men pull at their beards. "What did she say?"

Honora shakes her head for answer.

"She thinks I've deserted her," David Martin says. His face reddens as if he has divulged a shameful secret, and then he tells us about his leaving. It sounds in his telling like some remote event, a decision made long ago by someone he had heard about but never known.

Still Honora seizes his news. "I'm so glad," she says. "I wish we had something to celebrate with."

"Do you think Johanna really is going to do something?" I ask Mr. Martin.

"She gets fired up," he says, "but she fizzles."

"And flares up again," I say.

The ringing phone startles us. "That could be your call from San Francisco," Honora says. "I'll get it." She jogs across the room to her office—a funny, shambling dogtrot. She moves exhaustedly, like a runner whose legs have given out long before the finish.

It turns out to be a wrong number and a signal to disperse.

"Well, when will you go?" Honora asks Mr. Martin.

"Oh, not till the end." He laughs. "I always stay till the end."

"Good," Honora says. "I wasn't worried about you," she adds. "Maybe I had a premonition you would decide to go."

"I'd like to think so," David Martin says. "I'd like to think you knew it all along."

* * *

Late in the afternoon Honora asks me if I would stay the night. "Just in case," she says.

I say I will, and we go to make up a bed for me in one of the empty rooms.

"This was Mr. and Mrs. Martin's room," Honora says, smoothing the stiff bottom sheet all the way around her side of the bed. "Charlotte Martin died in this bed."

We shake the top sheet up in the air, each of us holding

an end. The sheet billows up like a sail catching the wind, then collapses softly onto the bed. "She called him a shitass the week before she died," Honora says. "Do you want the sides tucked in?"

"I don't like that feeling," I say.

She straightens up and looks at me. "I love it. It makes me feel safe."

She moves away from the bed, lifting up the garish tangerine-colored spread that is folded up on the orange chair in the corner. "You're not going to stay, are you, Clara?"

"Whatever I do," I say, "I won't go till you're finished here."

"This is such a ugly spread," Honora says. "Used to, you couldn't even find a spread so ugly. And the green ones are worse." She places the folded spread at the bottom of the bed and sits down beside it. "I could call Johanna's mother now, before supper.

"Suppertime," she says. "My brother and I had our worst fights at suppertime. And Alice and me when she was coming up. Frank proposed to me at suppertime." She puts both hands down on the bed and hoists herself up as if it is some effort. "You could tell some stories about suppertime, Clara."

"It's the middle of the night in Antwerp, Honora."

* * *

Honora woke Mrs. Jessup to give her her supper, and she told her that she was going to call her daughter in Antwerp, and would she like to speak to her.

"Mrs. Jessup didn't say anything, of course," Honora tells David Martin and me. "She just ate her supper and then she slid back down in the bed and closed her eyes and fell asleep."

Honora goes into her office to place her call to Antwerp. David Martin and I play blackjack and wait.

When Honora comes out of her office, she says, "Well, it's done."

"You sound as if you've given something away," David Martin says.

Honora gives him a sharp look. "Maybe I did." She pulls a chair up to the card table and sits down. "She'll come," she says.

"When?" I ask.

"I told her how little time we've got," Honora says, ignoring my question, "and that I still didn't have a place for her mother. I told her I was thinking of a special boardinghouse but I hadn't found one yet, but I thought we could find that faster than a place in a regular nursing home. And I said she might like that a lot better. If we got the right one. But if it didn't work out, I would still keep on looking for something else. And she said, 'I don't know. I wasn't expecting this at all. I don't know what to do.'

"And then I said, 'Johanna's talking about taking her grandmother home with her.' And she said, 'Oh, my God.' And I said, 'She's upset. She might just be talking.' And Mrs. Green said, 'Johanna left New York and quit a job she'd had for four years to move in with a man she met on a seven-day vacation in Spain. She's thirty-eight years old and she acts like she's eighteen.'

"Then I said, 'Mrs. Green, your mother is worse,' and I told her Mrs. Jessup is sleeping most of the day, and then I told her her mother hasn't talked in three weeks. 'What do you mean?' she said. 'She just stopped talking,' I said. I told her it wasn't anything physical, that Dr. Milne said there's nothing organic. 'Then why?' she said. 'Why?'

"And then she switched and she said, 'I can't understand, Mrs. Bliss, why you waited till the very last minute to tell me you still don't have a place for my mother. I mean it's unbelievable. And you wait till tonight to tell me my mother hasn't spoken in three weeks. Johanna hasn't said one word about it in her letters to us. I just don't understand. The two of you have been in some sort of collusion.' Her voice was getting louder and louder. 'I had absolute trust in your judgment, Mrs. Bliss. You've violated that.' Then there was this long silence, and I said, 'Mrs. Green?' and there was no answer, but I could hear her breathing, so I just waited. Then I heard a man's voice in the background. I couldn't hear what he was saying, but I knew it must be Johanna's father.

"And then I said, 'I'm sorry, Mrs. Green. I'm so sorry.' And she said, 'It's me. I shouldn't be here. I should have stayed. I should have kept her with me in New York.'

" 'You couldn't do that,' I said.

"And she said, 'It was only for a year and a half, and I was going to come back for two weeks at Thanksgiving. I thought it would be all right. I thought it might even be good for Johanna.' 'It has been,' I told her, and I realized just then when I was saying it that I thought it was true.

" 'I'll come right away,' she said. Then the man, Johanna's father, said something again, and she said, 'Oh, God, Mrs. Bliss, I forgot. I can't come today. There's an air controllers' strike here.' And then the man said something again, and she said something back to him I couldn't hear, and then she got back on the line and she said, 'My husband will drive me to Paris tomorrow. I'll fly from there to New York. I should get to you tomorrow night or the following morning.'

"I told her that was fine, that was plenty of time, and I said, 'I meant to call you before.'

"And she said, 'Tell Johanna I'll be there. Tell her I'll be there as soon as I can.' "

* * *

David Martin excuses himself right after supper to go to his room, and Honora goes off to settle Hannah Jessup for the night. I curl up on the couch intending to look at the newspaper Mr. Martin left for me. Outside the window toward the horizon the low clouds are banked like hills. If I squint all I see is those clouds, a white landscape, like the dream of a hilly country outside an airplane window. I put the paper down and close my eyes. I have the sensation of falling. I'm in a plane diving down over a sparkling blue sea. There's music coming from somewhere— dance music. A man leads me to an aisle as wide as the porch of Green Mansions and takes me in his arms. I'm falling into the music, into the sea. There's a soft thud, an ending. We're on a sandy runway like a beach. "Come on, Clara," Honora is calling to me. She's standing arm in arm with my Aunt Celia, and the man is behind them, beckoning.

I shake my head. "I'm going on."

Celia laughs as if I'd said something wonderful.

"But we're here," Honora says. "Come on, Clara.

"Come on." Honora gives my shoulder a little shake. "It's late. It's time to get up and go in to bed."

* * *

The phone in the middle of the night shrieks like a siren. I race to the door of my room. David Martin is already in the hall. Honora, a black ghost in her long white nightdress, streaks past us as if she were on fire.

David Martin looks at me. "It can't be good," he says.

But in seconds Honora emerges from her office smiling broadly. She has one hand up in the air, hailing us. "It's your son," she calls out.

"Glenn?" David Martin says, pulling his robe around him. "Glenn's on the phone?"

"No, no," Honora explains, coming up to him. She is panting a little, still a little breathless. "It was a telex. He's in the United States. It was him calling from San Francisco. He's on his way to Seattle now for some kind of business and then he's flying here. He arrives at the airport here on Eastern flight 387 at 8:12 tonight."

"Tonight?" David Martin repeats it as if he can't believe it's true.

Honora laughs. She is vivified by the good news she brings. The moonlight falling in at the window at the end of the hall lights her up. She glows robustly like a near star on a clear night.

David Martin grins like a boy. "I'm not going to be able to go back to sleep."

"I'm wide awake," Honora says.

"We could play poker," David Martin says.

"Come on, Clara." Honora grabs my arm. "We'll go make us a feast, while Mr. Martin lays out the cards."

45

The room is growing light, and we are all numb with fatigue. There has been no conversation for the last hour, and we are all playing badly. But we are still dealing out the sticky cards, shoving the chips into and out of the center of the table, raising and calling and bluffing and folding and cutting and shuffling and dealing again.

Suddenly there is a loud banging at the door.

Honora jumps out of her seat, and the little towers of red, white and blue plastic chips she has stacked up in front of her clatter to the floor, bouncing on the linoleum.

She crosses the room in two running steps and pulls the door open. It's Johanna. She is dressed up in a white pi-qué sundress with a wide square neck. Her hair, just washed, is still damp. It curls around her face. Her skin too looks faintly damp.

"What are you doing here at this hour?" Honora asks her.

Johanna looks past Honora to the table where David Martin and I sit. She takes in the cards and the coffee cups and the paper plates dotted with crumbs.

"Glenn's coming," David Martin calls to her. "He'll be here tonight."

Johanna stares at him.

"His telex came in the middle of the night," David Martin explains. "We've been playing cards since then. Honora's the big winner."

"Is she?" Johanna says with an edge in her voice. But she takes Honora's arm. "I want to talk to you."

"May I sit down?" she asks as she and Honora approach the table. She is strangely formal, as if her white sundress and her white sandals and her shiny hair have altered her relation to us.

"Please," David Martin says, rising to pull over a fourth chair for her.

"I wrote to my mother," Johanna says. "I've been up all night."

I can see now that this is so. There are deep shadows under her eyes, and her voice is slowed down and thick. "I was writing the letter and planning things out."

"What do you mean?" Honora asks. "What are you planning?"

"I spoke to my boss, Mr. Hill, last night. I called him at his home and explained everything, and we had a very satisfactory talk." Johanna slurs the "satisfactory" very slightly. "He's going to give me my two weeks' vacation pay that I have coming," she says. "With that money com-

ing right away I can manage till I get everything orga-
nized. He said they could definitely use me on a free-lance
basis, and last night I looked at my closet really seriously,
and it'll work fine for a darkroom. I called a carpenter friend
of mine; he can do what little needs to be done for next to
nothing. I know somewhere where I can get a good deal
on secondhand equipment. Plus I have a little money saved.
If things are tight at first, I can manage. I'll have the work
from my job to start, and I'll get other clients. My darkroom work is very good."

Honora leans sideways in her chair, scooping up fallen
poker chips, stalling for time.

"I made a list of things I'll need to buy or have installed," Johanna says, watching Honora. "Like a wheelchair and a stable tray for eating in bed, and extra sheets,
and an egg-crate mattress. That's what you call it, isn't it,
the kind that goes on top of the regular mattress to prevent bedsores? I'll have to have metal grab bars installed
for the tub and near the toilet. And I'll need one of those
elevated toilet seats. I thought you might make me a list,
Mrs. Bliss, of whatever else you think I might need."

"Johanna," I say, "Honora called your mother last night."

Inexplicably Johanna laughs.

"She's coming here," David Martin says. "Your father
is driving her to Paris, and she'll fly from there. She'll be
here late tonight or tomorrow."

"I told my mother I'm bringing Han home with me,"
Johanna says passionately. She looks around the little ta-
ble, seeking out each one of us in turn, first Honora, then
David Martin, then me.

"Your mother will have left Antwerp before your letter
gets there," I say.

"I'm going to get my grandmother," Johanna says, rising up out of her chair like a queen in a play rising from
her throne. She towers over us.

"No!" Honora yells, leaping around in front of Johanna to bar her way. She grabs hold of Johanna's arm.

"Let her go," David Martin says. Honora falls back as if all her will and all her energy had consisted in his not saying that.

"You don't have to worry," Johanna says earnestly to Honora, to all of us. She is earnest and ardent and eager and certain. "I know what I'm doing."

Perhaps she does. Perhaps she knows something we forgot. She leads and we follow, Honora and David Martin and I, straggling behind her, worn out and sheepish and old.

Hannah Jessup is leaning back against her pillows so that she is raised up a little in the bed. She looks up at us with an expression of the fullest comprehension. I imagine she is going to speak. I imagine she is going to say, "I have been expecting you."

"You're awake," Johanna says, crossing the room in one long stride, leaving Honora and David Martin and me behind. She sits down on the edge of the bed, leaning against her grandmother's hip, nudging her over in the bed so she will have room.

Hannah Jessup doesn't respond. She looks over Johanna's shoulder at the three of us huddled together in the narrow doorway like refugees and smiles coolly, the way you smile at someone you have finally outsmarted.

"Han," Johanna begins. "Han, I know Mrs. Bliss has told you Green Mansions is closing soon. Well, I've figured it out."

David Martin sucks his breath in.

"I'm taking you to live with me," Johanna says. "I'm fixing my room up for you so you'll have your own private room, and I'll be right in the next room. It will be a home. A real home, Han."

The old woman laughs.

Johanna grabs her grandmother's hand, which looks as weightless as a bird's wing. She squeezes it hard, grimacing as if it hurts her to squeeze so hard. "You can talk, can't you?" she says, leaning up over her grandmother as if Hannah Jessup were the source of everything she prized.

"I can talk," Hannah Jessup says.

"Oh, Han."

"I don't want to go with you," Hannah Jessup says. She pushes herself up farther in the bed. Her nose is almost touching Johanna's. "Close your mouth," she says. "You look like a fish."

Johanna's face is as white and as blank as the wall. Honora and I step over the threshold into the room.

"You used to say that to me when I was a little girl," Johanna says.

"*Ach, Gott,*" Hannah Jessup cries out. "If you could hear how you sound. Go away, Johanna." She sinks back down in the bed. "I want to die by myself."

"You're not dying."

"If you say so, darling."

"But why are you so sarcastic? Why are you so angry?" Hannah Jessup turns her head away.

"You were a good person, Han," Johanna cries. "You were a good person."

"Go away," Hannah Jessup says.

"Don't you love me? Don't you love me anymore?"

"It's finished, all that," Hannah Jessup says. "It's something else now. I can't explain it to you, Johanna," she says with a kind of hopeless exasperation.

"But Mom is coming tomorrow, Han." Johanna grabs a fistful of her grandmother's nightdress. She is holding on so tight her knuckles are white. "She's coming right away. She'll be here tonight or tomorrow."

"Please," Hannah Jessup says. "I'm too tired."

David Martin brushes past Honora and me. He touches Johanna's shoulder. "Johanna. Come away, Johanna."

"NO!" Johanna lunges for her grandmother, pulling her up against her own body, falling backward with her on the bed. Johanna's head hits the metal railing at the foot of the bed. "It hurts," she sobs. "It hurts."

David Martin pulls Hannah Jessup out of Johanna's arms and lifts her back against the pillows. Then he picks Johanna up in his arms. He picks her up in his arms like a baby and carries her past Honora and me, out of the room.

* * *

When Honora and I come out into the lounge, Johanna is curled up on the black couch, her face to the wall. She is still sobbing. David Martin is sitting beside her. "Her head's okay, I think," he says. "Just a bad bump." He gets up to let Honora sit down.

Honora puts a hand on Johanna's shoulder. "Listen, Johanna," she says. "I want you to know your grandmother is okay. She's already back asleep. I'm going to call Dr. Milne to come by to check her just to make sure. Do you hear me?"

Johanna gives no sign that she does. "Right now," Honora says, "I'm going to get you something to let you sleep."

46

Johanna sleeps like a dead man, like someone plunged into the center of the black earth, where no sound, no light, can ever penetrate.

When she wakes up it is almost six. She opens her eyes. For a long moment she seems to drift, to veer away from this moment and the shadowy light back into sleep, but she sits up, drawing the blanket Honora had put over her while she slept around her. "What time is it?" she asks.

"Six o'clock," Honora says. "Time for supper."

Johanna passes a hand across her forehead as if she is brushing the last of her sleep away. She looks fully her age, as if all the years she had sloughed off before had come to rest inside her while she slept. "I've slept all day," she says.

"Could you eat something?" David Martin asks.

She shakes her head.

"Dr. Milne came by, and your grandmother's all right," Honora says. "And your father called while you were asleep. He said your mother got the earliest flight she could from Paris to New York and she'd be at Kennedy by seven a.m. tomorrow. She's got an Eastern flight from La Guardia that will get her to the airport here at 11:37 tomorrow morning."

"I see," Johanna says. She watches Honora so intently that it seems literally to be true, as if she saw everything that was going to happen in Honora's dark eyes.

When David Martin asks her if she will drive him to the airport to pick up Glenn, she says, "He really is coming?"

"He'll be here in two hours."

"And my mother is coming tomorrow morning," Johanna says, as if the two events are connected in her mind.

"I realize," Mr. Martin says, "it's an odd request under the circumstances, but I thought . . ."

"I want to do something," Johanna says. "I'll drive you to pick Glenn up tonight, and tomorrow morning I'll get my mother." She stands up, wobbling a little, like someone who's just discarded crutches. David Martin puts out a hand to steady her.

Honora asks her if she's certain she feels okay to drive, and Johanna assures her she does. "I'm just going to check on my grandmother before we go," she says.

Honora looks at me.

"I'm all right," Johanna says. "It's okay." She walks out of the lounge toward her grandmother's room.

* * *

Honora fixes a light supper for herself and David Martin and me. Johanna says she doesn't want anything, but she ends up drinking the broth Honora brings her. When we are through, Honora and I walk Mr. Martin and Johanna to Johanna's car.

It's cool outside, the first cool night of the summer.

"I can smell the cold coming," Honora says as she leads us across the parking lot in the dusk.

David Martin catches up with Honora, and Johanna falls back to walk with me. "Mr. Martin said I misread everything." She trails her hand along the length of an outsized sawhorse one of the workmen left standing free in the middle of the parking lot. "He was right."

"You wanted to save her," I say.

"I still do," Johanna says.

We walk on in silence.

"I thought I could make it work out," Johanna says suddenly. "You would never have thought that."

"I don't like to hope for what can't be. I'd rather imagine what might be."

Johanna looks over at me. "You want less than I do," she says. "Or maybe more."

Honora and David Martin have stopped beside Johanna's old car.

"What are you going to do when you leave here?" Johanna asks me.

"I'm going to go somewhere I've never been."

"That sounds wonderful to me," Johanna says.

"I'm going to wake up in a new town," I tell Johanna. "I'm going to walk out in its streets looking for a story and someone to tell it to."

Johanna stares at me.

The darkness is spreading around us like waves. We almost walk into Honora and David Martin, who are leaning against Johanna's car. It's too dark now to see what color Johanna's car is, but you can make out its shape and tell that it's seen better days.

Johanna opens the door of her car and rolls the window down, and David Martin walks around to the other side and gets in.

"Tell my grandmother I'll be here early tomorrow morning," Johanna tells Honora, settling into her seat. "I'll come to see her before I go get my mother."

"I'll tell her," Honora says.

"Well," Johanna says. She slams the door shut. She has to do it twice more to get it to shut right. Honora and I step back.

Johanna sticks her right hand out against the dash. Her head sinks down on the wheel. She stays that way for a long time. No one says anything.

At last Honora says, "Well, we'll see you all later."

"I'll see you tomorrow," Johanna says, and still hunched over the wheel, she flips on the radio.

As Honora and I walk back across the lot to Green Mansions, we hear the man singing his old song: "Take your shoes off, do not fear . . ."

And then, rising in the cool night, over the clatter and the wheezing of Johanna's car starting up, Johanna joining in: "Bring that bottle over here . . ."

Her voice, surprisingly clear, is full of everything she knows.

* * *

Honora and I sat outside on the wide steps of Green Mansions for a long time.

The night was full of sound and motion. The pines leaned toward us, hissing a little as they swayed. The last diehard cicadas were making a racket in the grass at our feet, and somewhere to the east of us the cars on the new length of expressway rushed by.

Honora said she would go see Mrs. Merriman soon. "I don't really know anything about that place, and that nurse sounded so cold. She might take it out on Mrs. Merriman that I lied to get her in there."

"I doubt she'd do that," I said.

"I can't stand to think of her living on and on in a place where nobody cares about her," Honora said. She crossed her arms across her chest as if she were suddenly cold. "And Mrs. Jessup has no place to go to. She has no place to die in."

"You still might find a place for her. You can keep looking."

"That's all I can do," Honora said.

We looked out into the night. We looked out at the dark shapes of the magnolias and the pines and the kudzu nothing can hold back.

I looked over at Honora. "I'll miss you."

"I dreamed your dream," Honora said. "Only it was me asking you why you wander instead of your father. We were sitting on the porch of the old house on Corporation Street. I was in the swing chair, and you were squatting on the top step. Hunkering. The way a kid would. Or a man. You had one hand up sort of shading your eyes, like you were trying to see something in the distance and the sun was in your eyes."

"What did I tell you?"

"What?" Honora said, as if I'd startled her.

"What answer did I give you?"

"You said you wandered to find out why you wander."

"I'll tell my father that next time," I said.

"You tell him you learned it from me," Honora said.

"I'll come back to see you, Honora."

"I had the impression you don't go back anywhere."

"I will this time. I'll want to know how you are."

Honora pulled her dress over her knees. "If you come back, I'll tell you."

Before we went back inside, I told Honora an idea for a story I'd been turning around in my mind. "It's about a great Swedish director," I said. "He had devoted his life to his films, and his images turned up in the dreams of butchers and bankers and beggars and thieves."

"What happened to him?" Honora asked.

"He fell in love with the brilliant Finnish actress who was his greatest leading lady. He fell in love with Ultima Thule, the most beautiful woman in the world."

"But she didn't love him," Honora said.

"He did everything in his power to make her love him," I said. "He gave her everything she asked for, and he gave her all his heart besides."

"She loved somebody else," Honora said.

"She loved a punk rocker from East L.A. She loved Tommy Rot."

"She loved that boy though he wasn't worth a thing," Honora said.

"The great Swedish director couldn't believe that Ultima Thule, who was so intelligent and so full of feeling, could love this puling boy. The great director could make a cloudy day sunny. He could paint the town red and the sea gold. He could stop time. But he couldn't make Ultima Thule love him."

"It made him crazy," Honora said.

"It finally made him crazy," I said. "And all that was left to him was to imagine that the darkness that fell over his mind might bring out a star for him to see by."

Honora considered it. "Well, it might," she said, and we got up off the steps and went inside.

Laurel Goldman lives in Durham, North Carolina. Her first novel, *Sounding the Territory*, was published to wide critical acclaim. *The Part of Fortune* is her second book.